Praise for FORGOTTEN

'A fascinating dive into the consequ... ... . and the passage of time, taking the concept of being "unrecognisable to the former self" to its apotheosis. All the characters are intriguing and their complexity is revealed alongside Ava's, and the reader shares in her fears. A beautiful novel worth a read for anyone also struggling with identity.'
Nita Delgado, Editor

'A refreshingly raw and conflicting journey with Ava as she is forced to pick up an unrecognisable life from where she supposedly left off. Complimented by the compelling thrill of law, *Forgotten* tackles friendship, motherhood, and sexuality in a completely smudged and delightful human way.'
Olivia Griffith, Reviewer

'Wise, warm and witty, *Forgotten* examines the metamorphosis of motherhood through the eyes of Ava, who wakes after an accident to find she's forgotten the past decade. Ava stumbles to reconcile the life she's woken into, complete with a new husband and a preschooler, with the woman she believes she is. The premise is relatable to the point of being visceral and poses the question that all mothers have asked themselves: What happened to my life? It encourages us to consider that, although our lives may never return to the way they were before children, if we have the courage and support, we may be able to build something richer. With profound themes and a light touch, Casey Nott delivers a story with well-drawn characters, authentic relationships and a narrative voice that reads like a best friend. An enjoyable and life-affirming debut that I will be recommending to all the mothers I know. I can't wait to see what this talented writer delivers next.'
Anne Freeman, Author of Me That You See

Praise for FORGOTTEN

'*Forgotten* is a charming and captivating read. Ava's struggle is relatable and grounded, while still encompassing much bigger questions. Nott has a strong voice, conversational while still holding weight, like a 3am deep and meaningful with a close friend. Funny, warm and heartbreaking in equal measure, I fell in love with this book and was "ride or die" with Ava right until the perfect and satisfying resolution.'
Samuel Maguire, Reviewer

'A woman rediscovering who she is but more importantly, what she wants, *Forgotten* tackles an impossible dilemma and will leave you thinking long after you read the last page.'
Kylie Orr, Author

'A captivating debut. Casey Nott is an author to watch. An empowering and heartfelt novel exploring identity and motherhood.'
Jodi Gibson, Author

FORGOTTEN

Casey Nott

HAWKEYE
PUBLISHING

First published in Australia in 2024 by Hawkeye Publishing.

Copyright © Casey Nott

Cover Design by Annie Liang

All rights reserved. No part of this book may be reproduced, stored in a retrieval system, or transmitted, in any form or by any means, without the prior permission in writing of the publisher, nor be otherwise circulated in any form of binding or cover other than that in which it is published and without a similar condition including this condition being imposed on the subsequent purchaser.

A catalogue record of this book is available from the National Library of Australia.

ISBN 9781923105546

Proudly printed in Australia.

www.hawkeyepublishing.com.au
www.hawkeyebooks.com.au

For my mother, Michelle, who made me believe I could do anything.

And for my children, to whom I tell the same thing.

ONE

AVA wonders if this is what it feels like to be dead. She's trying to move her lips into the shape of words but they remain fixed and lifeless, wanting to speak but rendered mute. Her head throbs in a rhythmic punishment, making it hard to think. Someone is stroking her left hand. It's soft and repetitive and familiar. It must be Seb. He must be sitting with her, willing her to live. She wants to see him too. In this moment she can't think of anything she wants more than that. Despite her best effort, opening her eyes proves futile. A soft mechanical hum and sporadic beeps exist on her periphery. Are those beeps for her? Sounds are blurry and when she does hear a voice, it's muffled and the words land around her. If only the voice would talk to her and tell her she's okay. Is she okay? She wants Seb to talk to her and say anything. Anything at all.

Though she's barely cognisant, her mind muddles through memories like a wobbling kaleidoscope. Nothing is linear and everything she remembers feels far away. Combing through her mind keeps her tethered to life. If she can think, then she's alive. She manages to hold on to one scrap of memory and plays it over and over for comfort. She travels back to before they were married. To the beginning. The soft waves bobbed against them as they paddled the canoe around inlets and through secluded rock pools. Seb sat in the rear, controlling their direction, whilst she offered the occasional limp paddle and he teased her for being lazy. The view of the coastline was hers to soak in, vast and unencumbered. Her laugh peppered over the top of the waves as he shepherded them back to the desolate sandy beach. They'd melted into one another on top of wet sand and his lips were as salty as they were urgent. She could never give Seb anything less than all of her attention, and she liked that about him. She wanted to be wherever he was. That's all she still wants. She can't slip out of life and leave him behind. She just can't. As she wills herself to cooperate, fatigue overpowers her ragged body and she fades back to the edge of existence.

~

It's the rhythmic beeping she hears first as she flirts with consciousness. As her senses sharpen, the smell reminds her something's wrong. The aroma is a clinical mix of disinfectant and malaise that you can only get in a hospital. It's the kind of smell that makes Ava wish her mother would stroke her hair and comfort her as though she were a child, despite the fact that she was now a thirty-year-old woman. Her tendency to reach for her mother when things are difficult is a childhood crutch that persists, and Luci's particular brand of gentle stoicism has always been a comfort. She can smell something else that she can't quite place. It wafts around her, floral and musky. A perfume? Her mother? With Luci swirling through her, sleep sucks her into another vortex of forgotten time.

Ava's eyes are still shut, but in her mind she's walking through a meadow. The high grass and wildflowers caress her legs as she sashays through, searching for a path that doesn't appear. The sun is gentle as fluffy clouds dance across the sky. There's a figure she can't quite make out in the distance. It's a man but she can only see the back of him. She tries to run to get closer but the grass is too high and it tangles around her feet, forcing her knees to the ground. She gets back up and sees there's a woman walking with him. She shouts but nothing comes out. Her mouth is nothing but a silenced void. The grass begins to sprout around her, growing taller and eventually entwining above her head. The world darkens as the earth swallows her and she crumbles on top of herself to cry. Gasping for air, she splutters through a tube in her mouth and bats at it with her hand that is suddenly alive again. Her eyes cleave open as a nurse in creased blue scrubs approaches and the beeping around her gets louder and faster.

'It's okay, you're in hospital, you're okay,' the nurse offers, squeezing her hand and removing the tube from her throat as she struggles to catch her breath. Her lungs are tight with each breath and the shooting pain along her right side intensifies with every inhale.

'Shh, slow breaths,' the nurse coaches at her side, and Ava mirrors her rhythm until she begins to find a sort of calm.

Four more people rush into the room and exude a flurry of excited concern over her. Apparently she wasn't the only one worried that she was dead. A woman appears next to her with a mass of dark curly hair and thick red glasses. She has a stethoscope and a clipboard and introduces herself as Doctor Fowler.

'Can you tell me your name?' Dr Fowler asks.

'Ava Durant,' she manages, swallowing the dry lump in her throat.

'It's good to talk to you, Ava. We've been very worried about you.' The doctor smiles, letting Ava unclench a little. 'Do you know how you got here?' Dr Fowler asks.

Ava shakes her head.

'Don't worry, this is normal after trauma. You were in a car accident and you're safe now. Try to breathe slowly,' Dr Fowler reassures her.

Ava repeats the words *car accident* in her head. She can't remember when she last drove. Then her thoughts turn to Seb; has she hurt him too?

'My husband?' Ava asks, her voice breaking.

'Yes, the nurse is calling him now. He'll be relieved to see you, he's been here every day. So has your sister. I'm sure they'll be here soon.'

Freya has been here? This fact is surprising, but Ava figures that trauma has a way of forcing people's hands. Sinking back against the pillow, her eyes get heavy again and a warmth rushes through her, knowing that Seb and Freya are close. She knew she could feel her family.

She runs her fingers reflexively over her left hand. It's bare.

'My wedding rings…' she mutters to herself, but the nurse

overhears and assures her they've been in a safe. When she brings them back to her, they slide out of a labelled paper bag along with her necklace, clinking together on the bed. The necklace was her grandmother's. A simple diamond pendant that she wore everyday like a talisman. Ava rolls the rings over in her hand, cold and foreign. These aren't hers. The nurse assures her that she's the only woman in the ICU. It's not possible that they were mixed up. The nurse says sometimes people get confused in the ICU and suggests she try them on. Ava slides them onto her finger and they fit like they were made for her.

~

Freya freezes in the doorway when she sees Ava. Her face is red and puffy and her clothes are dishevelled, suggesting she left home in a hurry, but Ava couldn't be sure. Dishevelled is kind of on-brand for Freya. Her curly auburn hair is untamed and her black Ray-Bans sit firmly amongst the mop. It's been ages since she's seen her sister but she looks pretty much the same, albeit a bit weathered from her perpetual suntan lifestyle. Ava had been forced to say *no* to her the last time she wanted to borrow money because Seb thought it was a bad idea. Freya hadn't spoken to her since, freezing her out in a childish sulk.

The awkwardness that hangs over Ava is suddenly broken when Freya rushes over to the bedside and flops over her in an effusive embrace, sobbing into her. She wraps her arm around her baby sister as relief washes over both of them.

When they finally untangle themselves, Freya sits back and looks at Ava through her glassy eyes.

'I'm sorry about the money. Seb didn't want me to; I should've helped you. I'm sorry we fought.' Ava hangs her eyes, not wanting to witness Freya's hurt.

'What? That was ages ago. Who cares about that anyway? I'm just glad you're okay.' Freya shrugs as if it's no big deal.

Ava's foray into near death has apparently wiped their slate clean, and although she's happy to have her sister back, it's like winning by default.

The door to her room clicks open, interrupting her thoughts, and Ava looks to see Tom paused in the doorway. His eyes linger on her for a moment before he walks into the room. He looks different somehow, but his smile is broad and she sees his eyes welling up. He gives her a searching look and she can't help but furrow her brow. What's he doing here? Why isn't Seb here yet?

'Tom?' she mutters.

'Hey, you.' His voice is trembling but soft.

Ava looks to Freya, who is holding her hand, for some kind of explanation, but Freya remains smiling and confident.

Ava starts to speak in a slow voice.

'What are you doing here?'

Freya and Tom turn to glance at each other and back to Ava.

'What do you mean, Ava?' Freya asks her.

'Where's Seb?'

Tom's eyes drop and Freya looks nervous.

Freya jumps in, filling the silence that is now awkward.

'Er, I just rang him, I'm sure he's not far away. I'll go call him again. We'll leave you to rest.' With that, she motions for Tom to leave the room with her, leaving Ava in uneasy quiet. Something's not right; what are they not telling her?

Her heart pangs for Seb and she knows in her gut that he isn't okay. He's dead. She knows he's dead. That's why Tom's here, to break the news.

A hum of quiet yet urgent conversation goes on outside the door but she can't make out the words. Adjusting herself to hear them better causes a swift pain in her chest, forcing her back against the pillow with a loud groan.

Freya rushes back into the room.

'Are you okay?'

'My ribs...' Ava gestures.

'Okay, I'll get the doctor. Wait here...' Freya adds, then glances back at Ava's raised eyebrow and weak smile, not immune to the irony of that sentiment.

Dr Fowler re-enters the room with a smile that doesn't seem genuine. Freya follows behind her and sits next to her sister's bed to hold her hand.

'How's your pain out of ten, Ava? Ten is the worst.'

'Eight,' Ava breathes.

Dr Fowler makes a note before instructing the nurse to fetch some morphine for Ava's drip. Mercifully, it doesn't take long to kick in and her breathing steadies again.

'Ava, can you remember anything at all before the accident?' she asks, putting her pen down.

Considering her answer, she draws in a few long, slow breaths. The last thing she remembers is having dinner with Seb. They'd walked home the long way, holding hands. The weather was mild and she hadn't taken her coat. They'd laughed together at some joke Seb had made, which she can't recall now. She relays this to the doctor before voicing her fears.

'Where's my husband? You said you called him. He's dead, isn't he? You have to tell me.' Ava rubs her sore head in frustration.

'It's okay, let's take this slow. Your husband isn't dead.' Dr Fowler pauses, and Freya squeezes her hand a little. 'You were in a serious car accident. You've suffered a severe head injury and some internal trauma and fractured ribs. There was some internal bleeding but we believe that has now been resolved. We need to do a few more cognitive tests to assess you. Is it okay if I ask you some questions?'

Ava nods and lets out a sigh. Her head is aching and it hurts to move. All she can do is breathe, yet that, too, is torturous.

'Do you know today's date?' Dr Fowler quizzes.

'Er, August...the sixteenth maybe? I'm not sure how long I've been here...' she trails off.

'That's okay, it's the thirtieth, but that's okay. You've been here for nearly two weeks,' Dr Fowler smiles. 'And year?'

'2008,' Ava answers. Dr Fowler makes notes on her clipboard.

Responding to several more inane questions about her full name, age and address as well as who the prime minister is and historical events including WWII. She rattles off her answers in between stilted breaths.

Dr Fowler finishes her questions and moves to the side to read over her notes, encouraging Ava to rest. She leans her head back further into the pillow, which has an annoying plastic rustle and scratches the back of her neck. Freya holds her hand, letting her be quiet and catch her breath.

As the morphine drip takes effect, the pain in her chest dulls, along with most of her other senses. But she can move her arms, fingers and toes, so the doctors are confident she has avoided any catastrophic spinal cord injuries. She tries to focus on what the doctor is saying to her, but life is still blurry around the edges. A dull throb circles her head and though she does her best at their questions, nobody seems to be able to answer hers: *Where is Seb?*

'Freya?' she squeezes out.

'Yes, Ava?'

'Did he die? Are they not telling me that he died? Is that why Tom's here?'

Freya goes white and looks over at Dr Fowler, who gives a small nod and then moves to the side of the room and waits.

'No. He didn't die.' Freya's words are slow.

'Then where is he?'

'Ava, there are some gaps in your memory. You told Dr Fowler that it's 2008, and that you are thirty years old. It's not 2008 anymore. There are a few years you can't remember yet.' Freya keeps her voice gentle though her words are becoming terrifying.

'How many years?' Panic grips Ava's throat.

Freya glances at Dr Fowler, then looks down at the floor as if to steel herself.

'Ten. It's ten years later than you think it is. It's 2018. You're forty.'

Ava searches Freya's eyes for some kind of inkling that this is all a sick joke, but Freya's face is as bloodless as her own.

'What?' Tears start pouring down her cheeks onto the stiff hospital pillow. Questions bubble up and clog behind her throat, where she chokes back sobs. Her terror spikes, immediately evident for all via the heart rate monitor. What has happened to her life?

'Shh, don't worry, I'm here. You're safe, it'll be okay.' Freya wraps her arms around her sister but Ava's not sure how those words could be at all true.

Ava doesn't know how long she stays cradled in Freya's arms, but she can't move. The need to know more is crippled by fear.

'Do you want to ask me things?' Freya whispers in her ear.

'I'm scared. Tell me about you first. Are you still living in Byron?' Ava asks, letting Freya release her hold.

'I'm back in Melbourne now, I live in St Kilda,' Freya begins.

'Of course you do, still as cool as ever.' Ava smiles.

'Er, not *that* cool anymore. I'm a mum now actually.' Freya seems nervous.

Ava sits back to look at her as this revelation sinks in.

'What? That's amazing. I'm an aunty?' Ava's joy is genuine and Freya's eyes light up.

'Yep. Little Pip is two and she's wonderful and exhausting and motherhood is amazing and terrifying all at the same time.' Freya reaches into her pocket, pulling out what Ava assumes is a giant PalmPilot and flashing a photo up at her.

The screen reveals a tiny smiling girl with a cluster of auburn curls that match Freya's. Dressed head to toe in pink she looks a mini version of Freya.

'She's a doll. Congratulations little sissy, I'm proud of you.' Ava pauses. 'But what the hell is that thing?' Ava gestures to the PalmPilot.

'Oh, that's a phone. That's what phones are like now. Kind of like a little computer and camera and basically your whole life in your hand. Don't worry, you'll be addicted soon enough.' Freya winks at her.

'God, I've missed everything. Imagine you fat and pregnant without me to tease you,' Ava jokes, leaning her head back and trying to picture it.

'Don't worry, you did plenty of that.' Freya laughs.

'Are you married?' Ava asks.

'Ah, no. Boyfriend, but that's a story for another day.' Freya seems eager to move the conversation off herself. Ava steadies her breathing and asks the question she's not sure she wants the real answer to.

'Where's Seb, Freya? Why isn't he here?'

'Um, he and you, aren't...'

'No!' Ava bursts.

'I'm sorry. It was a long time ago. You both moved on.'

'No, we wouldn't... no. No.' Ava shakes her head, refusing to believe.

The assault of truth surges over her body. Seb was more than her husband. They'd learnt how to be grown-ups together. He kept her tethered whenever life overwhelmed her. He was part of her soul.

'But,' Ava begins, 'the doctor, she said that she called my husband. Who is my *husband*, Freya?'

She watches Freya take a big breath and lets it out slowly as if to brace herself before she speaks.

'Tom. You're married to Tom now.'

The words coming out of Freya's mouth mingle in her mind like a foreign language, making her body hot and prickly.

'Tom? I married Seb's best mate?' Ava shakes her head.

Her breathing labours and the room blurs, her eyes refusing to focus. Before Freya can impart any more truth bombs, Ava closes her eyes, succumbing to the full effect of the morphine drip. The reality of the day is too much to stay lucid for.

TWO

ALONE in the muted evening light of her hospital room, Ava picks up the phone next to the bed. She dials the first of the only two numbers that she knows off by heart. Maybe her mother will be able to offer some clarity.

The number you have dialled is no longer in service. Please hang up and try again.

Trying the number a second time elicits the same message. Weird. Her mother must have changed her number. Is it possible that Luci, the perennial Luddite, upgraded to the fancy smart phones that the whole world has seemingly adopted? Stranger things have happened, she supposes.

It takes her a few more minutes to build up the courage to dial the other number she knows. The person to which her heart belongs. Or *used to* belong. She dials before she can chicken out, and her heartbeat pulses in her ears as she hears it ring.

'Hello?' His smooth voice purrs down the phone.

'Seb,' is all she can muster as her throat closes up.

He sighs down the phone, but he doesn't hang up.

'I uh, I've been in an accident,' Ava offers.

'I know. Freya called me.' He pauses then asks, 'Are you alright?'

Hearing his voice ask her questions gives her new relief in this hellish reality.

'Well, sort of. I'm not going to die, but no, I'm not alright. I can't remember what happened to us, Seb.'

'I wish I couldn't.' Seb's voice is soft and she can hear hurt.

'What did happen to us?'

Hearing him take a deep breath makes her realise that she's holding onto her own.

'It was a long time ago, Ava. I had to move on. Hasn't Tom told you?'

'I haven't seen him yet. I wasn't ready. I want you to tell me…'

'You left me for Tom. That's about the crux of it.' Seb lets out another resigned sigh.

Ava shakes her head. The phone cradled on her ear grows hot.

'Why would I do that?' Ava is baffled.

'I've asked myself that question many times.' His voice is husky and pained. It sounds different, which is unsettling.

'Can I see you? Please?' she begs, her eyes wet.

'I dunno, Ava. I've worked really hard to move past this. I don't know if I can. I'm sorry.' She thinks she can hear him crying too.

They stay silent on the phone for a few seconds, and she can hear him breathing. She's still trying to think of something to say when the line goes dead.

~

Easing herself up in bed, Ava notices the pain in her chest has eased, but she remains careful. She surveys her new hospital room in the soft morning light. They'd moved her out of ICU and into a ward, where there is reprieve from the constant hum of ventilators and various other beeping noises. The room is less frightening, with a pink hospital coverlet over the bed and a large window at the end of the room overlooking the communal garden. The lush hydrangeas offer up a gentle dance though the window. Her eyes jerk back to the door when Dr Fowler bustles in, armed with her clipboard and a takeaway coffee, an intern at her heels.

After a routine examination, the doctor seems satisfied that Ava is now stable enough to try walking with the physiotherapist today. There will also be regular appointments with the neurologist for at least the next few months and Ava steels herself with a deep breath for the onslaught of this recovery. Dr Fowler seems to sense her burden and sits on the end of her bed while the intern disappears himself against the beige wallpaper.

'Ava,' the doctor begins, 'this is going to take some time. You've had a serious trauma and it's not only a physical process from here on out. I'd recommend some counselling to help you cope once you go home.'

Ava gulps at the mention of home. She doesn't know where her home is now. She doubts any medical professional is going to make it okay that *Seb* isn't her home anymore, but she offers the doctor a limp nod.

'Do you have any questions?' Dr Fowler asks with a tilt of her head.

'My memory... will it ever come back?'

'Maybe, maybe not. Post-traumatic retrograde amnesia is common after sustaining head injuries like yours. Some people recover memories in the weeks following the accident, but it's a case of wait-and-see for now. You might get some things back or nothing at all. I know it's frustrating.' Dr Fowler gives her a stiff pat on her leg, the rigidity of her cold presence clashing with Ava's warm body.

The facts make reality bleak. She's flying blind and might have to do so forever. The doctor scribbles a few notes before moving on to the next broken body on her list. Ava steeps in the silence until it feels like it's choking her. She flicks on the TV above the bed to distract herself with the inane chitchat of morning shows in an attempt to drown out these horrible new insights.

~

Freya arrives with a big bunch of lilies and puts them in the corner. Tom walks in behind her with his hands in his pockets, looking almost shy. It's comical on his tall frame and it doesn't suit him.

Ava is sitting up in bed, alert and eager, though she's cagey with Tom. Freya looks uncomfortable around them. He sits in the chair furthest from the bed and waits for Freya to sit down and read the room for him.

'Lilies are the flower of death, you know?' Ava says, glancing over to the corner with a smirk on her face.

'Oh, I know. I picked them specially.' Freya smirks back and Ava enjoys the teasing. It feels like old times.

'When are you going to bring little Pip in for me to meet her? I can't believe I'm an aunty!' Ava lights up a little.

'I still can't believe I'm a mother,' Freya retorts, but then seems to catch herself. 'Soon. I'll bring her in soon. She's a little two-year-old hurricane, so you'll need to get your strength up.'

'Did you sleep well?' Tom asks her, changing the subject.

'Not really. I'm still pretty sore.' She shifts awkwardly in the bed as if to illustrate her point.

She looks at him properly for what, in some way, feels like the first time. He looks different to what she remembers. Older, greyer, but also softer somehow.

'The doctors are amazed at your progress so far! Dr Fowler said she thinks you might be up walking by tomorrow.' Freya jumps in, upbeat, bordering on manic.

'Well, I'm trying hard.'

'You always do,' Tom says softly.

Ava is unnerved by Tom's advantage of knowledge over her. It's so weird that he's her husband. Tom was Seb's best mate; they were like brothers, and that's how she saw Tom too. He was part of the furniture of her life. She loved him, but he was background music. He's looking at her with broken eyes and it's wounding her for all the wrong reasons. If he was still just her friend, she could comfort him but now, as his *wife,* she doesn't know how. Instead, she changes the subject to something lighter.

'Can you give me Mum's new phone number?'

Freya whips her head around from where she's fiddling with the flowers. 'What?'

'I tried calling her last night, but it must be an old number. Where is she anyway? On a cruise or something?' Ava's surprised her mother isn't here bossing all the staff around in her authoritative fashion.

Tom and Freya look at each other and both of them turn pale. A hard knot forms in Ava's stomach.

'We were going to wait a few days to tell you...' Tom trails off.

Her face goes hot. She sits like stone, waiting for the truth she doesn't want.

Freya pulls a chair over to the side of Ava's bed and sits down, picking up Ava's hand as she does.

'Mum, um, she died, Ave. Nine years ago,' Freya manages.

The finality of the sentence hangs thick in the air and Ava has to focus on breathing as hot tears prick the backs of her eyes.

'But... I just saw her the other day... we had lunch at Graze...' Ava trails off, knowing she's caught in between realities, where nothing is simple. Ava wipes a furious hand over the tears flooding her face.

'How?' she asks, hungry for the evidence.

'Um, she had a massive stroke, and ah, she didn't suffer. She was swimming. Ironic, huh? Still fit and energetic, swimming at six on a Wednesday morning. She got out of the pool and collapsed. The ambulance came quickly and they did everything they could, but...' Freya's voice fades out.

'This is so unfair,' Ava mutters, her mind in a fog of implausible truth. Everything she loves the most has been taken from her and she can't remember any of it. The devastation of not getting to say goodbye to her mother or try and save her marriage flows out of her like water from a burst tap, and her whole body heaves as she sobs.

When the torrent of grief finally ebbs, she realises that Freya has climbed up off her chair to embrace her, whilst Tom is now at the edge of the bed with his hand resting on hers. It's warm and smooth against the tops of her fingers, but it isn't Seb's. She slides her hand out from beneath his under the guise of reaching for a tissue to mop up her face. He takes the cue and sits back in his chair, reluctantly shifting his hands to his own lap.

Freya still has her arms locked around Ava when Tom stands up and delicately offers to leave, promising Ava that he'll return tomorrow so they can talk. She's relieved as he departs, wanting her grief to be private and preserved for family. Tom isn't her family and she can't pretend he is. Not today.

~

When Ava sees him standing in the doorway, she has to catch her breath. She didn't think he'd come but is overcome with relief that he has. He's dressed casually, in jeans and a light blue Ralph Lauren polo shirt. She notices grey flecks in his dark hair and a few soft lines around his blue eyes that weren't there before. His frame is strong and largely unchanged though, and she's relieved to see that he's still Seb.

He walks over to the bed and she wishes she could stand up to throw her arms around him. He sits on the chair next to her and offers a weak smile as a greeting. She's disappointed he's not happy to see her.

'Hi,' she says, sounding small. 'Thanks for coming,' she adds.

'I'm sorry about Luci...' he seems genuine, but it's clear she's guilted him here with her own grief at the expense of his.

'I'm still in shock I think, with, well... everything.' She sweeps her arm in his direction.

'Yeah, it was a pretty bad time. Sorry you have to do it again,' he offers.

'I don't know how I'm meant to do any of this without you.' She lets her need drip off her, hoping that it will get through to him.

'You'll do just fine. You always have.' He pats her hand before moving it back to his own lap.

'What does that mean?'

'You never *needed* me. You never needed anybody. You're strong,' he explains.

His words jar with her memories. She needs Seb in the same way she needs water or oxygen. Her want for him is visceral and she doesn't understand how he can think otherwise.

'That's not true.' She meets his eyes.

'Ava, we don't need to go digging up our pain again.'

'There's no *again* for me. This is fresh pain. I've lost everyone. I've lost *you*.' She's crying again.

Seb gets up and sits next to her on the bed, draping his arm around her. She breathes in his scent of shampoo and cologne. He smells like home. Her head goes heavy against his chest and they stay quiet, neither willing to break the spell.

'I loved Luci too. I know this hurts,' he whispers, gently squeezing her shoulder.

'What about us, Seb? *That* hurts,' she whispers back, nuzzling further into him.

'We died too, I guess. I don't blame you anymore. But... I can't go back...' His words are soft yet wound like knives.

He pulls away and sits back down next to her and she dabs her eyes dry with the edge of the sheet.

'When did we last see each other?' she asks.

He takes a breath and rubs his brow. 'It must be a few years ago. We ran into each other in court just before you gave up practising and exchanged a nod in the hallway.'

She jerks her head at him.

'Gave up practising?' She flushes with the now-familiar foreboding.

'Uh, yeah. I don't know the details, but you left the big firm.' Seb shrugs.

'Am I working at another firm?'

'I don't know, Ava. We're not in touch. We're not *friends*.' He delivers the words slowly, but it's not malicious.

'So we just got divorced... and that's it? Out of each other's lives?' She's still incredulous.

'Well, yeah. That's pretty much how it works.' He gives her a gentle smile.

She's frustrated that her brain can't compute the reality of her divorce. She's not a fool. She's seen more than her fair share of feuding couples in court to know that *happily ever after* often means *I'll rip you to shreds in Family Court*.

'Did we sell the flat?' Her brain kicks in.

'We kept our own properties. I moved out of the Prahran flat.'

'Do I still have it?' She prods.

'I don't know, Ava. Have you even spoken to Tom about your life?' Seb's voice takes on a tinge of frustration.

'No. Everything's been kind of overwhelming.' She's embarrassed at the mention of Tom.

'Well, I suggest you do. I can't tell you this stuff. It's not my place.' Seb lowers his eyes to the floor.

'What stuff?'

'Your life. I'm not privy to your life anymore.' He lifts his eyes again and they look sad.

'But you know things?'

He nods.

'And you won't tell me?'

He shakes his head and she lets out a frustrated sigh.

She sits back in the bed and looks at him without the pressure of speaking. Here is the same man she married but for the few marks of age scattered over his face. His arms drape down by his sides. They're still strong and rippled with a hint of muscle through his shirt. Those arms were the place she sought comfort and where she was most desired. How is that gone? How is the same man so different?

'I can't give you what you need,' he says, interrupting her thoughts.

'Can't or won't?' She raises an eyebrow.

'Does it make a difference?' He shrugs.

Then she sees it. Or more accurately, she doesn't. He's not looking at her like he used to. The invisible power she had as his wife isn't there. She broke them and now it might not be fixable.

'Are you married?' She's suddenly eager for any detail about his life.

'No.'

'Single?' She's hopeful.

'No.'

Damn.

'Where do you live?'

'Ava, I... this isn't going to help you.'

She sighs in annoyance; she's no longer privy to *his* life either.

Seb smooths his hands over his thighs and stands. It's obvious his discomfort has peaked. 'I'm going to go…' he says, then adds, 'I hope you feel better soon.'

He doesn't hug her or kiss her goodbye, instead giving the hospital bed a wide berth as he leaves. With too much empty space in the otherwise small room, her chest tightens. The pain of losing her mother and her husband hurts more than the sum of her aching injuries.

~

After her encounter with Seb the previous day, Ava didn't manage more than a few hours' sleep. The constant twisting on the rigid hospital mattress has made her feel worse and there is less optimism in this new day. The hospital dressing gown is stiff on top of her body, as if it's been washed in trauma a thousand times. Her urge to move is strong and a young, fresh-faced nurse helps manoeuvre her into the chair next to the window. It's freeing to be out of bed. She lifts her legs up and down in an even, methodical motion, mimicking the instructions of the physiotherapist. Her feet are tight, clad up to the knee in hospital-issue compression socks, but she can move them. She can still move her body and that's what she intends to do, as if movement will somehow unshackle her from herself. A soft tap on the door steadies her legs as her eyes look up to greet her visitor. She sees Tom in the doorway and it doesn't occur to her not to look disappointed.

His sand-coloured hair looks damp and he's carrying a small tray with coffees. He offers a tentative smile as he sits down on the chair opposite her and puts a bag of pastries on her table.

'I thought you'd like a real coffee.' He tilts his head like it's a question.

Grateful, Ava pushes her sad cup of lukewarm instant away from her and takes the one he offers, noting the scribble on the side of the paper cup. *Soy flat white*, in loopy cursive scrawl. The fact that he knows things about her reminds her that she doesn't know much about him.

She knows his parents, where he went to school and that he lives for the Melbourne Football Club but she doesn't know what he likes for breakfast or if he prefers boxers to briefs. Thinking about his underwear makes her catch herself, so she shakes her head a little to regroup. She decides that small talk isn't a viable option. She needs some answers.

Ava looks at him and says, 'Tom. I need you to tell me what happened. How we, you know… got together.'

Tom, seeming to anticipate this, takes in a slow breath.

'I wasn't harbouring some great unrequited love or anything, it wasn't like that. We all hung out a lot, I was part of your family I guess, and I was there when things were falling apart. Luci died a few months after my dad died…'

'Jeff died? Oh god, I'm sorry.' Jeff used to give her and Seb rides home after many a drunken party at Tom's place back in their university days. Jeff and Jane were "cool" in a way that Luci wasn't.

Tom seems to have to remember that his dad's death was sad. He's had time to grieve the loss of his parent in a way that Ava hasn't yet been afforded.

'You and I were really devastated and Seb didn't get it, at least not in the same way. He was away a lot and things kind of… escalated.' His eyes slide away from hers.

'Seb and I weren't happy?' Ava probes.

'He was away a lot for work. I think you started to want different things.' Tom shrugs.

This isn't how Ava remembers it. She was as obsessed with work as he was. All they both ever wanted were work and each other.

'What things? We had everything…' The life she remembers is in colour, relegating this new existence to black and white.

Tom winces a little but she's unable to make room for his pain alongside her trauma.

'You were distraught. He didn't know what to do, so he didn't do anything. Seb wasn't good at the hard stuff,' Tom offers.

Wasn't he? Ava tries to remember what hard stuff even existed for them. Their life was fun. They were both a bit selfish but it never mattered.

'There wasn't any hard stuff,' she counters.

'Ava, I was there. He wasn't. You were fighting a lot.' He's challenging her with a familiarity that she doesn't like.

'Everyone fights, that's normal.' She attempts dismissal.

'Not for us,' he quips back.

'*Us*? What 'us', Tom? Christ, you're like my brother!' She's hot and red and mad. Tom's face falls and Ava sees the hurt etched on him.

Tom pauses and meets Ava's gaze, then speaks with a clear, pointed tone.

'Ava. I'm not your brother. I'm not the husband you remember either. But I'm something else now. Something we can't undo.'

She sits waiting in the swollen air between them.

'Ava. I am the father of your son.'

THREE

IT'S 2am and the dim night-light next to her bed keeps the room soft. Ava repeats his name over and over in her head, hoping it will thrust forward a barrage of memories. *Noah. Noah. Noah.* She tries saying it out loud but the name is foreign in her mouth. There are no memories flooding back, no slivers of recognition, just a stranger's name on her lips.

She looks at the photo Tom gave her. Ava herself is in the photo next to Tom, who looks relaxed in a casual green polo shirt and a wide smile. He has flecks of grey through his hair, which are the main hint that he's aged from the man he was in her memory. Other than that, he looks good, like he might still work out with some degree of regularity. She looks at herself in the photo, smiling and wearing a floral dress that she doesn't recognise. Her chestnut hair falls in soft waves around her shoulders and she's glowing with a relaxed ease, her arms wrapped around a little boy. *Noah.* In front of them is a dinosaur birthday cake with a big number four on top and he's beaming a big, dimpled smile. She wonders if she made that cake, though she can't imagine how she could have. Noah has big blue eyes and a mop of soft curls the exact shade of Ava's. In him, she sees herself mirrored. But she's still looking at a stranger. It's the kind of photo you expect to find in a frame when you buy it, showing you the prototype happy memory that can be immortalised within it. Finding herself embedded in this happy life is like a kind of torture. She can see her life, but she can't touch it or feel it, or even believe it. She stares at the photograph as if she's looking at a broken clock, expecting it to tell her the right time.

She and Seb fought about having kids all the time. He wanted to have three and she wasn't sure she wanted any. She was devoted to her job and desperate to make partner by the time she was thirty. *Was.*

She forgot to ask Tom about her job after she was blindsided by Noah. Surely she's made senior partner by now, maybe even knocking on the door of managing partner or CEO. It's a boys' club, she's well aware, but that hasn't stopped her wanting to be part of it. You can't change anything without a seat at the table and she is working her arse off for that opportunity. *Was* working her arse off. Being caught between the *is* and *was* has her untethered and desperate for answers. Ava closes her eyes in frustrated exhaustion and, with the photo still in her hand, succumbs to sleep.

~

Ava is unsteady as she tries to stand for the first time. The bubbly nurse by her side steadies her. The weakness throughout her limbs makes her heavy and cumbersome, but she clings tight to the nurse's arm and manages the few steps into the bathroom. It's her first proper shower in two weeks and even though she's seated in a plastic chair, water rushing all over her is heaven. She looks down at her body, trying to make it belong to her. Seeing herself naked for the first time is confronting. Aside from being bruised and scraped from the accident, it's a different body than it was ten years ago; not exactly chubby, but softer than it was. Ava notices a pinkish scar a few inches below her belly button. It looks old and feels hard under her fingers but isn't sore. The nurse holding the showerhead must notice her stroking her finger across it and informs her that it looks like a scar from a caesarean-section. Her body wears the evidence that she is Noah's mother even if her brain refuses to remember. What made her want a baby? The water rinses the thought as quick as it came.

When she's finished, she fishes some clothes out of a bag that Tom brought in yesterday. It's like rifling through someone else's luggage, but she tries not to dwell on that and gets on with making a decision. She picks out some soft, olive-coloured cotton trousers and a matching camisole that says "loungewear" on the tag, and a chunky grey woollen cardigan that feels expensive. Size twelve. She's gone up a size, which annoys her, but she attempts to shrug off the sticky, critical thought. The selection of clothes is illuminating, making it clear that she still has good taste and some money to throw around on whatever "loungewear" is. In her old life she mostly wore tailored suits for work and jeans with sneakers on the weekends. Sunday afternoon was about the only time she and Seb kept sacred to hang out at home and often those hours were swallowed by work anyway. Both of them were desperate to make partner, which meant every available moment was an opportunity to put in overtime. She's eager for Tom to arrive so she can ask about her job. Seb said she left the firm, which she can't believe. Maybe he's wrong.

As she continues looking through her things, she finds a smaller bag of various makeup and skincare paraphernalia and is gobsmacked by the number of products a middle-aged face seems to require. The nurse finishes dispensing Ava's medication and leaves her to it, and she's left alone wondering what "retinol" is and what it's supposed to do for her.

~

There's a soft knock on Ava's hospital room door and only after she answers does he enter the room. It's an odd formality for a husband, but it would have been awkward had he walked straight in, so she appreciates the gesture. Ava's sitting in the reclining chair next to her bed, and he looks at her a few seconds longer than she's comfortable with. Her hair is loose around her shoulders and she's bathing in the morning light.

'Hi. You look...' he seems to catch himself then says, 'like you.' He smiles all the way to his eyes and she blushes.

'The nurse helped me wash my hair and I feel kind of human again.'

He walks over to her and hands her a takeaway coffee cup, solidifying their new morning routine.

'I brought in some more clothes and stuff too. It might be a bit random, I wasn't sure what you'd want.' He gestures to the small duffle bag he's left on the floor next to her.

The jagged roll of the zip pierces the silence and Ava examines yet more foreign items. On top of mostly black and grey clothes, there are two pairs of Lycra pants adorned with bright swirly patterns, which cause her to pause and furrow her brow.

'Yoga pants. You work out most days,' Tom clarifies.

She's surprised, given her obsession with spin class borders on cult-like. Yoga is for older women who are afraid to sweat.

Rifling a little deeper into the bag, she pulls out a couple of pairs of lacy black undies, then quickly shoves them back into the bag, hoping Tom didn't notice. He smirks behind his coffee and she changes the subject.

'Can you bring in my laptop? I want to check my case load.'

His shoulders stiffen. 'You don't have a case load anymore.'

So it's true. Seb was right.

'I don't understand.' An involuntary held breath solidifies the tension in her body.

'You left law a few years ago.'

Ava swallows hard, her skin prickling all over. This is what Seb was alluding to the other day but didn't have the heart to tell her.

'Why would I do that? I lived for that job. I couldn't have… I was right in the middle of the Fallon trial…' Her realities are colliding again.

'You won the Fallon case and got them to pay costs too. Ten years ago. But you got passed over for partner again and again. All the years of missing out took a toll. Then when we had Noah, things changed. You tried to go back after maternity leave but they "cock-blocked" you from all the big cases. Those were your words, by the way. In the end you had a showdown with Gary and you told him to "go fuck himself" and left. Again, your words.' Tom sips his coffee as if all this is normal information.

Ava's mouth is hanging open now. Tom waits until he's obviously too uncomfortable and then speaks again.

'You lost the joy; the fire. Plus, they were a bunch of pricks that didn't care about you. You didn't want to do it all anymore.'

She tries to visualise what her life looks like without work at its core but can't. None of this is plausible.

'What do I do then? Swan around and do yoga all day?' Her tone is curt and Tom flinches like he's been hit.

'No, you do lots of things. You look after Noah, you're pretty involved in the community. You occasionally work for the community legal aid centre. You're really into gardening…' Tom stops once he sees her face get tighter with his every word.

'Tom, are you actually kidding me?' Her jaw stays tight.

'At this stage, I really don't think you're ready for me to kid.' His eyes stoop to the ground.

'But I was talented. Why did I throw it all away to stay home and plant daisies? I mean… what the fuck?' Her neck turns hot and scratchy.

'You didn't just wake up one day and "throw it all away". You got tired of putting in so much and getting no recognition. It was hard to watch.' Tom's tone is firmer now.

'Well, it's hard to hear that everything I worked for has been torched.' She folds her arms, sullen.

'It stopped defining you. I know you, Ava. Ten years ago, yes, you were hungry; making partner was *everything*. All you ever did was try to impress all those dicks that ultimately screwed you over in the end.'

'Why didn't I go to another firm? Why didn't I try harder?'

'You stopped wanting it. You wanted something else.'

'Yoga and kids?' There's a sharp edge to her voice now, and Tom looks uncomfortable.

'Yes. Ultimately, yes. You became someone who gave a shit about someone other than yourself. You wanted to be there for your son. *Our* son. Who you haven't even mentioned yet, by the way. You wanted to build something to suit our life.' He waves his arm, exasperated.

'Our life? Or *your* life? What do you do now, Tom?' She's argumentative now. He looks embarrassed and she narrows her eyes, sensing what's coming.

'I'm still at Tate & Fox.' The heat evaporates from his tone.

'Oh yeah? As what?' Her gaze is hard.

'Tax Partner.'

Ava scoffs and shakes her head.

'So you get to have it all and I don't? Hooray for feminism.' She throws her arms up in a faux "hallelujah".

'That's not fair.' Tom's voice is soft.

'Isn't it? How come you're living *my* dream and I'm stuck in this nightmare?'

'You're not the only one who's stuck in a nightmare! The accident changed my life too! I was happy, life was good. *We* were good. But now my wife thinks that I'm some scumbag holding her captive in a life she hates.'

Ava watches him for a few moments as he cradles his head in his hands, distraught. She knows this torture goes beyond her alone. The sting in Tom is evident on his face. He's her friend. She *knows* him. She doesn't want this for either of them.

'Tom, I know you're not a scumbag. I'm just confused. None of my choices belong to me anymore.'

He looks up at her, meeting her eyes as tears shine in his. 'Ava, do you really think me – or anyone else, for that matter – could have forced you to make a decision you didn't want to make? You're still the same person. You never do anything you don't want to do.'

Conceding that he's probably right, she nods. She's stubborn and headstrong and has never been great at compromise. She and Seb used to fight a lot as a result. The fights were often superficial, and on some level they both enjoyed the sparring, but their more serious disagreements were rooted in a blatant refusal to meet each other halfway. Maybe she and Tom are the same but she can't bring herself to ask him, afraid to peek at their intimacy.

'That's true.' She's softened her voice.

'I'm sorry.' He rubs his knees and shakes his head. 'I should have been more prepared to talk about this stuff. I keep getting blindsided, which is ironic given the circumstances.'

'I know it's not a choice, Tom.'

'Do you want to know anything else? Want me to call Sarah or one of your other old colleagues to get another perspective?'

'No. Thank you. Not now. I actually want to talk about Noah.' And she means it.

With that, the tension in the room lightens and Tom gives her a weak smile.

~

Ava's phone vibrates next to her. She looks at the screen for a few moments then picks up.

'Hello? Freya?'

'Yep, hi Ava, it's me.' Freya's reassurance steadies her.

'Oh good, I'm still working out how to use this thing. Tom gave me a crash course but it's a fair leap from my old Nokia.'

The pages of apps that she can't imagine having a use for make her head hurt.

'Ha, I bet. Don't feel bad, Tom still has to teach me how to use apps all the time.'

'How was school today?' Ava asks.

'Great, yeah. Good to see the kids, good to be back. I was teaching Shakespeare today, if you can believe that.'

'Barely.' Ava smiles, still computing that her little sister is a sensible schoolteacher now.

'How was your day?' Freya asks.

Ava exhales. 'It was a lot to process but Tom is being really kind.'

'He *is* kind.'

'Yeah, of course he is. It's weird to have him... love me like this.'

'Did you talk about Noah?'

'Yes. I um... I want to see him. Tom said that he'd bring him in tomorrow. Maybe you could come too? Then he'll have another familiar face. Tom said he might be a bit shy because I've been absent.'

Talking about Noah is still safely abstract. But the impending reality of meeting her child for the first time is making her chest tight.

'Yes, of course. Of course I'll come,' Freya says.

Ava pauses. The truth catches in her throat.

'I'm... I'm terrified, Freya.'

'Of Noah?' Freya asks.

Yes. And of Tom. And of all of it. 'Of disappointing him,' she says, a cop-out.

'You won't. He just wants to see his mummy. You like kids, Ava. Bundle him up in a cuddle and nothing else will matter. I promise.'

She can't escape the thought that this little boy will see right through her. He'll know that she's not his mother; at least, not the one he remembers.

'Hey, I'll bring something for back up. He loves dinosaurs and superhero stuff, I'll pick up a few things for you to give him, to help warm him up. You did that for him when Pip was born. Hospitals are scary for kids.' Freya fills the silence with reassurance.

Hospitals are scary for everyone, she thinks.

'My ideas all seem to belong to some other woman. A woman I don't know.' Ava sighs.

'What other ideas?'

'All of them. Have an affair, marry Tom, have a baby, quit my job that I loved. Now I'm some product of another woman's choices? It's not fair.'

'Well, you're right that it's not fair...' Freya trails off.

'But?'

'You're happy, Ava. Or at least you *were* happy. It's not like you're tormented by your choices. Nobody forced them on you.'

'You sound like Tom.'

'Well, he's wise like me.'

Ava lets out a small laugh but doesn't quite commit to it.

'Hey, look. I'll come in after work and we can talk about it some more, okay?'

'Okay.'

'I love you.'

'I love you too.'

Freya's love steeps her in the familiarity of time and family. What if she can't love Noah like that? What if she can't love him at all?

~

With her fingers hovering over the *send* button, Ava second-guesses herself and deletes the whole text. She's been trying to draft a message for about an hour but the words never seem good enough. He knows she's been in an accident; he knows she nearly died. He knows her memory is impaired and he knows she's in pain. He's seen her lying in a hospital bed. The void between them is undeniable but she can sense he still has feelings for her. Why else would he have come? But her fingers remain strangely paralysed. How do you formulate a text message that will bridge a chasm of hurt? She doesn't know, hence draft after draft of nothing.

She puts her phone down and gives up. She pushes Seb out of her mind, or at least to the dull edges. Her focus switches to Noah, with the enormity of their meeting tomorrow threatening to swallow her. She's trapped between wanting tomorrow to come faster and not wanting it to come at all. What if he can tell she's not the same? What if he's scared of her? What if she's scared of him? What if the lost years mean she can't be a mother anymore? What if she doesn't want to be a mother? In an engulfment of *what ifs*, Ava surrenders to a morphine-laced sleep to dream of the yesterdays.

FOUR

AVA oscillates between excited and terrified as she gets ready for Noah's arrival. She got up early to shower even though Tom said they wouldn't be coming in until 10am. The urge to be prepared is overpowering and she doesn't want to be caught on the back foot. Looking in the bag of neatly folded clothes, she's unsure what to wear. Again, it's like borrowing an outfit from a friend; a friend who's older and far more stylish than she is. Settling on some grey crushed linen trousers and a crisp white T-shirt, she adds her chunky grey cardigan on top, which has fast become her favourite item of clothing. The yoga pants remain undisturbed in the bag. She wants to look familiar to Noah, but also cover some of her nasty bruises and bandages so as not to frighten him. The only visible evidence from the accident is a small dressing on the cut above her right eye, but her loose hair hides most of it.

Grief pangs deep in her gut thinking of her mother and wishing she could be here for this. How can she learn to be Noah's mother without guidance from her own? How can she do *anything* without Luci's guidance? Her mother was her sounding board. Drawing her breath deep into her belly, she pushes the bubbling grief down as low as she can, saving it for later. She's getting good at that.

Today is for Noah. Everything has to be for him. Thanks to her eager preparation, she now has forty-five minutes to sit and be ready. Waiting. Waiting for Noah.

After unpacking and repacking her clothes, sorting her vast array of cosmetics and trying to watch some horrific morning television, it is five past ten. The sun through the window is warm on her back as she tries to relax on the small sofa, staring at the open door, her stomach churning with nervous energy. Freya had visited her last night to drop off the little present for Noah and to give her a pep talk. It had helped at the time but as the long minutes tick by, she's struggling to remember the advice she was given. Hearing Tom's voice waft into the corridor, she sits up straight to brace herself. Her hands go clammy and she's too jittery to stand for the occasion.

"Mummy!" Noah shouts, wriggling out of Tom's grasp and hurtling towards Ava in an exuberant four-year-old onslaught. She winces a little as he squeezes her around the waist, burrowing his head into her chest. When her initial shock ebbs, she lets herself inhale the top of his head, where smells of strawberry shampoo and peanut butter mingle. Freya shoots Ava an encouraging wink as she walks in behind Tom.

'Hey buddy, be gentle with Mummy, okay?' Tom says.

Noah releases his grip and takes a seat next to Ava, squishing himself tight against her body.

'Hi Noah.' Ava smiles, trying to keep tears back. Noah looks exactly like she did as a child and it's unnerving; like looking at an old photograph that's come to life.

'I've got a special present for you. Would you like to open it?' Ava asks.

Noah's eyes light up and he nods with enthusiasm as she hands it over. 'What is it?'

He rips open the wrapping paper and pulls out a Batman colouring book, some pencils and a small plush dinosaur. He beams at Tom, holding them up for him to see, and Tom offers excitement to match Noah's.

Noah looks at Ava and says, 'Thank you, Mummy.'

The name reverberates off her, making her stomach flip in nervous embarrassment as though she hasn't yet earned this mantle.

Noah begins frenzied colouring on the wheelie hospital table between them right away. Ava follows his lead and picks up a green pencil to begin working on a tree. Colouring is methodical and doable, distracting her from the gravity of the day.

'Freya and I are going to pop down to the café and grab us all some coffees. Is that okay? Noah, are you happy to stay here with Mum?'

Ava gives Tom a panicked look as Noah remains casual and says, 'Yep.'

'We won't be long.' His eyes are pointed at Ava whilst he proffers a reassuring smile.

Freya gives Ava a thumbs-up and she and Tom leave. Noah starts discussing which colour should go where. The ease with which Noah has warmed to her quells the panic and reminds her that *she* isn't a stranger to *him*.

After they complete the first page of the Batman book, Tom and Freya still aren't back and Noah says, 'Mum, I'm hungry.'

Looking around the room, bereft, she eventually locates a half-eaten packet of chocolate biscuits Freya brought in a few days ago. Judging by Noah's excitement level she wonders if maybe she's a mother who doesn't let him eat biscuits. It's too late to worry about that as Noah retrieves the biscuits from the bedside table, pulls one out for himself, and then hands one to Ava.

'Thanks, Noah. Do you like chocolate biscuits?'

'Yep,' he says with his mouth full, crumbs falling across his lap.

'Do we have biscuits at home?'

'Sometimes Nanna brings them for me.'

Tom's mum must be "Nanna", she notes to herself.

'She takes me to kinder cause you're in the hostible,' Noah continues.

'Yeah, I'm sorry that I've been away.'

'When are you coming home?' His expectant eyes meet hers.

Ava knows she won't be in hospital forever, but the question jars her a little bit because of course she'll have to go home to this foreign life.

'Um, soon, I think. When the doctor says that I'm allowed to.' Her words are sticky in her mouth.

'Okay. Can I have another biscuit?'

Ava hands him another biscuit from the dwindling packet.

'I think you forgot to say *please*, Noah.' Tom appears with his gentle admonishment and Ava wonders how long he's been standing there.

'Sowwy. *Please*, Mummy?'

'Hope these are okay?' She directs her question to Tom while passing Noah another biscuit and he waves his hand as if to say that it's no big deal. Freya hands her a hot takeaway cup, which is soothing in her hands.

'Mummy?' Noah's voice squeaks.

'Yes?' She still feels conspicuous, but it isn't unpleasant to be called *Mummy*.

'Did you know that the T-Wex was a carn-ah-vore? That means he eats people. But there were no peoples to eat then so he ate other dinosaurs coz he can run really fast!'

'Amazing! Sounds like you know lots about dinosaurs.' She smiles at him.

'You teached me from the big dinosaur book,' he explains.

Ava shoots Tom a blank look and he jumps in. 'Yeah, that's the book you've been reading at bedtime with Mummy.'

'Sorry, Noah. I've forgotten some things because I hurt my head a little bit.' She wobbles her head and smiles to illustrate her point.

'Is that why you have a band-aid on your head?' He points to her eye, not fooled by her attempt to cover up.

'Yeah. I've got a few band-aids to help me feel better.'

Noah slides over to Ava and wraps his little arms around her, gently this time.

'Here, Mummy. I cuddle you to feel better.'

Ava takes his cue and slips her arms around him, breathing him in and letting a couple of tears roll down her cheeks. 'Thanks, Noah. That makes me feel heaps better.' And she's pleased to find that it does.

~

The two hours that Ava spent with Noah that morning flew by and she didn't want them to leave. Her thoughts were more torturous when she was alone. Tom promised to come back in the evening and bring them some dinner, giving her a night off hospital food. Freya volunteered to host Noah for a sleepover so they could have time to talk. As the minutes tick closer to Tom's arrival, her nerves swell. It feels like a date. She only has vague memories of first-date nerves and doesn't quite know what to do with them. She wishes things were different and that Noah was Seb's child. As if it would be easier to fall in love with Noah if half of him belonged to Seb. The thought of having to fall in love with her own child is tormenting enough without layering the guilt about her feelings for both her husbands. Her old betrayal is still a seeping wound, and the only antidote that she can think of is to call her mother. Luci would know what to do. Luci would tell her what she needed to hear. The grief is thick in the back of her throat and gentle tears roll down her cheeks. Alone, with nobody to pretend for, she lets them flow without wiping them away.

There's a soft knock on the open door, where Tom is standing holding a paper takeaway food bag and watching Ava cry. She wipes her eyes on her sleeves before looking up at him.

'Oh, babe, are you okay?'

She doesn't react to being called *babe*.

'I'm... no, not really.'

Tom puts the bag of food down on the small table next to the bed and sits down with her on the couch, waiting for her to talk again.

'It's just been a lot. Mum is still constantly on my mind and sometimes it's just... I wish I could talk to her,' she babbles.

Tom puts his arm around her and she leans into it without pausing to think about it first.

'I know. You said a similar thing ten years ago,' Tom says.

'I did?'

'Of course. You always went to Luci for advice. You and Seb weren't in a great place and you didn't know what you'd do without her.'

'What did I do? You know, to cope?'

'Well, you and I got drunk a few times. That didn't help our grief, but it helped us talk about it.'

'Seb didn't support me?'

'He was travelling a lot for work and you were kind of alone. Freya was living in Byron Bay then too and wasn't around for long after the funeral. You drifted a little back then. You still called her a lot. You were worried she was getting stoned all the time and didn't want her knocked up in some hippy commune."

'Is that where she got knocked up?' Ava can picture a swollen-bellied Freya in a floaty tie-dye dress, walking barefoot on the beach.

'Nah. She was back in Melbourne by then, with a musician boyfriend. Jarred somebody. We only met him a few times and he was long gone by the time Pip was born. You weren't super keen on him.'

'That sounds more diplomatic than I probably was.' She smiles at him.

'Hungry? I got sushi from your favourite Japanese restaurant. Thought it might help bring back a memory or two.'

Her stomach gurgles, expectant, as the aroma of gyoza wafts from the bag

'Thanks. I'm starving, sushi sounds great. Should we go and have it in the garden? I need to get out of this room...'

Tom helps her walk slowly out to the patients' garden as she holds onto his arm, the weirdness of touching him negated by necessity. They pick a bench under the flowering crabapple tree and it feels good to be outside. The early evening sky is dappled with light and it's still mild with no breeze. Finally outside again, she exhales all the way to the pit of her belly and her shoulders sit low and comfortable. Tom pulls out an array of food they'll never get through, and she appreciates his effort. They sit next to each other, balancing bento boxes on their laps. It's easier to ask the questions she needs to while they're not looking directly at each other.

'So,' she pauses to chew, 'Seb was gone, Freya was stoned in Byron, and you and I were... hanging out, getting drunk?'

'Not exactly. We all used to hang out all the time: Seb, you, me and Jemima.'

'Oh yeah, Jemima! How is she?'

Tom turns to her and shoots up a raised eyebrow.

'Sorry, stupid question.' She gives him a smile.

'Jemima and I broke up a few months before Dad died. She broke up with me, actually. Said I had "commitment issues".' He uses air quotes and smiles.

'Did you?'

'Well, yeah, but only 'cause I obviously didn't want to commit to her.' Tom winks at her and the air softens around them.

'I liked Jem. I'm glad she wasn't more of my collateral damage.'

'You say that like we were callous villains.' His voice sounds hurt. 'Were we?'

'No. God. No.' He rubs his temple and thinks for a minute. 'We were drowning in grief. And we had nobody to share it with except each other. You and I were working in Bourke Street then, a few blocks apart, and we'd meet for a drink after work. It was completely normal, we were just mates. When Seb was in town, he'd be there too.'

'I remember those nights. It was like uni never ended.' She can see it in her mind: all of them high on the fumes of youth.

'University with pay cheques, you used to say.'

'Living the dream.' She laughs and notices how natural it sounds.

As Tom relays the past, she can see it sitting there like a scene in a snow globe. They were young, bulletproof kids, oblivious to the inevitability of life being shaken up.

'Were we meeting a lot? Without Seb?' Ava probes.

'It was a standing Friday night engagement. Whoever was around came along. Sarah and Nick used to come along sometimes. It was casual.'

'So… how, then?'

'Luci died and you weren't coping well. You stopped wanting to come out or do much of anything. Seb was on a major case in Brisbane and was basically living there, coming home maybe every second weekend.'

'I suppose Seb wasn't great emotional support at the best of times,' Ava concedes. Seb didn't like to be uncomfortable in the murkiness of his own emotions, let alone other people's.

'Things had been a bit off with you two. You didn't discuss it with me in any detail but it was obvious that you weren't in a great place. I didn't pry. I wasn't actively trying to fall in love with my best mate's wife.' Tom stabs his sushi roll with a chopstick.

Her cheeks flush at the mention of love. She can't stop now though, and keeps going, hoping for a light bulb to go off.

'Then how did you?' She keeps her gaze fixed ahead of her.

'We were united in this shitty grief and we talked about all kinds of things. Death, life, things we were scared of. It was liberating, and because we were just mates there was no pressure, and it was simple honesty. It helped us both.'

'And...'

He turns inward slightly and she's forced to look at him. He looks embarrassed too.

'I'd like to say, first, it's very weird to tell you this story. I've never told anybody this – well not in this much detail – because... because I've never had to.' His eyes close as he shakes his head.

'I agree. This is super weird.' She smiles and he lets out a deep breath she hadn't realised he was holding.

'Okay. So one night, we'd both worked late in the city. You'd brought me in as a consultant on a fraud case you had.'

'Oh, what case?' Ava interrupts him.

'Ava, please.' He raises an eyebrow to as if to say this is hard enough already.

'Sorry.' She lowers her eyes. It's clear to both of them that the lawyer in her is still very much alive.

'Christ.' He rolls his eyes and sighs. 'It was a money laundering fraud, big investment group, got a lot of press.'

'Ooh. Did we win?'

'Ava! Jesus.' He pauses again then says, 'Yes. Of course we won. Now may I continue, or would you like the billable hours too?'

She stays quiet and nods although she'd actually love to know what they billed.

'We'd worked late and we grabbed a cab home together. That's when I was living in Prahran right near you and Seb. We decided to go back to your place and order some dinner. It wasn't sinister, more like an old habit. We spent a few hours sitting on the balcony, talking and having a few drinks, but we weren't hammered or anything. It was late, probably midnight, and you turned and looked at me and said something.'

'What?'

He flushes a little before meeting her eyes and not looking away.

'You said, *I want you to kiss me.*'

Ava can picture her flat in Prahran with its art deco arches and exposed brick kitchen with fancy new appliances that she rarely used. She can picture the large lounge room and Baltic pine floors, the soft cream shag-pile rug and expensive slate grey couch that Seb never liked. She can picture the double glass doors that led onto the balcony, which was just large enough for two wicker chairs and a lone pot plant that, despite continuous neglect, never died. She can see all of that in vivid colour but she hasn't got a picture of sitting on her balcony with Tom, asking him to kiss her.

'And what did you say?' Ava asks him.

Though her face belies her calm voice, she doesn't break Tom's eye contact. They're sitting close but not touching, and she notices how he smells. It's a pleasant mix of cologne and a soapy, freshly showered scent.

'I didn't say anything.' He continues to hold her gaze. 'I just kissed you.'

It would be a lie to say she didn't find Tom attractive. He is tall, with floppy, sandy hair, blue eyes and strong features. He's well put together and polished in a way that suggests private schooling and a nice family. She had actually noticed him first when she'd met him and

Seb at university all those years ago. Seb's confidence and the way he commanded the room had overpowered any residual attraction she'd had for Tom, and her fleeting desire had dissolved. Sitting here though, on this bench, close enough to hear each other breathing, she can't say that she feels nothing.

Ava breaks the eye contact and fidgets with her food a little before changing the subject. 'I meant to tell you; I spoke to Dr Fowler today. We talked about my rehab plans and she thinks I'll be fine to go home next week. I'd have to come in for physio appointments and stuff, but she thinks I'm well enough to leave hospital.' She rambles a little but Tom takes her new lead.

'And how do you feel about that?'

She looks him in the eyes again and decides he knows her well enough that pretending isn't necessary.

'Shit-scared.'

'Me too.' He pokes at his food.

'Really?' Relief floods through her.

'Of course. I don't want you to come home and hate your life or feel like you're living in a stranger's house with a stranger of a husband.'

'You're not a stranger, Tom.'

'Thank you, but you know that's not what I meant.'

'Well, I think I need to try. I'd like to try to be…' She wants to say *Noah's mother, your wife, somebody who practises yoga*, but instead says, 'try to be whoever I am.'

'We'll do this together. You're not alone.' His tone is certain.

'Thanks.' She reaches over and takes his hand and they sit in the quiet, wishing for the unsaid things.

'So,' Ava says eventually, breaking the silence. 'What *did* we bill on that money laundering case?'

Tom lets out a laugh and puts his arm around Ava in a gentle squeeze. 'God, I've missed you.'

~

It's been half an hour since Tom gave Ava an easy hug and left to go home, and Ava can't fight the urge to pick up her phone. Her finger hovers over the number and she takes a deep breath before she relents and presses it. He answers on the first ring and the words catch in her throat as she speaks.

'Hi, Seb.'

FIVE

IN order to prepare Ava to go home in her strongest possible way, Dr Fowler suggests that she should meet with the hospital psychologist. Ava's sceptical, knowing that she can't talk her memories back into existence and feeling irreparably lost without them. Recalling the counsellor her mother had taken her to as a child to 'talk about her feelings' after her father died makes her chest hurt. Talking about her grief back then didn't make him any less dead, or their family any less broken. It simply hurt. But the urge to leave the hospital, to start getting her life back, compels her to agree despite the futility of the exercise. If she's going to learn how to be Noah's mother, she needs to be close to him. Going home with Tom is the only real option, but the thought of it makes her rigid with unease.

Kelly Anderson's office doesn't do much to relax her. It's clinical in the way that hospitals are, with stiff faux-leather chairs and a utilitarian desk between them. A lone pot plant sits in the corner but it's too small for the room and the large, plastic, too-green leaves indicate that it's fake. The harsh fluorescent lighting bounces off the linoleum floor and makes everything look haphazard and cheap. Kelly seems to clock Ava's disappointment with the environment and assures her their future sessions can be undertaken in her Brighton office, closer to home. Ava bristles at her use of the word *home*. Tom's told her about their big house in Brighton, though she still struggles to place herself in that upper-middle class, suburban Mum life. Kelly tilts her clear-framed glasses back into position and rests her pen beside her leather notebook before asking Ava how she's feeling. It's an unsurprising, pedestrian question given the myriad of emotions swirling within her, but she supposes they have to start somewhere. She tells Kelly that she doesn't know. It's a cop-out but she doesn't feel like baring her soul yet. She's afraid of what she'll have to see.

They meander around Kelly's broad questions regarding what Ava remembers about her life and how it's changed before reaching the crux of the session.

'How do you feel about going home with your husband?' Kelly asks, pen in hand.

All Ava can think is, *he's not my husband*, but she doesn't want to say it out loud. She doesn't want to discuss Seb in here either. She doesn't want the psychologist to know that she's been talking to him, texting him and thinking about him. All the time. She needs to be able to get to know Noah and she can't do that if she's with Seb. She'll have to work out all the other stuff later but for now she decides to fake it a little.

'I mean, I'm a bit nervous, but it's not like Tom's a stranger, he's my friend.' Ava keeps her voice light and Kelly scribbles notes in her book. She won't let herself be too honest, lest she falls into the trough of grief just below her fragile surface.

'It's normal for you to be nervous, you're grieving a great deal right now,' Kelly offers, though Ava wasn't seeking validation. 'But I want to be clear that you don't have to go home right away. The hospital can make arrangements if required.'

The thought of a state-funded halfway house for those who can't remember who they are fills Ava with dread. She decides to perk up for fear of being committed or barred from making her own choices.

'No, I feel safe with Tom. He's my family. I want to go home. I want to try and see if it will bring my memories back.' Ava smiles as her mouth says the right words.

Kelly seems satisfied with this and makes a few more notes before wrapping up the session, seeming happy with both Ava and herself. She schedules a follow-up session for next week, about which Ava pretends to be pleased. Therapy seems like it's going to involve a fair bit of pretending, mostly to herself.

~

Bracing herself as she steps up, Ava feels Tom slip his arm around her to help her into the car. He's gentle as he lifts her into the big white Range Rover, which still has its new car smell and looks immaculate inside. It's a far cry from her small Mazda, which, despite having been brand new, gathered a few parking lot dints and was loaded with various remnants of life that she intended to throw out but never did. He shuts her door for her before walking around to get into the driver's seat.

'Nice car. Is it new?' she asks.

'Got it last year. I did have it cleaned last week; you still treat your car floor like a rubbish bin.' Tom teases her.

'This is *my* car?' The surprise makes her voice squeak.

'Yep.' He's nonchalant, as if luxury cars are a regular household item.

'If this is my car, what car was the accident in?' Ava lowers her voice so Noah can't hear her from the backseat.

'That was in my car. We'd swapped for the day, I was dropping yours off for a service.'

'Sorry.' She winces.

Tom tilts his head to the side. 'Ava, please. It's just a car. And anyway, I love buying cars. My new one is already on order.' He smiles at her, before turning to Noah in the back. 'Okay, everybody ready?'

'Yep!' shouts Noah from the back seat. 'Sing the *Buckle Up* song, Mummy!'

Her face falls a little before Tom chimes in and sings the song for her. Noah joins in from the back as they drive off and head home.

The drive is pleasant and they wind through wide, leafy streets lined with huge houses. There are lots of other Range Rovers – ridiculous urban cars for people with too much money – but despite herself, she's enjoying the luxury more than she'd care to admit. She and Seb had earned decent money but they'd ploughed most of it into their mortgages and the occasional nice holiday rather than expensive cars. Thinking about mortgages reminds her about her flat.

'What happened to my Prahran flat by the way? Was it sold in the divorce?' She remains casual, not wanting to distract Noah from his iPad or upset Tom by talking about the past.

'Ah, no actually. You got Prahran in the settlement, and he kept his St Kilda flat. It was all pretty neatly tied up.'

'Oh. Did I sell it when we moved here?'

'No, we kept it. It's leased. It's a good little earner, plus you really loved it because it was the first place that was yours. Kept it to be sentimental.'

'I did love it.' She looks out the window at the Brighton mansions that are a world away from her two-bedroom art deco haven.

Tom moves his hand to rest on top of hers and says, 'You love this house too. You picked it. I thought it was too big but you talked me around.'

'I'm still bossy then?'

'You're still *you*, Ava.'

This is both reassuring and hard to believe but she gives Tom a smile anyway.

Tom turns the car into a double driveway as a black, timber-panelled gate slides open to reveal a large, manicured front garden with a lush lawn and a mature cherry blossom tree in the centre, thick with early spring buds. The house itself is a double-fronted Edwardian, painted crisp white, with bay windows and an expansive veranda. Sculpted pot plants straddle either side of the front door and a small green bike rests against a wooden bench seat. It's immaculate and impressive. Ava tries to take it all in while they wait for the garage door to roll up.

'Wow,' she whispers under her breath. The size of the house knocks the wind out of her and it's hard to believe this is real.

'Yeah, you've worked hard on the garden. It was half-dead two years ago.'

'*I* worked hard on the garden?' She's incredulous.

'Well, we have Steve, who does the lawns and pruning, but you do most of the planting. I'm not very good at visualising the way you are. We go to Bunnings most weekends; you always have a garden project on the go.'

Ava's never been inside a Bunnings store, only ever walked past for a Sunday morning hangover sausage with Seb. She's speechless that she could accomplish anything like this, having never taken an interest whatsoever in gardening, or living things in general. Her stoic little balcony pot plant was the only thing she'd ever kept alive, and that was despite her, not because of her.

Tom parks the car and releases Noah from his car seat, letting him bolt through an internal door leading into the house.

'Are you ready?' Tom asks her.

No, she thinks, but she steels herself with a quick deep breath and nods, following him through the door. The entrance hallway is bright, with a sitting room off to the side. The soft brown leather couches look brand new, and the room looks like it's set up for a magazine shoot. Tom notices her staring.

'Oh yeah, that's the "good room". None of us are allowed to go in there, which is why it looks like that,' he explains.

'It's lovely.' She walks past the mantlepiece, running her hand along the frames of smiling faces, pausing at the last one to catch her breath. It's a posed shot, with her mother in the middle, flanked by herself and Freya, standing outside their country house. Their younger faces are bright and unmarred by time. This photo sat on her bedside table in her Prahran flat and was the image that her mind said goodnight and good morning to. Now its pride of place is in her grown-up "good room". Tom doesn't say anything as she continues to walk through the room.

The high, ornate ceiling is regal with its striking beaded chandelier in a soft grey colour.

'Like it?' He asks.

'Yes, it's stunning.'

He lets out a little laugh. 'That's what you said to me three months ago when you ordered it. You said it was an "impressive statement piece" that would "tie everything together".'

'You don't like it?'

'Oh no, I like it, I guess. "Impressive statement pieces" aren't my area of expertise. It made an impression on the bank statement though.' He smiles.

'Do I spend lots of money on stuff?' Guilt rises as she's suddenly aware that she no longer has an income of her own.

'I don't police your spending if that's what you mean. You don't need my permission. We don't operate like that. Money isn't a big issue for us anyway. We're doing okay.' He's warm and genuine so she doesn't push further and they step back into the hallway.

She feels like she's being taken through an open house as she follows him down the hallway and into a huge open plan living and dining area with high ceilings and lots of oversized windows. Her favourite leather armchair sits adjacent to a sofa that she doesn't recognise. The armchair was a housewarming present from her mother when she'd moved into her flat. She has to fight the urge to curl up in it and hide under a blanket, which was her favourite coping strategy when life felt hard. Instead, she turns towards Tom and takes in the space. It's fresh and modern and looks like a lavish addition to the original house. There's a generous kitchen with white cabinetry and marble benches to one side and big glass doors leading out to a covered courtyard and seating area on the other. Noah has let himself out the back door and she can see him jumping on the trampoline, which sits on a lush, green lawn. She sits down on one of the six stools at the bench and Tom puts the kettle on.

'Holy shit, Tom.' She sighs, shaking her head a little.

'Too much? Should I have shown you pictures first?' He's floundering in concern.

She shrugs and shakes her head, knowing that nothing could have prepared her for this. Her childhood was spent in a humble weatherboard home where she and Freya had shared a bedroom. A necessity that never bothered either of them, even when teenage Freya would ransack her wardrobe and steal her makeup. Ava loved how they would whisper to one another in the dark, a sisters' covenant for shared fears and kept secrets. Her mother had done the best she could after their father died and Ava never felt like she missed out, but it's obvious from looking around that Noah's life is different.

'Sorry, I... um. there's no rule book for this.' He clears his throat and tries to press on with what is obviously a pre-prepared plan for the day. 'I thought you'd probably have questions, legal questions mostly, so I pulled out some papers for you if you want to have a read. Divorce papers, Section 32 on this place, Luci's will...' He trails off.

She's impressed that he's being this thoughtful and seems to know exactly what she's thinking, which is heartening and overwhelming at the same time.

'You know me well.' She meets his eyes, and he shrugs and his cheeks pink a bit before he turns, busying himself with the kettle.

Tom hands her a cup of English breakfast tea, made with a splash of milk – exactly how she likes it – and she follows him outside into the gentle spring sunshine.

~

The first afternoon at home passes with relative ease, and Ava is surprised at the normalness of it all. Noah was content playing outside for most of the afternoon and seemed to enjoy it most when Ava was in his eyeline for various renditions of 'Mum, look at me!'. He had boundless energy and she wondered how she was ever going to keep up with the kid. Tom cooked them all dinner on the barbecue and they ate outside on the large wooden table under the shade of the flowering jacaranda that billows over the side fence from the neighbouring house.

Later, while Tom is upstairs giving Noah a bath, Ava ensconces herself at one end of the oak dining table and starts going through the paperwork that Tom has collated for her. It is comprehensive, which is unsurprising given how meticulous she knows Tom to be as a lawyer, and she appreciates the effort. Luci's will sits to one side of her but she can't bring herself to read that yet. The divorce papers are the ones taunting her the most, the subject of both curiosity and fear. She is about to reach for them when Noah bounds down the stairs with damp hair, dressed in Batman pyjamas.

'Okay buddy, say goodnight to Mummy,' Tom says, following him down the stairs.

'I want Mummy to read me a story,' Noah pleads.

'Sure, I can do that,' Ava jumps in.

She follows them up the sleek timber staircase, which is complete with glass balustrades connecting the upstairs floor with seamless elegance. There is a large rumpus area at the top of the stairs, with Noah's bedroom at one end of the corridor along with a spare bedroom and a bathroom. Ava and Tom's bedroom is at the other side of the rumpus area, though she hasn't lingered in there beyond a cursory tour when Tom showed her the ensuite and where her side of the wardrobe was. Pushing that out of her head for now, she follows Noah into his bedroom, watching as he retrieves a large book from his bookshelf and jumps onto his bed.

Tom finishes adjusting the covers with practised ease and motions for Ava to perch herself on the side of the bed.

'Okay, what book have you picked, Noah?' she asks, taking a seat.

'The dinosaur book. We're up to this page, remember Mummy?' He pulls out a bookmark and points to the page with enthusiasm.

Ava smiles and makes a mental note to read the start of this book to herself some other time so she can learn all the dinosaur facts too. She gets comfortable and transports them back to when diplodocuses and triceratopses roamed free. Noah is quiet while she reads, and by the time she reaches the end of the chapter, his eyes are heavy.

'Goodnight, Noah. Here's Goose.' Tom kisses him on top of the head and gives him a final tuck. Ava notices "Goose" is a bear and gives Tom a quizzical eyebrow.

'Top Gun,' he whispers to her, and she smiles in acknowledgement, grateful for a cultural reference she can remember.

'He's seen it?'

Tom's eyes go wide, 'No, he's four. I just named the bear.'

She feels silly for asking the question.

'Cuddle, Mummy.' Noah's little voice is soft.

Ava leans in and lets him squeeze her until his little arms go limp, signalling that he's finished.

'Goodnight, Noah,' she whispers.

Noah snuggles down into the covers with Goose tucked under his arm. Tom flicks on the dim night-light next to his bed before he and Ava shut the door behind them and go back downstairs.

'Is it always that easy?' she asks.

'Oh, not always, but he was pretty exhausted today. Plus, you're back...'

A rush of acknowledgment bundles in her throat, knowing that Tom has been doing all the heavy lifting at home. It's something akin to guilt, or maybe it's dread, knowing how unprepared for motherhood she is.

'He's a good kid, Tom.'

'You deserve a lot of the credit for that.'

'You're a good dad, I can tell.' She means it. She can't remember her own father very well, but Tom's ease and warmth make him seem like a natural even from her naïve vantage point.

'You do lots of the grunt work. I come in for the glory.'

'Oh, I doubt I'd let you get away with that.'

'Well, you do get pissy with me if I miss bath time. That's kind of the deal during the week. I get home in time for family dinner and do the bath.'

'Who cooks dinner?' she asks, hoping it's not her.

'We share. You mostly do the weeknights when time is tight. I take over on the weekend.'

'I'm amazed that I've learnt to cook edible food.' Ava's idea of cooking dinner is buying a roast chicken and a premade salad.

'You have a lot of recipe books that you treat as binding contracts. If it says *cut your finger and bleed into it*, you'll do it.'

She laughs, knowing she's never had any intuition in the kitchen beyond being able to set off the smoke detectors.

'Don't worry about that stuff yet anyway. Mum is happy to help out while we try to work out our new normal. She loves feeding people.'

'Oh, Jane is a gem, I always liked her.' Ava can remember plentiful banquets at Tom's place with Jane at the helm when they were lowly undergrads.

'She's a pretty big fan of yours too. You two gang up on me all the time. She likes the chandelier too.' He smiles and his eyes drift to the piles of papers on the dining table. 'You still reading?'

'Actually, I might finish up and read it another time. I'm pretty tired.'

'Sure. I've got some work to do, I'll be in my office for a while if you need anything.'

He pauses, looking at the floor, suddenly uncomfortable.

'Um, also,' he continues, 'I'll… sleep in the spare room tonight, the one next to Noah's room. Give you some time to get used to your new surroundings.'

'Are you sure?' She hides her relief, not wanting to make him feel terrible.

'Absolutely. Baby steps.'

She smiles and nods at him. He turns and heads for his study as Ava gathers the papers she's strewn across the table back into a neat pile. She turns to head up the stairs to her room but has second thoughts. With a quick glance down the hall to check that Tom isn't watching her, she scoops up the pile and takes it with her.

SIX

AFTER waking, it takes Ava a few seconds to remember where she is, as she surveys the unfamiliar ceiling above her. A dull pain radiates under her ribs, prompting her to reach for the painkillers on the bedside table. The alarm clock next to her informs her that it's 6:03am, and she figures she might as well get up and face the day. Her body becomes less sore once she's moving around, and the hospital physio told her the morning is the best time to do her prescribed stretches anyway.

She eases herself up to the side of the bed and notices the pile of paperwork on the floor. That assault of information kept her up pretty late last night. She doesn't dwell on the facts now and decides to ask Freya about it later when she gets the chance. She walks into the long dressing room at the far side of the room. This space is apparently all hers. Tom has a smaller, yet still generous, walk-in wardrobe next to the ensuite. There is ample hanging space and shelving on either side of her robe, with a large, circular, emerald-green velvet ottoman in the centre. She grabs a waffle cotton robe off the hook near the door and puts it on over her silk pyjamas to take the edge off the morning chill. She creeps through the upstairs lounge room, careful not to wake Noah and Tom as she heads down the stairs to the kitchen.

Inside the spacious butler's pantry sits a large and complicated-looking coffee machine. Whilst she stands there, weighing up if hunting for a jar of instant is a better solution, Noah's small voice startles her from behind. He looks up at her, bright-eyed in his crumpled Batman pyjamas.

'Hey, Noah.' She uses a soft voice, not wanting to wake Tom.

'Did you have a good sleep?' Her face is over-animated like she's an actor in a low-budget advert.

'Yep. I'm hungwy.'

'Hmm, me too. What do you normally have for breakfast?'

'Pancakes pwease.'

'You know what? I'm not a very good cook, but I learnt to make pancakes when I was at university. They're the one thing I'm good at.' She smiles at him and he beams back at her.

Ava, Seb and Tom had been part of a university charity drive raising money for some noble cause that she can no longer recall. They'd teamed up with a bunch of students to run a pancake stall on campus one morning and she'd never forgotten how to flip a pancake. It was her one cooking accomplishment. Seb used to love her Sunday morning pancakes. They'd eat them in bed and not care when maple syrup dripped onto the sheets.

Glancing around the pantry, she shakes Seb out of her mind, wondering where she's going to find everything she needs, and spots some glass canisters on the shelf. They're well-stocked and complete with printed labels. Her alter-ego's meticulous attention to detail has made this task impossible to screw up. She grabs the flour and sugar and goes in search of the fridge. The kitchen cabinetry is vast, but she can't see a fridge anywhere. She turns to Noah, who's propped himself up on a stool at the bench.

'Noah, I can't remember where the fridge is, can you help me find it?'

'It's there.' He points at a cupboard behind her.

The sleek black handle swings open to reveal a massive integrated fridge, which is also well-stocked and organised. 'Oh, that's right,' she says to Noah, before smiling and making a silly face, and he giggles. She locates the eggs and milk and adds them to her collection of ingredients on the bench.

Noting yet another confused expression from Ava, Noah jumps down from his stool and runs around to pull out a large drawer under the stove to help her find the mixing bowls. In it is a plethora of baking implements, including bowls, trays and cake tins of all shapes and sizes.

'Look, Mum! Can we make dinosaur cookies later?' He waves a T-rex shaped cookie cutter at her.

A flutter of panic rises before Tom drifts into the room surveying the benchtop. 'Noah, I think you might be being a bit cheeky this morning. Pancakes are just for the weekends, buddy.' Tom's scolding is gentle and he ruffles Noah's hair as he walks past him.

Tom has a jersey robe draped around him, and although he's wearing pyjama bottoms, the sliver of chest tells Ava he's shirtless underneath. She decides he must still go to the gym a lot, then catches herself and reroutes her thoughts back to the pancakes.

'Well, I've found most of the stuff now. I can do it, it's no big deal.' Ava shrugs.

Tom smiles his gratitude and locates a pan for her before going into the pantry to pilot the coffee machine.

Noah is a keen apprentice, watching her every move and asking to stir the mix. After Noah's satisfied that the batter has had a thorough mixing, she gets to work at the stove, churning out breakfast. Tom and Noah set the table with cutlery and an array of condiments and they're ready and waiting as Ava sets down a big stack of pancakes for them to help themselves.

'Um, wow,' says Tom.

'I know. I'm actually quite proud.' She's satisfied with the accomplishment after weeks of hospital-bound malaise – though relieved to sit down – and takes a big gulp of the coffee Tom has made for her.

'Yum. The complicated coffee robot makes an excellent drop.' She closes her eyes to savour it.

'These are delicious,' Tom says with his mouth full, and then the table falls quiet as they all tuck in.

'What's the plan for today?' Ava asks, and goes on to add, 'Freya texted me last night saying she'll pick Noah up for swimming lessons.'

'Monday afternoons you two take the kids to swimming. Noah

finishes kinder at lunchtime. Mum's going to drop him off this morning and I'll pick him up; I'm going to work from home as much as I can this week. We've got sports day at Noah's kindergarten tomorrow and I've got to be in court Wednesday, but that's mostly under control.'

'Maybe I should write all this down.' Her brow furrows as the information goes in and then out of her head.

'I've synced our calendars, it's all on your phone. But Mum and Freya will help us, at least until you're feeling a bit better.'

She wonders if he really means *until you're back to normal*. The wife. The mother. The doer of all the things in the family calendar. How much of her old self is even left at the end of each day? Her remaining pancake goes cold in front of her as she drains her coffee cup.

~

Tom's proficiency in the morning routine is high. He stacks the dishwasher, gets Noah dressed, packs Noah's lunchbox and showers and dresses himself all before 8am. The Tom she knew ten years ago grabbed breakfast on the way to the office, which made him perpetually late, and didn't get out of bed before noon on weekends. Amidst Tom's apparent organisation, Ava showers and blow-dries her hair before slipping on a light floral dress, ready to show up for her first day as a mother. When she's ready, she lingers on her reflection in the mirror. Her face now bears soft lines around her eyes and she can see a few grey hairs scattered through her roots, but that isn't what's making her look different. Her eyes are different. She can't pinpoint how, exactly, but as she looks herself in the eye it seems as though a stranger looks back at her.

As she comes back down the stairs, Tom stops to look at her.

'You look... dressed up.'

This is meant to be a compliment but Ava can't decide if it's somehow wrong, and she looks down at the dress she's picked, self-conscious.

'Is this... not something I'd wear?' Her cheeks flush pink.

'No, no, it is. I guess I'm just used to seeing you in workout gear during the week.'

'Oh.' She feels silly, aware that she doesn't know herself anymore.

Tom steps towards her and tilts her chin up to meet his eyes with a gentle hand. 'Hey. You look amazing. Do whatever feels right, everything will be okay.'

She nods and steps back a little, not ready for him to touch her like this. The doorbell rings, offering an interruption, and Noah rushes to the door, screaming, 'Nanna's here!'

Jane walks in and sees Ava standing in the kitchen and her eyes fill with tears. She walks straight to Ava and envelops her in a warm embrace against her squishy body, her chunky beads rattling between them. Ava hugs her back, inhaling Jane's lavender scent, but aches with the fact that this is someone else's mother, not hers. Jane looks older, sporting a short crop of styled grey hair which Ava thinks suits her more than the blonde foils she used to get.

'Oh, darling, I'm so glad to see you.' Jane holds Ava back from her face, tilting her red-framed glasses down and examining her in a sort of motherly assessment.

'It's lovely to see you too, Jane, how are you?' Ava gives her a warm smile.

'Much better now that I see you here.' She smiles, then turns to Tom. 'Sweetheart, I have some bags of food in the boot, can you please bring them in for me?'

'Sure, Mum.' He takes her keys and heads out to the car with Noah in tow.

'Thank you for everything, Jane. It looks like you're keeping us all afloat here.'

'It's what mothers-in-law are for, pet. Now, you don't have to pretend with me. *How are you?*' Jane seems to see both the Ava of new and old as she looks at her.

'I'm trying,' Ava admits, not wanting to dissolve into too much honesty.

'I'm sure you are. This must be difficult.' Then she lowers her voice and says, 'I loved Sebby very much too.'

Ava tries not to react to the mention of Seb's name, but she's sure Jane can see the flicker in her eyes. Ava can still remember how he smelled when she saw him in the hospital, and that memory simmers as she tries to live in this new life. Thankfully, Tom bustles back into the room to halt her thoughts.

'Bloody hell, Mum. There's enough food for an army here,' Tom says underneath arms laden with bags. Noah trails behind him, straining with a hessian bag full of fresh fruit.

'I think you mean, "Thank you, Mum".' Jane smiles at him and he gives her arm a squeeze as he goes past her to load the food into the fridge.

'There's a chicken casserole in that blue Tupperware that will keep until tomorrow night unless you want to freeze it. I also went to the market and got some fresh fish that will need using in the next couple of days.'

'Jane, you're amazing. Thank you for this,' Ava says.

'Darling, it is my pleasure. Right, I'll take my little peanut off to kindy. Go get your bag and hat, sweetheart.' She gives Noah a warm smile and he rushes off to do as he's told.

'Mummy! Where are my blue shoes?' Noah shouts from the top of the stairs.

Tom and Jane are whispering by the front door, oblivious, and Ava darts her eyes around the room for shoes.

'How about these?' She holds up a pair of green-and-white striped sneakers for Noah's approval.

'Noo! I want the blue ones!' His lip drops and he's on the verge of tears.

Navigating the stairs as fast as she can manage, Ava begins the hunt for shoes in Noah's room. Rows of plastic tubs against his bedroom wall have no discernible system of order, with toys, books and a few rogue items of clothing scattered throughout. Everything except blue shoes.

'Where do your shoes normally go?'

'I don't know!' he yells, red faced.

A pile of shoes in the wardrobe offers up a bevy of still-unacceptable footwear until he finally agrees to wear bright red dinosaur-themed wellingtons and traipses down the stairs with Ava trailing behind.

Noah slams himself into Ava to hug her goodbye and plants a wet kiss on her cheek which she finds a bit gross but tries not to. A proper mother wouldn't think kissing her own child is unpleasant. It makes her a fraud. As she waves goodbye from the doorway, she notes the blue shoes placed neatly by the front door.

The chaos of the morning lulls, Tom retreats to his office, and Ava finds herself alone in the dining room. A rush of wind makes Ava glance out the window at a couple of pots that have fallen off a rockery in the outside courtyard. It's only once she reinstates them that she recognises her old plant from her apartment balcony. She props the hardy succulent back up, tucking it in against a bigger pot to protect it from the turbulent morning. Marvelling that it's still alive, she wonders how many more storms it will be able to weather.

~

Freya is punctual picking Noah up for swimming lessons, and although Tom told Ava she didn't have to go and watch, she wanted to anyway. With no idea what to expect, she finds herself enjoying watching Noah and Pip bob around in the water, despite the oppressive tropical climate of the indoor pool. Noah's exuberance is infectious, and she makes sure to watch the entire time as he stops to wave and shout, 'Look at me!' at regular intervals. Freya is seamless in organising the kids in and out of their swimsuits and Ava's heart swells as she watches her baby sister being such a good mother.

Once back at Ava's house, the kids immediately plonk themselves on the sofa, and Freya navigates the TV gadgetry to something called "Netflix", finding them a movie to watch.

'So nobody has DVDs anymore?' Ava asks.

'No need. Everything is streamed direct now. Nobody even has a DVD player anymore.' Freya clicks on *Toy Story 3*, which makes Ava shudder. Seb had dressed up as Woody for a Halloween party they'd thrown once. She'd been Bo Peep and Tom was Buzz Light Year – they'd been given a discount for renting the themed costumes. The three of them were so close; now, all the shared memories make her stomach gritty.

Following Freya into the kitchen, she tries getting her head around the fact that you can watch anything at the touch of a button. Will Noah be worse off missing out on the thrill of renting five weekly movies for five dollars at Blockbuster the way she did when she was a child?

'Should we order in tonight?' Freya asks as she sits next to Ava at the big bench.

'Jane left some fish. Tom said he'd "whack it on the barbie".' Ava lifts her arms in a non-committal shrug.

'Ah yes, Tom's specialty. Okay, we can make a salad.'

Freya navigates around the kitchen with ease, and before long has washed and peeled and chopped various produce, conjuring a big bowl of salad. She then has a quick hunt in the pantry and produces some potatoes and a large spaceship-looking appliance.

'I'll make some chips in the air fryer; that way, the kids will at least eat one vegetable.' Freya smiles triumphantly. Ava examines the air fryer with confused suspicion.

'You love a gadget. You're only a Thermomix away from a walking stereotype.' Freya laughs, and Ava doesn't even ask her to explain the joke that's at her expense.

'I need to talk to you.' Ava's tone is serious, and Freya looks up from her potato peeling to wait, expectant.

'I read Mum's will last night. I want to talk to you about the trust.'

'What about it?' Freya goes back to chopping but the air between them shifts.

'Are you upset? That your share of her estate has been locked up in a trust?'

Freya sighs and throws the chopped-up potatoes into the air-frying spaceship before answering. 'No. I mean, yes, I was at the time. But not anymore.'

'Upset with me as well as Mum?'

'Well, yes, Ava. I was obviously upset with you too, you wrote the trust deed.'

'Yeah, I figured. It looks like it'll wind up soon anyway, then you'll be free to do what you like with it.'

'Yes, my mother decided I could only be trusted to be an adult on my thirty-fifth birthday.' Freya sounds hurt rather than angry.

'I'm sorry. I have no idea why she wanted that done.'

'I think you do know. You suggested it to her.' Freya's voice is pointed, making Ava reel back in her seat.

'That's not true, Freya,' Tom interjects from the side of the room and they both flick their heads around, not having noticed he'd emerged from his study.

'Yes, it is. Mum wouldn't have thought that up by herself,' Freya retorts back at him.

'Seb wrote the will and set up the testamentary trust. Ava only found out about it when Luci died,' Tom counters.

'What? Why the hell would he do that?' Ava asks.

'He said that Luci asked him to, and she didn't want to involve you in it because you were a beneficiary. She probably didn't want you two having a conversation like this.' Tom keeps his voice measured, taking the heat out of the room.

Why her mother kept her in the dark and put her in the horrible position of being the trustee for Freya is puzzling. She wasn't crafty enough to come up with that on her own.

'Why would Seb agree to do that?' Ava shakes her head, baffled.

'Because he's an asshole,' Freya says under her breath.

Ava and Tom look confused, and Freya goes on, 'He was jealous. He hated Ava and I being so close. He probably did it to piss me off.'

Ava can't believe Freya feels like this. Sure, Seb and Freya would spar, but it was sibling-like banter, all in good fun. Wasn't it?

'No, that's not true, Freya. Seb loved you; you were his family too,' Ava counters.

'Ava, you were the only one who couldn't see him for who he

was.' Freya's eyes are sad.

Ava shakes her head, unable to reconcile the Seb that she knew with whoever Freya seems to think he is.

'Why were you angry with me? If I didn't know anything about it?'

Freya blushes and says, 'I didn't believe you. I thought you got Seb to write it up so you could say it wasn't your idea.'

'Why have we never discussed this? In ten years?'

'After I moved back from Byron I'd calmed down. You do a good job managing the trust and I was able to live off the income and go back to uni to get my teaching degree. It wasn't like I was never going to speak to you again. I was hurting about Mum being gone more than anything.'

Closing the gap between them, Ava walks around the bench to Freya and they hold on tight to one another in an ocean of old and new grief. A heavy weight sits on her chest knowing that she played a part in hurting her baby sister. Tom slips outside to heat up the barbecue, leaving them to have their private moment.

'Please don't worry about this,' Freya says. 'I know you did the best you could.'

Freya's platitude does nothing to unclench her tight chest. Not remembering is nothing but copping out under a technicality. Life is now a constant bewilderment and she doesn't know how to clean up all the murky water she's left in her wake.

SEVEN

THE morning sun is gently dappled on the path ahead, squeezing through the leafy oak trees as Ava and Tom walk through the community garden with Noah running ahead. He slept in his football jersey last night, pumped up by the excitement of his kindergarten sports day. A short stroll down the gravel pathway reveals a large field, which has been set up with various activities resembling a small obstacle course. There's a long trestle table to one side, set up as a drinks station. A group of adults are milling around it while small children run about with abandon. Noah bolts over to the action and joins in a chasing game. Tom takes Ava's hand in his, giving it a little squeeze as they approach the group of mingling parents. His hand is warm against hers and her tummy flips with something akin to first-date nerves – or perhaps Seb-laced guilt; she can't be sure. The group of strangers immediately fall silent as they see them approach, and Ava's neck is sweaty against the collar of her shirt. It's worse than the first day of high school but she paints a smile on her face as a small woman with perfect blonde hair approaches her.

'Ava! Oh, it's so good to see you up on your feet. Gosh, we've all missed you. How are you?' The small woman is effusive in her concern, which doesn't help Ava's twisting gut. Is she friends with this woman? The exchange is uneven.

'I'm okay, thank you... ah...' She looks at Tom to insert the small woman's name for her.

'Ava, this is Meredith, she's Zephyr's Mum,' Tom explains.

'Hi Meredith, nice to meet you.' Ava smiles.

'Oh yes, of course. Gosh, sorry, I should have introduced myself.

Oh dear, where is my head today? Sorry Ava, lovely to meet you too.' Meredith is manic and Ava finds herself relieved that Tom is still holding her hand.

'Tommy!' a voice booms from behind them and Tom swings around.

'Hey, mate, how are you?' Tom is enthusiastic as he shakes hands with a tall man in a navy suit.

'Can't complain. Ava, good to see you,' says the big voice with kind eyes.

'Ava, this is Jeff,' Tom says then gestures to the tall, dark-haired woman next to him, 'and his wife, Rachel. Their son Harry is Noah's friend.'

Rachel is casual in skinny jeans and a relaxed white shirt and Ava's initial impression is positive. When Rachel steps forward, Ava can see that her eyes are glassy. She prepares herself for a hectic Meredith-style onslaught but Rachel gives her a warm smile and says, 'So good to see you, Ava.'

Before the parents decide to assault Ava all at once, Tom ushers her to the side and says, 'Let's find a place to sit on the grass before you're totally under siege.'

Rachel offers them a spot on her picnic rug and Ava is grateful to sit while Tom and Jeff stand behind, chatting about their latest cases before drifting into football territory.

The teachers round up the children into some kind of order, spreading them around the various activities, while the parents watch and cheer for their mini athletes from the sidelines. Ava notices that Meredith maintains the same enthusiasm level and is cheering for Zephyr with consistent vigour.

'So that kid's name is *Zephyr*?' Ava asks Rachel in a hushed tone.

'Yep, as in, "a light breeze". That kid is more like a hurricane though.' Rachel pops up her eyebrow and Ava lets a little laugh escape.

'I'm glad you're here today. I needed someone to roll my eyes with.' Rachel smiles, leaning back to rest on her elbows.

'I'm out of my depth. They'll all be rolling their eyes at me.' Ava squirms a little.

'Let them roll. The Ava I know wouldn't care all that much anyway.' Ava is reassured by Rachel's candour and is relieved to have an ally out here in the wild.

Ava observes the gaggle of parents clustered to their left, occasionally stealing glances her way but making a concerted effort not to stare.

'Why are they avoiding me like I'm some kind of leper?'

Rachel glances behind them, making sure Tom isn't listening, before saying, 'Tom sent a message to the WhatsApp group. He gave everyone a heads up on your injuries and asked people to go easy today. Thought it might be overwhelming.'

Ava doesn't know if she's annoyed or grateful that Tom is smoothing the path of recovery for her. It's all very curated and she's a bit peeved that he thinks she can't handle this.

Firstly, though, she needs to catch up. She asks Rachel to show her what WhatsApp is and how to use it. Once she locates the kindergarten chat group, she flicks through reams of messages ranging from reminders about book week costumes, bake sale reminders, birthday party invitations and the random chit-chat in between. Her own participation in the group is consistent but not overbearing. Her own primary school boasted one weekly newsletter that always ended up crumpled and forgotten at the bottom of her school bag. Constant communication with everyone about every*thing* is obviously king now. Rachel shows her how to turn notifications on and off if the need should arise, the undertone being that it definitely will.

The sports tournament finishes with a brief medal presentation, and Noah beams at her as she claps along with the throng of parents. Once the teachers corral them into an orderly line, Noah waves a confident goodbye and trots off, happy, holding hands with Harry.

Tom walks away out of earshot to take a call while Ava helps Rachel fold up the picnic rug. She can see him rubbing his temple and he looks pained. He walks back over as they finish packing up.

'I've got to get into the office, everyone's panicked about

tomorrow,' he says.

'I can drop you home, Ava, if you like?' Rachel interjects with her breezy offer.

Ava smiles in agreement and Tom gives her a quick look, making sure she's okay for him to leave. He promises to pick Noah up on his way home and gives her shoulder a squeeze goodbye before he departs. To her surprise, her stomach falls a little as he leaves, but she's determined to show him that she can manage by herself.

Rachel suggests they stop for a coffee and Ava is more than grateful for the offer. She still can't work the machine at home, despite Tom's tutelage, and has been thinking about her next caffeine hit for the past hour. She's realising that watching kids get tired is exhausting stuff.

Rachel takes them to a nearby café with a small outdoor courtyard dotted with pots of painted wooden sunflowers set amongst lush greenery. It's bright and fun and Ava likes the non-pretentious vibe straight away. They order and Ava lets out an audible sigh as she leans back in her seat.

'You were great this morning. That must have been weird,' Rachel says. There's no trace of condescension in her voice.

'There's not a lot that isn't weird at the moment.'

Rachel leans forward, resting her elbows on the table and her chin on her hands. 'Are you alright? I mean, are you *really* alright?'

Ava swallows down the lump in her throat. The genuine concern from Rachel today and Jane yesterday is confronting. These women know her better than she knows herself right now. It's all become too much to shoulder alone and she decides she needs to trust someone that has at least some objectivity. Someone who didn't know her *before*.

'Not really, no.' Ava pauses and Rachel lets her take her time without needing to fill the silence. 'Tom is trying so hard and being supportive and kind. But… I don't feel what I'm meant to feel.' Ava scrunches her face up as though she's licked an unpleasant ice cream flavour.

'I totally understand. If someone had dumped me into my current life ten years ago, I wouldn't have recognised myself either.' Rachel reaches across the table and gives Ava's hand a little squeeze.

Rachel's insight validates her own reservations. It is an unrecognisable life.

'I didn't want to have kids… well, not ten years ago anyway. Being a mother is a big shock. Even though Noah is a great kid.' Ava shrugs, wishing she could summon more warmth for Noah.

'Yeah, I remember you saying that years ago,' Rachel says.

'Have we been friends a long time?' Ava asks.

'We met at mothers' group when the boys were one month old, and I guess we kind of bonded over not quite fitting the mould somehow. Not around here, anyway. I was still entrenched in corporate life, same as you, and we weren't overly maternal. I don't want to say *accident* but neither of us exactly planned our pregnancies,' Rachel explains.

'You're a lawyer?'

'Accountant. I do freelance consulting now, which I fit in around Harry's stuff. Jeff's a lawyer, partner at Roberts & Fritch.'

'No wonder we're all friends.' Ava smiles.

'You, Tom and Jeff are a real pain in the arse once you get going thrashing out case details.' She laughs, takes a sip of coffee, and continues. 'I guess what I'm saying, though, is it never came naturally for us. This life.'

Ava can tell Rachel has made her own sacrifices for motherhood and wonders if the two of them are the exception or the rule.

'Why did I give up my career?' Ava asks.

'We both tried to go back to work around the same time but the hours were crushing. I think you just hated not being able to do it all. Then after losing the baby, you just wanted to be with Noah.' Rachel sips her coffee.

'What baby?' Ava gives her a blank look.

'… oh God,' Rachel says in a small voice. 'I thought they would have told you. You should probably ask Tom.'

Ava raises an eyebrow at her and Rachel takes a deep breath and continues.

'Two years ago, you lost a baby – a little girl – at twenty-five weeks. Violet. You named her Violet.' Rachel's eyes well up with tears but Ava can't match her emotion. She understands the sadness but her memory loss protects her from it being anything more personal. As if it only happened on the pages of a book. Rachel brushes her hand over her eyes and goes on, 'Ava, are you sure you want me to be the one to tell you about this?'

'Yes.' Ava would prefer that Rachel tell her, not wanting the pressure to react in a certain way for Tom.

'You were obviously very fragile. Losing Violet was awful, but you also had an emergency hysterectomy due to blood loss. They had to do it to save your life. You were grieving one baby as well as any future babies.' Rachel reaches into her bag and fumbles for a tissue.

All the hypothetical babies she could have had with Seb, the ones that she wasn't sure she wanted, are gone. That picture of a family with him is gone. Seb can't be the father of her children and that's what hurts the most. Ava swallows hard and pushes her sunglasses down over her eyes.

'I'm sorry, Ava. I can't believe my big, stupid mouth. Tom will never forgive me.'

'It's okay. Thank you for telling me,' Ava manages.

There is some minor relief with this new information. At least she can now blame grief for making her abandon her career, which somehow makes more sense.

She also doesn't have to pretend to want any more children. Noah will be the extent of her mothering career, though she can't yet tell if he's the linchpin in her new life or the wedge.

~

When Ava gets home to the empty house, she's flooded with relief. Being allowed to exist alone in this space is calming, and with nobody watching her or asking her if she's alright, she can finally breathe properly. Although it's foreign, she likes the house. The neutral palate and pops of tasteful art are exactly what she would have picked. The furniture is sleek, yet comfortable, and the careful addition of oversized rugs and soft lighting illustrate that nothing is accidental here. Black and white photos are mounted throughout, providing a constant reminder of a passage of time she didn't get to walk through. Snippets of the past are, of course, peppered throughout the home via her travel knick-knacks and old photographs, but they're out of context and re-imagined in this grown-up vignette. Stopping to look at her and Tom's wedding photo that sits proud on a walnut end-table in the corner of the lounge room, she runs her finger along the edge of the frame. They're looking at each other rather than the camera, and her hands reach up to rest loosely around his neck. Their faces are young and glowing. The pain of not remembering is persistent. Nowhere is safe to be and everything she looks at is a reminder of what isn't real anymore.

The ringing of her phone breaks into her thoughts and she goes over to her bag to fish it out. Freya's name flashes on the screen.

'Hey,' Ava answers.

'Hi, how are you feeling today?' Freya's voice is perky as usual.

'I'm good. Are you alright? I've been worried that you hate me. Or hated me. Or something…'

'I told you, it's fine. I don't hate you, never hated you. Well, except when I was thirteen and you wouldn't let me borrow your clothes.' Freya seems light and Ava is relieved.

'You took whatever you wanted regardless,' Ava deadpans.

'Yeah well, then you became a lawyer and wore suits, so the urge went away eventually.'

'You took some jeans out of my wardrobe yesterday!'

They laugh together and Ava asks, 'Are we okay?'

'Yes, of course. I'm just calling to see how you went at the sports thing today.'

'Did Tom tell you to ring and check on me because he's worried and he didn't want to do it himself in case I thought he was being overprotective?'

'No,' Freya says in an exaggerated fashion that Ava takes as a *yes*.

'It was good. I think I made one friend. Rachel.'

'Rachel is your best mate. She's awesome, I love her.'

Ava's relieved that it was okay to relax for Rachel and finds an inkling of trust for her new self.

'Yeah, it was easy to talk to her. I miss talking to my friends. I tried calling Sarah but she hasn't got back to me yet.'

'Oh yeah, Sarah. You guys lost touch a bit when she moved to Sydney. I think you may have visited a couple of times but it wasn't the same, too far away.' Freya's voice is vague.

'We were so close,' Ava mumbles, pondering the demise of their friendship.

'Kids. I barely see any old friends these days. Anyway, I have to get moving to my next class. Glad you're okay. I'll come over Friday and we can take the kids to the park.'

They hang up and Ava cradles her phone in her hand. Her past has been literally reframed on these walls and she's desperate to dig up old memories. She scrolls through her phone contacts to find Sarah's number and tries calling it again.

~

Ava is curled up under a blanket watching TV when Tom finally emerges from the study where he was working for most of the evening. He plonks himself next to Ava on the couch, clearly exhausted.

'Long day?' she asks and he smiles, rubbing his eyes.

'What about you? How was your day?' He turns to look at her.

'Pretty good. It was nice to have Rachel to talk to. I do have to tell you something though.'

'What?' Tom's concern is immediate.

'Rachel told me about Violet and the hysterectomy. She didn't mean to. She didn't realise that I didn't know.'

She lets Violet's name sit between them, hoping that Tom won't be too crushed.

Tom rubs his head and says, 'I'm sorry. I wanted to tell you but

I'd given you enough terrible news. I couldn't find the right time…'

'It's okay, I understand. I just wanted you to know that I know. And I wanted to ask if you're okay. I'm sure it was a horrible time.' It occurs to her this is the first time she's bothered to ask Tom if he's okay.

He swallows hard and seems to weigh up his answer before his face sinks a little.

'It was the worst thing that's ever happened in my life. Well, with nearly losing you in the car accident, also right up there.' The wound seems closed enough that Tom can talk about it, but his eyes look dull. 'You nearly died after Violet was born. She was stillborn and you were rushed to the theatre straight away. I sat in a room for about an hour waiting for them to tell me if you were alive or not.'

Sorrow is etched on his face. No wonder he treats her like she's fragile. She is.

'I'm sorry you had to go through that.' Ava's cheeks are wet with tears and Tom guides her into his arms.

'All I cared about was that you were okay. We had already lost the baby, I couldn't lose you too.'

Lost the baby. The phrase rattles in her mind. It seems far too trivial a way to describe it.

'Are you sad that I can't have any more children?' Ava whispers, a little bit afraid of the answer.

'We made peace with it. You and Noah are enough for me. More than enough.' He kisses the top of her head where it's pressed against his chest. 'Are you sad you can't have more?' he asks her.

She can't tell him the truth. That Noah would be easier to love if he were Seb's child. That the loss of her career wouldn't sting as much if she was in Seb's arms now. That more children with Seb might be okay, but any children with Tom are inconceivable.

'I'm not sure what I feel.' She stays vague to avoid the truth.

Tom gently rubs her arm while they sit in this ambiguous emotional landscape. Tom eventually asks, 'Do you want to see her?' which prompts Ava to jerk her head to look at him.

'We have a photo album,' he explains. 'The hospital had a photographer take some photos of her and us together before they took...' he stops, unable to go on.

Ava nods through hot eyes and Tom goes and retrieves a small white book from the cabinet off to the side of the room. He hands it to her before sitting back down. The front of the book reads *Violet Grace 24~07~2016*, in soft pink letters. The pages are filled with beautiful shots capturing the tiniest baby that she's ever seen. There are images of perfectly-formed fingers and toes and a face that resembles a sleeping doll. The photo on the last page of the book makes her catch her breath. Violet is wrapped in a white knitted blanket, cradled in Ava's arms, with a toddler-sized Noah on Tom's lap next to them. They're all smiling for the camera. Looking at herself, she sees the forced smile and the agonised eyes. The loss. But it's pain that doesn't quite belong to her. Next to her, Tom rubs at his tear-streaked eyes; witnessing her friend in pain is what hurts. She wraps her arms around him and they hold onto each other in a mix of confusing comfort.

EIGHT

THE comfortable couch in Kelly Anderson's Brighton office is a joy for Ava to sink into, and a far cry from their initial meeting in the sad hospital consulting room. The whole room is inviting and plush and Kelly sits opposite her on a black leather Eames recliner, notebook on her lap, looking poised to psychoanalyse. Verdant plants are carefully positioned around the room in vibrant coloured pots and Ava finds herself wondering who waters them, as if it's a thing that matters to her. The whole space pays homage to every movie-scene therapy session that Ava can conjure. She uses the room as a tool for her brain to think about other things, thus avoiding what she's afraid to say. Her darkest thoughts about her life are safe if they're only in her head. Kelly won't let her cop out, though, and once they skirt around pleasantries and general *how are you coping?* questions, she homes in on Ava's soft spots.

'How does it feel to be a mother?' Kelly asks and Ava lets in a sharp breath. She doesn't know how to answer the question given that she's feeling a myriad of things, none of which seem like definitive therapy-worthy answers. Her obvious discomfort prompts Kelly to follow up with, 'There are no right or wrong answers,' which doesn't make Ava feel better. She's afraid of the truth and what it could mean.

'I feel like a visitor at home. Like I don't know where anything is or what I should be doing with Noah.' Ava shrugs as she lobs the information to Kelly.

'You can't be expected to know things. It will take time. We can work on some strategies here for you, and Tom could come to a session, if you like?'

The thought of Tom being in therapy with her, seeing her so exposed, makes her heart sink. He'll see through any façade. She's not ready for that kind of intimacy with him.

'I'm just sad. About the end of my marriage and losing my mother. It's not Tom's fault, but he's not my…' Ava trails off.

'Husband?'

Ava shrugs.

Tom is, of course, behaving like a doting husband. He asks her thoughtful questions and listens to the answers. He cooks meals and organises groceries. He drives her to appointments and helps her manoeuvre herself in and out of the car. He's respectful of her boundaries and has been firmly ensconced in the guest room. He's taken the lead on parenting Noah, which she concedes is a necessity given that she's a novice. He acts, for all intents and purposes, like a husband.

'He's my friend. That's the Tom I remember,' Ava says while Kelly scribbles a note.

'Why not be his friend then? Less pressure than husband. Just work on that for now,' Kelly suggests.

Despite her preconceptions that therapy is some kind of indulgent waste of her time, Ava agrees this is a good idea. Tom was one of her best friends. They'd often meet for a casual lunch or drink after work without subtext or awkward innuendo. She'd seen him pass out underneath her and Seb's dying Christmas tree one New Year's Eve. He'd picked her up from the airport when Seb was working. They'd laughed together, cried together, teased each other, supported each other. They were a family. The three of them. She's not sure if she and Tom can be a family without Seb, or if she even wants them to be, but she is sure she doesn't want to lose her friend.

~

Ava is happy to walk the short distance home after her therapy session. Rachel had taken Noah to a special dinosaur exhibition at the museum with Harry, so Ava seizes the opportunity to make the most of her morning alone.

Her local café is en route to home and she sits in the corner next to a window, close to the entrance. The hum of the coffee machine and the clinking of plates and general kitchen noises drown out the muffled conversations happening around her. She has an ulterior motive too – and he's due to walk through the door at any moment. This is meant to be for Freya, but all she really wants is an excuse to see him again.

Seb walks through the café door and tilts his black Ray-Bans up onto his head before spotting Ava at the nearby table. He's wearing a suit but he still looks cool, as if he somehow sits above all other corporate clones, privy to something that's elusive for most. He flashes a half-hearted smile as he slides into the chair opposite her, the scent of him wafting across the table and igniting all the wrong memories.

'Twice in one week. Not something I thought I'd ever say.' He raises a quizzical eyebrow as he leans back in the chair, waiting for Ava to show her hand. Before she can respond, a bouncy waitress appears to take their order. They each order a coffee and Seb points to a pastry in the display window across the room as an afterthought before she disappears back behind the counter.

'What's up?' he prods.

'Freya's trust – I'm about to unwind it for her. I have some questions.'

He flicks his eyebrows up in way that has always irritated her. It's as if he's fifteen, trying to dodge a conversation with his mother. It's one of many behaviours she would make concessions for due to the fact that she thought he was sexy. She still does, of course, which is also irritating, but for different reasons. Deciding to ignore him, she carries on with her questions.

'I'm going to get Tom to file all the paperwork. I'm not asking you to do anything. But I need to know – why?'

'Why what?'

'Why did you set it up for Mum? And why didn't you tell me about it?'

'Because Luci came to me and asked me what I thought she should do. She wanted to help Freya, who, if you recall, was making some pretty terrible decisions back then. She wanted to gift her money to get her into rehab or help her buy a house or something. I set up the trust as a backup first, then we were going to sort out the other stuff. But she died before we could do that.' Seb's eyes turn sad.

'Why didn't you tell me?'

'I was trying to protect you. You can't be objective when it comes to Freya, you know that.' He takes her hand across the table and the warmth from his fingers runs through her.

'Freya was hurt. She thought *I* hurt her.'

'Freya hurts herself all on her own.'

'What does that mean?' Ava's defences prick up.

'She always wants saving. And you always save her.' He shrugs, taking his hand back.

The waitress arrives and deposits their coffees, wordless but with a broad smile, and Ava sits back in her chair and lets his words land on her. Is he right? Does she always save Freya? Freya was never linear like everyone else. She was free and easy-going in a way that Ava was sometimes jealous of. Responsibility eluded her, and maybe Ava stepped in occasionally to help her little sister but that's hardly *saving* her.

'I thought… I thought you loved her like I did.' Ava mines her memories, hunting for evidence that Seb is wrong.

'Nobody could love Freya like you.' He takes a big bite out of his custard tart.

'I don't know what's real anymore,' she says, half to herself. 'I can't remember a huge chunk of my life and what I can remember seems like it's wrong.'

'Sometimes people remember what they want to remember.'

'Do you think I'm *choosing* this?'

'No. I'm saying memory is unreliable at the best of times. You know this, Ava. That's why eyewitness testimony is usually as useful as a bag of dicks.' He shovels the rest of the pastry into his mouth and drains his espresso. He seems different today in a way that she can't quite pinpoint. He's aloof, or he's trying to be.

She lets a sigh of resignation escape her lips, knowing he's right and that rehashing the past is futile. She decides to offer up some truth and see what happens.

'It's nice to see you. I know I'm not supposed to say this to you, but seeing you makes me feel kind of normal, like I can be myself.'

Seb lets out a little laugh and says, 'It's kind of the opposite for me.'

'I'm sorry. I'm *really* sorry that I hurt you.' She's wants to say that to him over and over until he scoops her up into his arms and loves her again.

'It's like you're apologising on someone else's behalf.'

'I am.'

He breathes out a long breath and meets her eyes before talking again. 'We can't do this again.'

'Are you sure?' She does nothing to quell the need in her voice.

'Yes,' he answers quickly. Too quickly, she thinks.

The subtext of what he's really saying is not lost on her but she's not convinced he totally believes it himself. Without speaking, he takes a crisp twenty-dollar note out of his wallet and puts it on the table, then gets up and stands silently for a few seconds, continuing to hold her gaze. He turns and walks out of the café, not looking back, and leaving the door ajar as he goes.

~

For the remainder of her morning, Ava attempts some light gardening to distract herself from the hovering thoughts of Seb. After planting some seedlings that Steve, the gardener, had brought with him, she tries her hand at the coffee machine. With her confidence high after yet another crash course on how to operate it this morning, she makes some for herself and Steve, who is on a pruning frenzy in the backyard. She liked Steve instantly; his casual demeanour and non-intrusive questions put her at ease. He even brought her a new pot plant blooming with bright pink chrysanthemums after hearing she'd been in hospital.

As Ava approaches him in the backyard, he puts down his secateurs to take the hot coffee out of her hands.

'Thanks.' He beams a big smile, showing perfect teeth and a chin dimple before asking, 'Where would you like the magnolias planted? I've got the eight you asked for in my trailer. Sorry about the delay.'

The only magnolia that springs to Ava's mind is the classic movie with Sally Field and Julia Roberts. *Laughter through tears is my favourite emotion* rings unbidden in her mind, complete with a Louisiana drawl.

'Sorry, Steve. I don't know what a magnolia is let alone where I should put one.'

'Oh, sorry, I thought we discussed it a few weeks ago.' He scratches his head.

'No, I'm sure we did. I have amnesia from my accident. There's a lot I can't remember.' It's the understatement of the century, with magnolias the least of her concerns.

There's an awkward silence, both of them unsure what to do next.

'I just can't really return them, given they were a special order.' Steve drops his eyes and scuffs his boot along the ground.

'I'll pay for them, of course,' she catches his drift. 'And I'm happy to plant them... somewhere,' she says with a sweep of an arm around the garden.

Apparently they are 'White Caviar Magnolias', perfect for a hedge, so they agree to have them planted in the front garden, along the fence line, before chatting briefly about the location of a new raised vegetable garden that she'd also apparently asked him to build. Then she leaves him to it, relieved there are no more decisions to make. If she were ten years younger, she'd have probably quite fancied Steve with his chiselled stubbly jaw and big arms in his sweaty work gear. Now that she's older and a suburban mother she feels a bit gross even noticing that he's attractive. Her new brain hasn't quite caught up with the fact that she's middle-aged now and she still shocks herself when she catches her aged face in a mirror. She goes hunting for some chips in the pantry to boost her mood but all she can find is a packet of "lightly salted kale chips", which taste about as good as a dry ball sack. Whoever had the audacity to call them "chips" should be fired.

The doorbell interrupts her lame snack and Ava lets Rachel in. Noah and Harry bubble around them with excited energy, high from their dinosaur encounter. Noah can barely catch his breath as he relays what they saw and how big a diplodocus is in real life and asks if she knew that a T-Rex mouth could crush a car, if cars had been around then. Ava manages to corral them into the dining room as the dinosaur facts swirl around and the air is peppered with little boy laughter. Then, as quickly as they bustled in, they run out the back door, heading for the trampoline.

'Christ, they're a lot, aren't they?' Rachel is smiling but the sentiment is real. Ava smiles back at her presuming this is a rhetorical question.

'Thanks for taking Noah with you, I'm pretty sure you've blown his little mind.'

'He was no trouble. They had a ball. Also, I let them have an icy-pole on the way out; sorry if I've overdone the sugar.'

'Am I uptight about that stuff? Is he not allowed junk food?'

'Oh no, you're normal. You use bribes like the rest of us. You're way better at making homemade snacks than me, though. Did you have a good morning?'

'Yeah, it was nice. I even did some gardening, which apparently I'm good at.' Ava smiles and shrugs her shoulders.

'You are good at it! Look at this oasis.' Rachel sweeps her arm towards the backyard before changing her expression to serious and lowering her voice. 'Um, also, I feel terrible about telling you all that stuff yesterday. I hope I didn't upset you or Tom too much.'

Rachel looks uncomfortable and Ava thinks back to last night, when she and Tom were wrapped in each other's arms. It was a solid step towards getting their friendship back.

'I'm grateful you told me, and I think Tom is too. I don't think he knew how to break the news.'

Rachel releases her held breath and relaxes a bit.

'I had a coffee with my ex-husband this morning.' Ava blurts out of nowhere.

'Oh wow, the first time you've seen him. How was it? ' Rachel's eyes go wide.

'Well... I actually saw him a few days ago. He came to see me before I left the hospital. I needed to ask him some more questions.' Ava plays it down.

'How was it?'

'Weird. Do you think I need to tell Tom that I saw him?'

'What would you tell him?'

'I have no idea. But I feel guilty.'

'Maybe you *like* Tom?'

'I've loved Tom for years, but not in that way.' Ava pauses to find the right words and goes on. 'When I'm with Seb I feel like I'm betraying Tom, and when I'm with Tom it's like I'm cheating on Seb. I still feel married to him.' Trying to explain it out loud feels odd.

'I don't think you need to tell him.' Rachel waves her arm, nonchalant.

'Seb basically said he can't see me anymore, so there's nothing to tell.' The disappointment of his dismissal still stings.

'Exactly. You're entitled to some privacy in this process – it's a pretty unique situation.'

Letting Rachel's advice settle over her, Ava lets the noise in her head fade out a little. Unloading to Rachel is coming naturally, making space for the things that feel too real for therapy. After chatting yesterday, Ava felt an innate trust in Rachel. It was like the friend version of muscle memory, aided by the fact that a friend softens the edges of misdemeanours in a way that a psychologist never would.

'Oh, before I forget, do you think you could do me a favour?' Ava asks. 'I need some financial statements for a trust prepared. I'd pay you, of course.'

'Happy to do it. Unhappy to be paid to do it.'

'At least let me make you a coffee to say thanks for this morning. I've finally mastered the robot.' Ava winks at her and Rachel laughs, making Ava aware of how much she misses the sound of her own laughter.

~

Tom looks exhausted as he walks into the dining room and Ava knows immediately that it didn't go well in court today. Noah jumps up from the table where he and Ava are in the middle of a dinosaur puzzle and leaps into Tom's arms, instantly softening his tired father. He's patient listening to Noah recount the details of his day, which are largely centred around his visit to the museum and Steve the gardener letting him hold his drill. Noah runs off to find his map of the museum and Tom slumps down on the chair next to Ava, giving her shoulder an affectionate squeeze as he does.

'How was your day, babe?' he asks, and she tries not to notice that he called her *babe*.

'Better than yours by the look of it. It didn't go well?'

'Dismissed. Client is pissed. Tomorrow's meeting with the other partners should be fun.'

'Sorry,' she offers with a head tilt.

'It's not important.' His words don't match his rigid body and she notices that this is the first time he's appeared stressed.

'Are you hungry? Jane dropped us off bolognaise sauce and I even managed to make some spaghetti that was edible. It's still warm on the stove.'

'Thanks. Looks like you're discovering your inner Nigella,' he jokes as he heads over to the stove to dish himself up a bowl.

'I wouldn't go that far, but I tried. Oh, before I forget – I'm going to wind up Freya's trust. I'll write it all up, but can you file it for me?'

'Isn't that for next year?'

'Yeah, but there's a clause in there allowing the trustee to wind up at their discretion. I'm going to do it early, as a surprise.' Ava is adamant.

'Is that a good idea?' His tone implies that it isn't.

'What do you mean?'

He comes back over to the dining table and sits down with his bowl of pasta. He pauses for too long before speaking again.

'Freya is in a pretty good place right now but she's only had her job for a year, Pip is still little, and she's still finding her feet again. I'm worried this might destabilise her.'

'How would being able to buy a house for her and Pip be destabilising?'

'Because you assume that's what she would do with it. And don't forget she's dating "Derek the douchebag".' He uses air quotes to emphasise the nickname.

'Those are my words, I presume?' She grimaces.

'Yep,' he replies with his mouth full.

Ava sighs and rubs the side of her head, which is developing a light throb.

'Maybe Seb's right…' she says without thinking.

'Huh?' Tom jerks his head up and she realises what she's said.

'I, uh, I spoke to him today. I rang him to ask about the trust.' Regret pulses through as she hears herself water down the truth.

Before Tom can respond, Noah bounds back into the room to show Tom his map and guidebook and launches into yet more dinosaur facts. An implicit agreement forms to shelve the discussion for now, and a knot twists in the pit of her stomach for the remainder of the evening as they meander through the bath and bedtime routine. It's only after she finishes reading Noah his bedtime story and comes back downstairs that they have space to talk about Seb, the big fat elephant, who, for Ava, is permanently in the room. Ava sits down on the sofa next to Tom and waits for him to speak.

'I wish you felt like you could talk to me about Seb. You don't have to keep it a secret.' He meets her eyes and he looks hurt. She appreciates the sentiment, but it's not possible to grieve about losing Seb with Tom.

'I saw him. I asked him to come and see me in hospital before I left. And I saw him again this morning so I could ask him about the trust.' Unloading the truth is both better and worse.

'Thanks for telling me.' Tom's tone is genuine and that makes her guiltier.

Ava's still trying to think of something to say when Tom asks, 'How did it feel to see him?'

Her internal battle simmers in her core and she levels her eyes at him to let him see. To let him glimpse her pain. To let him be her friend.

'Awful. It felt awful. I miss him.' She decides that she can't shield herself from Tom; it's too exhausting. Her sorrow is real and it's too tiring to pretend it isn't. So many things are lost – Seb, Luci, Violet and all the memories in between.

He reaches out and takes her hand, rubbing his thumb back and forth over her knuckles in a soft rhythm. His tenderness is instinctive and Ava finds herself liking it, which adds to the mire of her confusion.

'I know what it's like to miss him too. I missed him for a long time. Still do sometimes.' Tom offers his own truth, bridging the great divide a fraction.

There's something in the way Tom delivers that information that prompts her to ask, 'Have you ever told me that? Do we talk about him?'

'No. You were angry with him before you and I… well, before we became *you and I*. It never felt like my place to rummage through the remnants of your marriage. You didn't seem to want to talk about it anyway, and you definitely didn't want to hear me tell you that I missed him. That friendship was the price I paid to have you, and I'd pay it again, tenfold.'

Ava finds Tom's ability not to pry into the details unfathomable. How could Tom not want to know this stuff? How could he not ask her?

'I would have wanted to know all the gory details,' she muses, which makes Tom laugh.

'Oh, I know that for sure.' He smiles at her.

'Why didn't you want to know?'

'It was a complicated time. I didn't want to lose the magic of falling in love with you by talking about Seb.'

Ava's confusion sits adjacent to Tom's devotion. It's sobering.

'I'm sorry I didn't tell you I was going to see him. It felt wrong not to tell you.'

'Did you get what you needed from him?'

Ava can't tell how loaded this question is, but she can sense that Tom might have a fracture in his self-assured armour. She decides it's truth-or-die at this point.

'I don't know what I wanted, it just felt good to see him. I know who I am when I'm with him. Or at least I used to.'

Tom must sense the shift and lets his guard down too.

'You know, I can tell when you're the real you and when you're trying to be the 'new you', you know? I like it when you tell me how you really feel.'

'Does that mean I don't have to learn to cook or do yoga?'

Tom laughs and says, 'See? There you are.' He smiles, gives her hand a little squeeze and continues, 'Ava, I couldn't care less if you cook or do yoga. Just be *you* and we'll figure out the rest as we go along.'

Though she appreciates Tom's blind acceptance of her, she realises she's scared to be herself and live in this life. If she can exist in her new reality, won't that mean her old life is over?

NINE

THE hovering clouds dissipate to reveal warm spring sunshine, which subdues the morning chill. Ava removes her cardigan, willing the sun to thaw her insides. The cuts on her arms have largely healed and the bruising has faded. The physical evidence of trauma is leaving, yet her heart may ache forever. She's determined to make today a good day, though. She leans back into the park bench with Freya next to her, watching Noah and Pip play in the nearby sandpit.

'What a day, hey?' Freya muses, tilting her head back and shutting her eyes.

'You may have underdressed a tad. Got a plumbing job later?' Ava flicks up her eyebrows in jest.

'Excuse me, you rude cow! This is called a *boiler suit* and you know nothing about fashion and you wish you were as cool as me.' Freya pokes her tongue out.

Freya is definitely cooler than she is, though she can't pretend to understand this current outfit: a sage-green boiler suit with a floral panel down the front where the zip goes, cinched at the waist – which she supposes makes it flattering, at least as far as boiler suits go. Freya can't wear jeans and a T-shirt like a normal person; she always has to show off. Also, to Ava's annoyance, Freya pretty much looks good in anything. She's blessed with their mother's long legs and lean frame where Ava has always had to work hard to keep her waist from widening.

'Do you think you could take Noah to swimming on Monday without me? I'm having lunch with Sarah and might not get back in time.'

'Sure. Great that you finally got in touch with her. How is she?' Freya asks, opening her eyes again.

'Yeah, she's good. We only had a quick chat, but she's back living in Melbourne. It was nice to hear a familiar voice.' It felt like home to hear Sarah's voice. Like going back in time, cocooned by the fact that nothing had changed.

'I'm glad. Careful with the spade, Pippy!' Freya yells over to the sandpit.

'They seem to play well together. Do we do this regularly?'

'We usually keep Fridays available to hang out. You like to "expand their minds" at museums or creative play centres, whereas I prefer to go out for breakfast or dump them in the soft play at IKEA.'

'Said the teacher.' Ava smiles, shaking her head.

'I like them to just play and enjoy the company, they're both on their own a fair bit.'

Ava wouldn't have pictured her sister with children but she's clearly a natural.

'Do you want to have more children?' Ava probes.

Freya takes a sip of her soy latte, considering her answer.

'I don't think so. I'm not sure I'm that good at it. Plus, I don't think Derek wants to anyway.'

'Ah yes, the elusive Derek. When will I meet this boyfriend?'

'He wants us to move in together.' Freya fidgets with her sunglasses and wipes them on the leg of her pants.

'You seem... unexcited? Unsure?' Ava guesses.

'It's just... I let it happen, the Derek relationship. He's kind of like the human equivalent of warm milk before bed. Comforting and helps you get to sleep.'

'Wow, sexy.' Ava scrunches up her face.

'Reliable.'

'Also sexy.'

'Regular.'

'Christ, Freya, he sounds like a bowel movement. Is he at least a bit sexy?'

'I've done sexy. I've done dangerous. I've done the tortured artist, full-of-shit dickheads that don't commit or turn up on time, or don't turn up at all. Regular is kind of nice for a change. Not everyone gets a *Tom*.'

This halts Ava, as Freya probably intended, and she takes a slow sip out of her own coffee cup to catch her thoughts.

'I'm sorry. I only want you to be happy.' Ava seeks Freya's eyes.

'I know,' Freya says with a sigh, 'but seriously, what even is that? "Happy"? Like, I'm a thirty-four-year-old single mother, part-time teacher and full-time hot mess. I have a nice-enough man who likes me and buys groceries and doesn't do drugs. Maybe this *is* happiness for me…' Freya slumps down in her chair as if this isn't the first time she's thought this.

'I'm not a happiness expert, but I think maybe you can want more. That it's okay to want more.' Ava gives Freya's hand a little squeeze.

'Wanting more has always left me disappointed,' Freya says as she gets up to help Pip into the swing, then gives her a big push.

Pip's eyes pop as the swing goes up followed by sheer delight and surprise as it swings back down again. Her soft curls blow around as she shrieks with abandon. That's happiness. Somewhere between little girl delight and grown woman disappointment, Freya somehow learnt to expect less and not question why. It's hard to watch her little sister hurting. She can't stand by and let her be miserable. She can help. She *will* help. Seb's words echo in her head. *You always save her.* She wishes his voice would fade. She wishes she could really mean that.

'Who wants to go and get an ice cream?' Ava shouts across the playground and Noah's eyes bulge out of his head as he jumps up and down, shouting, 'Me! Me!'

'Ava! It's nine-thirty in the morning! Who even are you?' Freya shouts back, laughing.

'I'm trying to be happy.'

And she is. She really is.

~

Noah's been doing laps up and down the hallway on his scooter when

Ava hears a thud quickly followed by a retching sound. Springing up from the couch, she races down towards the front door where he's keeled over and covered in vomit. Her thoughts race as she tries not to panic. She hates vomit. The smell alone is making her queasy. She knows she'll have to clean this up with Tom not yet back from a meeting, but she can't bear to touch him. Noah starts to weep in his puddle of sick and she manages to pat his back a little while maintaining an arm's distance from the muck on the floor. The last time she had to clean up someone else's vomit was when Seb had too many Jägerbomb shots on a buck's night and threw up all over himself in their bed. Her solution was to throw the bedding out and buy new stuff, and she didn't speak to him for the whole of the next day. Knowing that's not an option here, she somehow corrals Noah into the downstairs bathroom, leaving a trail of sick in their wake.

She puts him into the shower fully dressed, hoping to wash off most of it before undressing him. She pumps the water on at full pace and Noah screams out, furious, 'Mummy, it's *cold!*' She is frantic at the tap to adjust the temperature whilst he continues to scream and writhe around under the spray. She tries not to retch as a mix of water and vomit splatters onto her cashmere sweater and face. Whilst trying to coax Noah's T-shirt over his head without touching him too much, Jane appears behind her.

'Oh, darlings, what's happened?' Jane steps forward next to Ava, assuring her that she will handle it, and sends her upstairs to change. Grateful, Ava steps over the remnants of vomit on the floor and heads up to her bedroom. Is motherhood always this gross? Her stomach isn't strong enough for the unpredictability and she doesn't know how she's going to do this. She throws her sweater into the laundry hamper and washes her face and hands, getting the water as hot as she can tolerate. She takes her time picking a new top, cowering in her room, so she doesn't have to go back down and face the clean-up. Eventually, she steels herself and heads back downstairs. Jane is talking to someone in the laundry and although it's hushed, she can hear one side of the conversation. 'Yes, darling, I know that but she's not ready for this, it's too much… you're not being fair to either of them.'

Not wanting to hear any more of the truth, Ava clears her throat, making herself conspicuous, and goes to the sink to fill up a glass of water. Jane flicks on the washing machine before coming back out to the kitchen.

'I'm sorry, pet, I didn't mean for you to hear that.' Jane looks away, embarrassed.

'No, I'm sorry. Thank you for stepping in, I was useless. You're right, I'm not ready for this. I don't know what I'm doing.' Ava's throat tightens admitting to her own incompetence.

Jane steps forward and wraps Ava into her arms like she's a child. Ava wishes her own mother were here to teach her how to do this. How to be selfless. How to manage the spot fires of parenting. How to be a mother.

'Nobody knows what they're doing, you know? We all just make it up as we go,' Jane whispers in her ear.

Ava knows she means to be comforting, but the thought of no roadmap – no clear instructions for a lifelong job of service, with someone's actual life on the line – makes her more terrified. Although reluctant, she lets Jane go and has a gulp of water to recalibrate.

'Is he okay?' Ava asks, guilty that she didn't ask sooner.

'Of course. Poor little poppet probably ate a bit too much before whizzing around.'

'I bought him an ice-cream earlier…' Ava's guilt intensifies.

Jane shrugs and says, 'These things happen. He threw up in my car last year and I considered setting it on fire to get rid of the smell. This one wiped up easily. Most things are fixable, darling.'

Most things. Not her memory, though. Not her life.

While Jane busies herself in the kitchen, Ava goes over to join Noah on the couch. He's wrapped in a blanket, an empty bucket perched next to him. He wriggles in close against her body without taking his eyes off the television. Their breathing falls into a relaxed synchronicity and she lifts her arm up so that Noah can burrow into her. It's the biggest lesson she's been able to glean so far: proximity is important. Perhaps even the most important thing.

~

The last slice of warm afternoon light hits the dining table as Ava sifts through some of the magazines Jane brought over. The jolt of her iPhone vibrating to life steals her attention.

Meredith: *Ava! 'Lacy Luxe' party tomorrow night at my house. Bubbles and nibbles provided, just bring your credit card! M x*

Ava reads the text twice, hoping it will make more sense the second time, but it doesn't. Is this a party she agreed to before the accident and Meredith hasn't quite grasped the reality of her brain injury? She almost wonders if Meredith has had a brain injury herself, but mostly she wonders what the hell *Lacy Luxe* is.

She's still trying to unmuddle her thoughts when another text arrives.

Rachel: *FYI, I'm not going to M's lingerie party*
Ava: *I was wondering what 'Lacy Luxe' was!*
Rachel: *Polyester undies for women with no imagination*
Ava: *LOL*
Rachel: *Coffee Monday after kinder drop off?*
Ava: *Yes :-)*
Rachel: *Remind me to teach you about emojis*
Ava: *????*

Rachel then sends a barrage of little pictures, mostly faces and animals, some vegetables and other random things including a bus and a cricket bat. Ava figures this is another fad that's come along during her memory fog and adds it to her mental list of stuff to learn in order to assimilate into the current decade.

Her phone pings again.

Rachel: *Here's the insta page for Lacy Luxe, FYI.*

Rachel sends a hyperlink and signs off with a yellow kissy face. Ava cements her resolve to master these *emojis*, which seem to be part of the modern vernacular now. The enormity of all the unknown things is overwhelming. Jane is in the kitchen making dinner with Noah and must overhear her sighing into her phone.

'You alright, pet?' Jane asks.

'Do you know how to use "emojis"? Or what "insta" is?' Ava asks, plonking herself on a stool.

'The Instagram is for young people, but I like the little emoji faces, I can show you those.'

Jane fishes her phone out of her handbag and points to a little smiley face button, unlocking a smorgasbord of tiny pictures that are apparently for when words are not enough, or maybe for when they're too much. Jane seems to favour a laughing/crying face, which means something is very funny, or – if the face is on an angle – that it's really hilarious.

'Some of these are weird,' Ava says scrolling though, baffled by the vast choices from food items to transport and an inordinate amount of monkeys.

'Don't worry, pet, you'll get the hang of it. You were the one who taught me, after all. Tom is impatient with me; children are mean to their own parents.' Jane smiles as she says it but Ava is immediately transported to trying to teach her own mother how to use her new email address. Finding Luci's lack of technical aptitude tedious, she was impatient and rude. Now she'd give anything to go back just for a moment with her.

Ava's eyes betray her, prompting Jane to ask, 'Something I said?'

'I wasn't very nice to Mum when teaching her techy things.'

'Oh, darling, I'm sorry. I shouldn't have said that,' Jane admonishes herself.

'No, it's okay. I just miss her.' It's the first time she's said it aloud without bursting into tears. The hurt is beginning to sit beside her.

'Of course you do.' Jane pats her hand a couple of times in a sort of acknowledgement that someone else's mother is a poor substitute for her own dead one.

'What are you making, Noah?' Ava turns her attention further down the bench where Noah is standing on a wooden step-stool. There is flour everywhere.

'Nocki!' he shouts back at her, smiling with flour on his nose.

'No-no is my chief gnocchi roller,' Jane says, ruffling his hair.

'It's like living in a restaurant.' Ava smiles.

'*You* taught *me*, pet,' Jane says, smiling, while Ava's face contorts to confusion and she shakes her head in quiet disbelief.

How did she become a person who could make gnocchi from scratch? She doesn't even know how to cook it out of a packet. It's something she loved to order at her favourite Italian restaurant, where the tablecloths were red gingham and the lighting was low, fairy lights strung up all over the walls. It was *their* place. It was a private pasta oasis in a busy life where they went to be together. She read that it recently burnt down, and now she's standing in the ashes.

To get a little breathing space, she leaves Jane in charge and goes upstairs to run a bath. The afternoons have become long and her aching muscles seem to wear out if she doesn't rest. Having a rambunctious four-year-old exacerbates her fatigue, making her further question how she's ever going to be any good at this. Her new self seems to be everything to everyone, an unfathomable transformation. In her own head, she's too selfish. If she's honest, she *wants* to be. She wants to be greedy with her own time, and whilst that seems to be somewhat possible in this grace period her family is allowing her, the expectation is building. They want her back. They want her to be *better*.

Supine in the bath with water lapping around her, calm escapes Ava. A tide of building anxiety rises from the pit of her stomach and squeezes her chest. Her lungs are all of a sudden unsatisfied with every new breath and she is claustrophobic within her own body. She gets out of the water to stop the drowning sensation and tries to catch her breath. She's wrapped in a towel, kneeling face down on the bathmat, when a soft tap on the door jolts her panicked thoughts.

'Ava? It's me,' Tom's muffled voice says through the closed door. 'You okay?'

'No,' she replies in a meek voice.

'Can I come in?' he asks.

'Yes.'

Overcome and spent, she lets him see her brokenness.

Tom grabs another towel and drops to his knees to wrap it around her shoulders, then braces his arms around her to quell her trembling body.

'Are you hurt?' he asks.

'No. I just... I can't breathe...'

'Okay, don't talk. Try and take slow breaths, I'll do it with you.'

Tom stays calm, and soon her breath falls in step with his and her heart stops exploding out of her chest. She's unable to tell if it's been seconds or minutes that they've sat on the bathroom floor, but she can finally feel her lungs fill again and doesn't want to break the spell by moving.

'Is that a bit better?' he asks.

'Yes.'

'I think you might have had an anxiety attack.'

'I don't know. I've never had one before.'

'Actually, you've had a few. Mostly after Violet, but you haven't had one for ages.'

She sits up to look at him, gripping the towel around her chest.

'Thank you for helping me,' she says.

His eyes look hurt in that moment and she worries she's said the wrong thing.

'What?' she asks.

'You keep thanking me for the most basic things I do for you. You've... forgotten me.' His eyes turn glassy and it's clear she's not the only broken one on display, sitting on the cold bathroom tiles.

She knows that he isn't being cruel – it's a statement of fact beyond Ava's control – but that doesn't stop the shame dripping off her.

'Sorry,' is all she can muster through hot, wet eyes.

He shakes his head through his own tears and they cry together, knowing the truth and hurting themselves with it. Who they were is gone. A pile of rubble where a bridge once stood.

'I'm going to see if Mum can take Noah for a sleepover tonight.

I think we need to have some time alone.'

She nods but can't seem to stop her tears.

~

It's dark outside when Ava and Tom finally get a chance to talk. The barely-touched homemade gnocchi has been relegated to Tupperware containers in the fridge and the house is quiet but for the background hum of the dishwasher. Ava is cross-legged on the edge of the big sofa and Tom chooses the armchair under the beige lamp. He looks quite beautiful under the soft light, his sharp yet delicate features punctuated with sad eyes. He's stopped trying to hide those eyes from her and it hurts her more than she would have expected. She's pretty certain she'll cry again if she tries to speak, so she waits, letting him go first.

'I think we may have tried to run before we could walk. It wasn't fair to expect you to come home and slip back into life. I was… hoping for a miracle, I guess,' he says.

'I think I was too. I hoped memories might flood back, but it's been harder than I thought,' she admits.

'I want to get you some more help, to take the pressure off. Give you some time.'

'Okay.'

'Mum can help us more if you're comfortable with that?'

Ava nods, knowing Jane does a better job than she does anyway. If Luci can't be here to teach her how to be a mother, maybe Jane can. Ava feels like she's set down a load of baggage, but remains heavy. She knows the other barrier they're facing isn't quite so fixable, and Tom appears to be searching for the right words.

He clears his throat, 'Also… you and me. I know you're not comfortable with me yet…'

'Tom, it's not that—'

'Ava, please,' he interrupts her with an imploring hand and she goes quiet.

'I know I'm not Seb. Which is ironic because that's one of the things you liked best about me.' He lets himself joke and it diffuses some tension.

'I want to go back a few steps and try and make this new for both of us. Maybe take you out on a date? If you'd like?'

He looks like a teenager, tentative and a bit sweaty. She finds his vulnerability disarming.

'Well, I'd have to check my calendar...' She smiles at him but he still looks nervous.

'How about tomorrow night? If you're free, of course.' he asks, faking confidence.

'I'd like that.'

His shoulders deflate and it's reassuring to see this side of him. She thought she was the only one who was unsure and nervous all the time. After watching Tom being unflappable most of the time, it's hard for her to pinpoint exactly what his flaw is. Ava unashamedly wears her flaws as armour, insofar as they can be considered flaws at all. Workaholic. Selfish. Blindly ambitious. If she were a man, these attributes would be assets. She keeps searching for the broken bits of Tom, knowing he can't stay perfect forever.

TEN

AN ideal Saturday morning used to consist of languid hours in bed followed by brunch that could last well into the afternoon. Instead, Ava is clad in Lycra, lying on a rubber mat next to Rachel in a light-filled studio. She agreed to Rachel's invitation this morning in an attempt to regain some kind of routine in her life and also to distract herself from the nerves about her date with Tom. As soft rainforest music plays in the background, she remains unconvinced that this is the best way to do it. The room is full of women about her age and, whilst Rachel assured her this wasn't a yoga class, her scepticism swells when the teacher introduces herself as *Fern*. Fern welcomes them to "Bliss Body Studio" and encourages them to "find their centre" before she begins, which prompts Ava to roll her eyes at Rachel, who just smiles and shuts her eyes, presumably in search of her own centre. The class turns out to be mostly long stretches and deep breathing with some goal visualisation and "bliss moments" thrown in for good measure.

Despite her initial reservations, she finds Fern's sporadic monologue soothing, and the experience isn't totally unpleasant. As the class progresses and she contorts herself into various stretch positions, she's aware of how unfamiliar her own body is. Time has rendered it stiff yet wobbly in a way that's rude and unsolicited. It's certainly not feeling like a "bliss body", not that Ava knows what that would entail anyway. It sounds more fitting for someone deep in the throes of an orgasm. Something in her stomach flips as she skims over that brief sexual thought. She hasn't been game to think about sex at all, but her desire is certainly not dead, only lurking. She won't let herself think about sex with Seb because it was good and she doesn't want to dwell on just *how good*. She also can't think about sex with Tom because that's still forbidden, even though she decides he'd probably be good at it too, which leaves her in a quite literal no man's land. Before she can mull over her lack of sex in any more depth, Fern thanks them for "sharing their energies" and invites them to "carry their bliss throughout their day".

The throng of women roll up their mats and stack them by the door as they head out.

'Brunch?' Rachel asks.

'Ooh, yes please,' Ava replies, optimistic that her life has retained some of its old perks.

The small café a few doors down from the Bliss Body Studio is humming with the easy Saturday morning crowd and they pick a table with a bit of shade.

'So, are you in touch with your "bliss body"?' Rachel asks with a smile, and Ava rolls her eyes at her.

'I don't think you get a bliss body over thirty-five.'

Rachel laughs in agreement, 'I just like to get out of the house for a couple of hours by myself and let Jeff take over on the weekend.'

'Fair enough. Now, I need your help,' Ava says in a serious tone.

'With what?' Rachel matches her tone with concern.

'I have a date with Tom tonight and I haven't been on a date in a million years.' Ava grimaces.

Rachel laughs, 'Christ, you're too serious! I thought you wanted me to hide a body with you.'

'Would you have?' Ava deadpans.

'Absolutely,' Rachel replies, without hesitating.

'Good to know.'

'You know, I haven't been on a date in a million years either. I'm not sure I'm going to be very helpful.' Rachel frowns.

'Well, I'm nervous. Really nervous.'

'That's probably a good sign. If you didn't care you wouldn't be nervous,' Rachel offers.

It is a pretty high-stakes date. The dates of her past were mostly awkward dudes fumbling with her bra hooks after cheap dinners. Even she and Seb didn't really date. They hooked up after a few boozy uni events and kind of fell into a relationship. Maybe things can be different with Tom. A beginning that's not comparable to Seb. Something new.

'Okay,' Rachel switches gears, 'how would you have normally prepared for a date?'

'Obsess over it all day until I was so strung out I could barely eat.' Ava shovels a mouthful of scrambled eggs into her mouth before saying, 'Clearly the latter is a problem I've overcome with age.'

'Well, how about we go for a little shopping trip and get you a new outfit? There's a little boutique not far from here that we like.'

A smile creeps onto Ava's face and she says, 'You're a bad influence, aren't you?'

'I try.' Rachel smiles back at her.

Though it's not quite "bliss", the knowledge that Rachel has her back amidst all the newness is not nothing.

~

Shopping with Rachel turns out to be more fun than Ava had anticipated, and she leaves the shop with two new dresses, a pair of slouchy silk pants, three tops that compliment her new curves and a silver-sequinned bomber jacket that is utterly indulgent and glorious. Her gut twisted as she swiped her credit card to pay the twelve hundred dollars she'd racked up but, as if reading her thoughts, Rachel had whispered, 'This is okay, trust me,' making her relax a little.

Back home in her bedroom, they're behaving like they're seventeen again, trying on clothes and giggling. Rachel helps her work through her wardrobe and try out different combinations to find some looks that she's comfortable with. They gather up four bags of clothes that Ava either doesn't like or don't fit properly. She figures that, at the very least, Freya would like to sift through them, and the rest will be bound for charity.

Ava sits on the large ottoman in the walk-in wardrobe, admiring the new space they've created where she can be at home with clothes that are more her style.

'Thank you for this,' she says in a quiet voice.

'Anytime. I've hung your date night outfit right here so you're good to go,' Rachel says, gesturing at the clothes where they sit limp on their hangers.

'I'm nervous.' Ava flops her head into her hands and takes in a long, slow breath.

'It's going to be fine, you're going to look great. Try to relax. This is Tom. He's not some uni douchebag who works part time and smokes weed on the weekends. It's *Tom*,' she says, expectant for recognition that Ava can't give her.

'That's why I'm nervous. I could deal with some stoner who doesn't know his arse from his elbow, there's nothing at stake.'

'Ava, this is your life. You need to trust yourself. Trust the Ava who made this decision in the first place. You're still the same person.'

She gives a thin smile as Rachel reiterates what Freya and Tom keep telling her. Is she really the same or do they all just wish she was?

Ava flops back onto the ottoman with a resigned sigh and says, 'Oh, fine. But if being myself backfires, I'm blaming you.'

'Duly noted. Now go and have a shower. Your bliss body is all sweaty.'

~

Adding the finishing touches to her makeup, Ava pauses in the unforgiving bathroom light to examine the fading bruises on her face. Makeup has covered up any remnants of visible trauma and for the first time she can see the outline of her old self. Before she can dwell on any imperfections, she hears the doorbell ring, which is weird for this hour on a Saturday. When it rings a second time, she shouts from the landing for Tom to answer it, but he doesn't respond. As she makes her way past the kitchen and towards the hall, flustered, it rings a third time. She shouts 'coming!' then curses the size of the house under her breath.

The thick oak door creaks on its hinges, swinging open to reveal

Tom holding a bunch of lemon-yellow tulips. He's wearing a pale blue checkered shirt with an open collar paired with dark jeans, and she's aware straight away that he looks good. Leaning in close, he gives her the flowers, the scent of woody cologne and fresh shampoo wafting over her.

'Hello there, you,' she says, both touched and a bit self-conscious that he's made such an effort.

'You look… wow. I should have asked you out on a date years ago.' His eyes freely comb over her.

'Oh, this old thing?' She smiles, her cheeks flushing. After agonising with Rachel about which outfit to wear, she picked the black silk trousers with a lacy black top, showing just enough cleavage to reiterate that this is definitely a date.

Tom's entrance breaks the ice and Ava is able to relax a bit as they drive to the beachside restaurant, Mood. It's high end, with careful lighting and plush décor, completed by stunning water views. It is obvious Tom has put thought into the evening. Once they are seated at their table by the window and the waiter disappears, her nerves creep back; they have to sit and look at one another.

'You okay?' he asks.

'Yeah. No. Yes, just… nervous.' She decides truth is the only way with Tom.

He suggests a drink and she responds with an enthusiastic nod. Tom looks up for the waiter, who materialises in prompt, expensive-restaurant fashion. He brings them a bottle of wine and they choose some entrées to share. Once they're sipping the crisp pinot gris and picking over some squid and tuna sashimi, she can breathe properly again.

'I eat more than I used to,' she says with her mouth half full.

'What makes you say that?'

'I'm always eating, and today I had to buy some slightly bigger sizes than I was used to.' She blushes a little.

'Well, I think you look as sexy as ever. How was your day with Rachel?'

Being called *sexy* rolls through her like melted butter into toast. Tom's validation is unnerving yet not unwelcome. She sips her water, trying to be normal.

'It was good. A non-yoga class that felt very much like yoga, brunch, shopping. I've slipped into Brighton life I guess. Sorry about the credit card,' she says, averting her eyes.

'Ava,' he pauses, waiting for her to look at him again, 'you don't have to apologise for going shopping. I'm not your parent.' There's a sensual quality to his voice as he makes his point; it's as if he's daring her to take charge.

'Seb could be weird with money. Old habits die hard, I guess.' The slivers of truth about Seb are unpleasant in her mouth.

'I remember. It took years for you to relax about that stuff.'

'Well, by the look of this handbag, I definitely loosened up.' She smiles and holds up her black Chanel handbag, which she and Rachel found in a drawer today.

'Actually, I bought you that. I wanted to give you something special when Noah was born. This is the first time I've seen you use it. You were always saving it for a special occasion, worried it was too precious to use.' Tom shrugs, and Ava swallows a lump in her throat. She can't imagine why she shoved this bag in a drawer and never used it.

'Sorry, Tom. Sometimes I think I'm a bit thoughtless. But I promise to use this gorgeous bag, I love it.' She beams at him, meaning it. She's always had a weakness for handbags.

'I'm glad.' His eyes brighten.

'Do we do this often? Date nights?' she asks, changing the subject.

'I'm sorry to say not much anymore. We've gotten a bit distracted and lazy at the whole romance thing. But I'm really glad we're doing it again,' he says with a warm smile.

'Me too. It's nice to give your poor Mum a night off cooking. I think she's worried that you and Noah will starve now that I've apparently lost all ability to cook.'

'Nah, she loves it. I think she likes being needed these days. She was a bit lonely after Dad died and once Noah came along a bit of spark came back into her. Stacey doesn't have any kids so all of Mum's grandparent love gets poured into him.'

'Of course she doesn't, she's a teenager!' Ava gasps at the suggestion Tom's little sister would be a mother.

'She's twenty-nine and got married last year,' Tom says. 'I walked her down the aisle,' he adds proudly.

Ava shakes her head, caught out again, 'I can't believe little Stacey's all grown up.'

'Andrew's English and they live in London. Mum was basically hanging onto her legs at the airport. So Noah's even more special now that Stacey's not around,' Tom says, sadness at the edge of his eyes.

'She's so good with him. It's lovely he's got such a good grandma.' Ava's eyes shine a little as she says the word *grandma*.

Tom reaches across the table and holds her hand as he says, 'Luci would've been good too.'

Ava smiles and nods in quiet agreement, then shakes it off, trying to keep tonight light. The gloom hovers over them, omnipotent, but she wants to look at their life without the fog of tears.

'Let's talk about something more fun. Tell me about our first date?'

'Well, we didn't *date* per se,' he looks a bit embarrassed as he takes a glug from his glass of wine, 'we were kind of busy with… indoor pursuits in those early days.'

'Like Scrabble?' Ava raises an eyebrow.

'Probably more like Twister.' He laughs and winks back at her, making her blush and hold her face in her hands as if the embarrassment of talking about sex is contagious.

She composes herself and says, 'Okay, Casanova, once we made it outdoors, what did we do together? What would a weekend look like?'

'Well, we ate out all the time due to both of us having an aversion to actually using our kitchens. We used to walk everywhere: parks, city streets and sometimes beaches down the coast. You would find these secluded little walking trails on Tripadvisor and we'd set off for an adventure. You wanted new memories for us, ones that were just ours. You said that a few times.'

Listening to Tom talk about their life is strangely abstract yet familiar. She can't remember it, but it feels true. He feels true.

'Do you think you can go another round of memory-making?' she asks.

'What do you mean?' He looks confused.

'I don't want to be on the back foot all the time, not remembering anything. I want to make some new memories again. Completely new ones, for the three of us… if you want to?'

'I'd love that,' he smiles, looking relieved.

They find some ease in the new and in the promise of the undiscovered. For the first time, looking at Tom isn't awkward. They chat without pretence and enjoy a repartee that is practised and unforced. As they order dessert, Tom's phone blasts in his pocket and breaks the reverie.

'God, sorry, it's Mum. I left it on in case she needed us,' he explains in haste, then answers it. 'Hi, Mum? No, no it's okay, tell him we'll come now… it's fine, I don't want him upset. Okay, see you soon.'

'Everything okay?'

'Noah woke up screaming from some kind of nightmare. Mum said he's upset and won't go back to bed. He's asking for you. I think we should go and pick him up, he's had a rough few weeks,' he explains.

'Of course, let's go get him.' Ava doesn't hesitate.

'I'm sorry, we haven't even got the dessert yet.' He looks disappointed.

'It's fine.' She waits for him to look at her. 'I was hoping for a second date anyway.' She smiles as she stands up to put her jacket on.

He helps her lift her jacket up over her shoulders and whispers in her ear, 'Me too.' The warmth of his breath makes her heart quicken. Her bravery slips, turning her cheeks a warm pink. She's glad to be facing away from him.

~

When Ava and Tom arrive at Jane's house, they find Noah nestled on the sofa with a blanket covering him. He looks so small, and the urge to hold him takes over as she hastens to sit next to him, leaving Tom and Jane whispering to each other in the hallway. Noah shuffles across onto her lap, burrowing his head into her, and says, 'I had a bad dweam.' She strokes his hair, looping her fingers through his soft curls, hoping to banish any imaginary demons. Tom comes over and carries him out to the car, leaving Ava to walk out with Jane.

'Sorry, Jane,' she offers as they head back to the car.

'Darling, don't be sorry, these things happen. He's a sensitive little possum.'

The guilt creeps around her like an eerie mist. Noah's caught in the middle of her turmoil without any real context as to why. Not knowing what to say, Ava nods, swallowing hard. Jane pulls her into her soft body for a hug and Ava briefly rests her head on her plush velvet dressing gown, finding Jane's musky scent an instant comfort. It's nice to have a mother when you need one, even if she's someone else's.

'I'll see you Wednesday, sweetheart. But do call me if you need anything in the meantime.' Jane radiates her warm smile, illustrating that Tom's kindness is no accident.

By the time they finish the ten-minute drive home, Noah is asleep again in the backseat. In a feat of stealth, Tom lifts him out of his car seat and transfers him into his bed without even so much as his eyelids fluttering. Ava waits in the open doorway while Tom tucks him under the covers and creeps out of the room.

'I feel bad leaving him alone,' Ava whispers to him.

'Don't worry. You could very well have a four o'clock visitor, though I hope not. It took us months to break that habit last year.' Tom rolls his eyes.

The night with Tom has stirred something she wasn't expecting it to. Pushing her nerves as far down as she can muster, she meets his eyes and holds them for a moment. Fuelled by a few glasses of wine, she's bold enough to explore.

'Would *you* like to sleep in our bed?' she asks. Before he can answer she adds, '*I'd* like you to sleep in our bed.'

Wordless, he takes her hand and leads her into their room before closing the door behind them.

ELEVEN

LOOKING out of the car window across rolling hills that are peppered with the vines of the wine country, Ava finds calm for the first time in ages. The day is green and lush, complete with a cloudless blue sky, making it feel as if optimism comes free today.

'Are we there yet?' Freya whines from the backseat.

'You know, I thought it might be the kids who were annoying in the car today,' Tom teases her from behind the wheel.

'Yeah, well, they're lightweights who fell asleep on me and now I'm bored,' she whispers with an edge of aggression.

'We'll be there in ten minutes,' Tom replies, and looks across at Ava for a brief second.

It was Tom's idea to go for a drive and have lunch at a winery, where there is apparently a small petting farm and tractor rides for kids. They asked Freya to join them in the spirit of making new family memories, though Ava is starting to regret it.

Noah and Pip wake up the moment the car stops in the carpark and they bounce ahead into the farm area with Tom at their heels while Ava follows behind with Freya.

'Can you be less of a pain in the arse today, please?' Ava pokes her sister in the ribs.

'What? I was bored.' Freya seems distracted but Ava doesn't want to delve into it now.

'Please make this fun. Tom is trying hard to give us some new memories. *All* of us, okay?' she squeezes her sister's arm a little bit, which she supposes could be construed as love or a warning.

'Sorry. I had a fight with Derek,' Freya explains.

'About what?'

'Nothing really. It started with me asking him to take the bin out and it kind of spiralled from there.' Freya kicks her foot into the gravel.

'Why are you wasting your time with him? Do you even love him?' Ava comes across more irritated that she intended.

'What? He's a bit lazy, therefore I don't love him? Is that what you heard?'

'I only have snippets of him in my mind. You've hardly given him a glowing endorsement.'

'I'm just tired. It's nothing.'

'Freya...'

'Come on, let's go in and ride a bloody tractor.' With that, Freya walks at pace, leaving Ava to trail in behind her.

Despite Freya's initial bad mood, they end up enjoying the farm, with the laughter from the kids softening Freya's edges and lightening the mood for everyone. Noah takes a particular shine to one of the guinea pigs and cries when he has to say goodbye. Tom placates him by saying they'll think about getting him a guinea pig for a pet. Straight afterwards, he whispers in Ava's ear, 'I will regret those words,' and she laughs.

It's nice to have Tom whisper things to her and include her in his secret parenting world of good intentions and loose promises. Noah peppers the word *Mum* across the day and she's getting used to the sound of it. She likes the way *Mum* is more than a name; it's a pertinent question, impatient for a response. A beacon to home in on.

Whilst Tom takes Noah and Pip for one last pony ride, Ava and Freya poke at the remnants of their lunches. With the conversation guarded and stiff, Ava decides to try to shock her sister in the hope it will mitigate her bad mood.

'I slept with Tom last night,' Ava offers, eating the last piece of brie off the cheese plate. Freya nearly chokes on her cracker.

'What?' Freya is wide-eyed and ripe for the details.

'Calm down. Slept. As in, laid down next to each other and slept.'

'Disappointing.' Freya shrugs and reaches for the last piece of stilton.

'It was lovely.' Ava floats back to the warmth of Tom's body next to hers. The smell of his minty breath as they whispered things to each other, cushioned by the darkness and safe under the doona.

'Did you at least kiss?' Freya is impatient.

'No. We just held hands and talked until we fell asleep. I haven't talked to anyone like that in years.'

'And you reckon Derek isn't sexy...' Freya raises her eyebrows.

'You know, *not* having sex is actually very sexy.' Ava is defensive now.

'Yeah,' Freya laughs, 'I'll tell my class that next time I'm teaching sex-ed.'

'There's nothing wrong with us taking it slow. I thought you'd be happy for me, instead you're just being a dick.' Ava slumps back in her chair, put out.

Freya huffs under her breath without responding and Ava realises that you're never too old to fight with your sister. She knows how this will play out; she's been arguing with Freya since forever. The many similarities that bond them are often their undoing. Stubbornness could render them both mute for days when they'd refuse to concede an argument. But Ava hates to waste time when she knows she won't win. It's how she feels about settling out of court: it's inevitable to save time, but beyond annoying – especially when she occupies the moral high ground.

'What's wrong? Just tell me,' Ava pleads.

Freya lets out a resigned sigh, twirling a loose curl around her finger.

'I found a text message on Derek's phone. I think he's cheating on me. I didn't want to drag you into my shit. And I'm happy for you and Tom, I'm just in a bad mood. Sorry.'

Ava moves to the other side of the table to sit next to Freya and put her arms around her. Freya rests her head on Ava's shoulder and takes a long breath.

'What did the text say?' Ava asks.

'"I had fun last night", then a winky face and a kissy face.'

'Ugh, those stupid emoji things again.'

'At least it wasn't an eggplant, I guess,' Freya says.

'Huh?'

'Seriously? Christ, I have so much to teach you. Cock. Eggplant is cock.' Freya rolls her eyes and finishes her wine.

'Well, that makes a lot more sense than it being an actual eggplant. I reckon you'd use the word "cock" with higher frequency.' Ava nods to herself.

'Anyway, he denied everything and said they were just friends, blah blah blah,' Freya continues.

'You don't believe him?' Ava tries to sound impartial.

'Nope.'

'Is it the end?'

'Yep. Annoyingly, you were right anyway. Derek was kind of a placeholder 'til something better came along. I didn't realise I was a placeholder for him too.'

'Do you want the last piece of cheese so you can eat your feelings?'

Freya doesn't reply but pops the last sliver of havarti in her mouth while Ava hugs her again, trying to fill her up with love. She has only ever wanted her little sister to have enough of everything. Enough love, enough friends, enough self-esteem, enough drive. Just to be... enough. Watching her sister in pain makes Ava uncomfortable, and she's never been able to sit in the discomfort with her. She's always believed that everything was fixable. It's probably why law was attractive to her; because she could fight and she could win. She could *fix*.

She holds Freya's hand as they all walk back to the car, not wanting her to feel alone but aware she's bordering on overbearing.

'Do you want to stay with us tonight?' Ava asks.

'No, I'll be okay. I told him to be gone by the time we got home.'

'Yeah, but you might be lonely. We could have a movie night?'

Ava's voice is too perky.

'Ava. I'm fine.'

Ava doesn't ask any more questions and the drive home is relatively quiet. She spends most of the journey musing on how she will help her sister, unable to sit idle while she's hurting.

~

The quiet that settles over the house once Noah is in bed is stark. His little voice is a reliable constant throughout the day, and the mood changes when he's not filling the big spaces. It's not an unpleasant shift, ultimately reminding Ava how much she's gotten used to him.

'Do you still fancy a movie night?' Tom asks as she sits down next to him on the sofa.

'Sure.'

'Classic or new?' he asks as he flicks around on a giant screen of options.

'Oh, I dunno. Show me one of my favourite ones, one that I can't remember. Then I know I'll love it and it will still be new.'

'Your favourite movie is still *The Notebook*,' he grins and adds, 'unfortunately,' with a faux pained expression.

'Ah, *The Notebook*, forever a classic.' She clutches her chest and smiles. 'But no. I want to try a new one.'

'How about *Bridesmaids*? I remember you saw that with some friends and liked it. I've never seen it. It will be new for both of us.'

'Perfect,' she says.

While Tom navigates around the TV screen to find the movie, she puts her hand on his and says, 'Sorry about Freya's shitty mood today. She's breaking up with Derek.'

'I thought something was up with her. What happened?' Tom asks.

'Cheated on her.' Ava shrugs as if their demise was inevitable.

'Dick.' Tom shakes his head then adds, 'I'm not sure she was that keen on him though.'

'That's what *I* said to her. Good. I knew I was right.'

Tom laughs, 'So long as you were right then.'

'You know what I mean. Anyway, thank you for today. Despite her drama, it was nice. *Really* nice.' She meets his eyes, showing him she means it.

'My pleasure.' He lifts her hand to his mouth, kissing it gently, and the warmth of his lips runs through her, forcing her to focus on slowing her breath.

The movie starts playing in the background but neither of them removes their gaze from the other. Their fingers are still threaded, her thumb stroking Tom's knuckles but the rest of her limbs remain paralysed. Her heart races in her chest as the prickles of desire move through her. Her body is betraying everything she'd wanted to be true about Tom, and for the first time she can believe it. She believes it could have happened.

A scream from upstairs pierces the moment and Ava lets go of Tom's hand. They rush up to Noah's room, where he's crying and screaming. Tom tries to stroke his head.

'No! I want *Muuuuuummmmmyyyyy!*' His small face is red and angry.

Ava stands in the doorway, not sure what to do. She's never seen him like this; it's at odds with the sweet, cuddly child she's gotten used to. Tom gestures for her to take over and looks a bit miffed that she's not reacting. In a reluctant daze, she walks over to the bed, taking Tom's place as Noah continues to shout, 'No, Daddy!' until Tom finally leaves the room to make him stop.

Noah's breathing is ragged as she holds him upright in her arms. *Proximity*, she repeats to herself in a mantra. Most of what he seems to need is to have her beside him. Like a poised servant ready to meet his needs as they arise. She's not sure where her needs are meant to fit in, though. Maybe she's not meant to need as much anymore. Or anything at all.

Eventually, Noah's head goes limp atop of her now-dead arm and she can tell he's gone back to sleep. She lowers him back onto his pillow and pulls the covers up, wedging Goose in next to him. His face is angelic in the soft glow of the night-light and she soaks it in, wanting to trace the plump edges of his cheek but too scared to touch him. A gentle warmth runs through her as she looks at him, but it's restrained. When does the life-changing flush of love come? When will she feel like his mother? When will any of this be real?

~

The cascading trees, set amongst the lush gardens overlooking a shimmering duck pond, are ripe with spring. Hot coffee in hand and watching the morning sunshine poke through a dissipating cloud, Ava wants to be able to get used to this life. She agreed to walk home with Rachel after dropping the boys at kinder, which naturally morphed into coffee and a wander through the park. Her senses are still heightened after last night, with Tom's touch somehow lingering on her. The thoughts in her head are manic and, like a teenager fully charged with dopamine, she needs to tell someone.

'Tom and I had a moment. Last night, we almost… I dunno what we almost did.' The words spew out.

Rachel turns to her with wide eyes and a big smile, waiting for her to keep going. Steadying her thoughts, Ava takes a slow breath, instantly glad she told Rachel instead of calling Freya. It's good to say it out loud, making it real beyond mere thought.

'What happened?' Rachel asks.

'We were watching a movie and we kind of locked eyes and he held my hand. I felt like we were about to kiss… then Noah woke up from some kind of nightmare and it killed the vibe.' Confusion dominates as she reflects on the ruined moment.

'You liked the idea?' Rachel fishes.

'I felt like I was about to cheat on Seb. But that almost made it better somehow. Illicit and naughty.' Her rampant guilt feels like something she should file away for her therapy sessions.

'How was it this morning? Was it weird?'

'No, it was nice. We had a coffee, got Noah ready. It was just sort of normal.'

'He's clearly hot for you, considerate, *and* he packs school lunches? Sounds like a perfect marriage.' Rachel giggles.

'Maybe. I'm hardly an expert but my marriage with Seb was

nothing like this.'

Rachel doesn't probe for details, instead leaving Ava time to gather her thoughts on her own.

'I just wish I had the bit in the middle. What drove in the final wedge? Seb wasn't perfect, but I was pretty happy. I didn't hate him or anything.'

She doesn't tell Rachel that she wishes she didn't find Tom attractive. Or that she'd like to run screaming back to Seb and beg him to forgive her. Or that it would all be easier if she wasn't Noah's mother.

'Give it some more time. It's amazing you've come this far already.' Rachel swirls the remaining coffee in her cup before finishing it.

'Thanks. And sorry I'm so needy. I feel like I'm constantly whinging to you.'

'We don't keep score. You don't need to apologise for needing a friend. By the way, I've finished all those trust financials, I'll email them over today.'

'Thank you. What do I owe you?'

'Nothing. I told you; we don't keep score.' Rachel throws her coffee cup into the bin next to her.

Ava starts to wonder if she's ever had a friend like Rachel, one who doesn't *keep score*. Most of her friendships have been symbiotic, even her relationships with Seb and Freya. Priding herself on her reliability, she was incapable of being in someone else's debt, always quick to repay whatever she'd taken whether that be a beloved sweater (Freya) or oral sex (Seb). Nothing came free, everything was transactional, and the slate had to be kept even. Perhaps it was an innate concept of fairness, but now she entertains the possibility that it was something else. Was she not worthy of being in someone's debt? The notion sits uneasy, like a splinter she can't expel.

~

With an hour to kill until her lunch with Sarah, Ava walks the two blocks to the beach, emboldened by the unseasonably warm sunshine.

Early spring means the shackles of winter layers can be removed, and although she knows the water will still be freezing, she wants to feel it against her skin. She runs into the gentle, lapping waves and dives straight under so she can't change her mind. The icy water bites at her skin but after the initial shock, her whole body comes alive. Nerve endings awaken and her lungs heave with cool air. After staying in for as long as she can tolerate, she jogs back to her towel on the sand and wraps her invigorated body up to ease the wind chill. An old couple walking past wearing puffer jackets smile and shake their heads at her as if she's mad. Maybe she is.

Back at home, the hot torrent from the shower washes off the sticky layer of salt and sand. She watches the water cascade down her uneven body. Her forty-year-old body. A body that has weathered life and begun to rumple at the edges. She doesn't feel old exactly, but she *is* changed. In an unapologetic way. The terrain of her body is like a map of unfamiliar lands. This body would have taught her things. Primal lessons that her memory has now forgotten.

Her phone starts ringing from the bedroom and she manages to towel off and reach it in time.

'Ava?' The unfamiliar caller asks.

'Yes?'

'Simon Green. How are you?' Simon's familiarity makes her stomach drop. Is this yet another relationship she has to lumber through and rebuild?

'I'm okay...'

Before she can launch into *I actually have a brain injury and no idea who you are*, he cuts her off.

'I'm just following up with you after you missed the interview a few weeks ago, are you still interested?'

'Sorry, what interview was that?'

'The junior partnership at our firm,' he says, sounding a bit put out.

Ava doesn't remember Tom mentioning this to her and it occurs to her: that's because he hasn't.

'Sorry, Simon. I can explain. Can you remind me what date the interview was scheduled?'

'The sixteenth of August.'

Ava's blood turns cold. That was the date of her accident.

TWELVE

AVA decided on Entrez Vous for lunch with Sarah, partly because it has five stars on the Hot Spoon restaurant app she's learning to use, and partly because it's walking distance from the house. She still isn't ready to drive and she's pretty sure Tom feels the same way. He hasn't said anything explicitly but she sensed that the trauma from the accident was still too fresh to even broach the subject of her getting behind the wheel yet. In any case, walking through Brighton's leafy backstreets in spring is a pleasure, and the more she uses her legs the better she feels. It also gives her time to stew on the phone call with Simon Green.

Green & Fraser was a mid-tier firm with a good reputation. She interviewed there as a graduate but eventually took an offer from a bigger firm. Back then it felt like bigger would always be better. Simon himself was a third generation Green and, according to him, was responsible for cultivating a cohesive and collaborative team environment. He explained that he had been the one to invite her in for an interview after connecting at some Law Institute function she'd attended with Tom a couple of months ago. He seemed concerned when she'd explained her accident and told her to call him anytime she felt up to it. The fact that Tom failed to mention she was courting an offer stings. She shelves it to deal with later, not wanting to sour her lunch with Sarah. To shift the stabs of anger, she practises the breathing exercises recommended by the psychologist. Her ribs expand as she breathes as deeply as her lungs allow. Mindfulness is what will curb her anxiety. Apparently.

Strolling along, she shifts her gaze to soak in the variety of houses, some more opulent than others, but all erring on the more generous side of real estate. The odd palm tree peppers the front lawns of the more grandiose residences, sitting atop meticulous green lawns and pristine flowerbeds. Walking past a fairy garden nestled in the base of a giant English oak, she makes a note to mention that to Steve and see if they can make one for Noah on their own front lawn. She smiles at the thought, enjoying it all the more due to the fact that it popped naturally into her mind. Thinking of Noah is becoming an extension of her existence, an unconscious habit. Though still an imposter in her own life, she hopes these tiny moments will morph her into a proper mother.

When Ava enters the restaurant, she spots Sarah already seated at a table next to the window, tapping away on her phone. She still looks the same as Ava remembers with her sharp blonde bob and an effortlessly-slim physique that Ava coveted. Still the epitome of a glossy lawyer, in her slick black tailored suit and white silk blouse. The addition of thin-framed black glasses is new, but they only serve to make her even more corporate-glam than she already was.

'Hey, you!' Ava gives her a warm smile as she approaches the table.

'Hey, Ava.' Sarah beams back and gets up to hug her.

Ava can't tell if the hug is weird or not – Sarah was never much of a hugger, but it seems necessary after all these years apart, even though Ava herself does not have that missing gulf of time.

'It's good to see a familiar face.' Ava hangs her denim jacket on the back of the chair as she sits down.

'I was sorry to hear about your accident.' Sarah tilts her head as if to emphasise her concern.

'Thanks. Yeah, I'm lucky that I'm mostly okay. Bummer about erasing bits of my brain though.' Ava gives her a half-cocked smile, trying to keep herself light.

'Will you recover fully?'

'They don't know. My brain is fine, no irreversible injury, but they can't explain the memory loss or tell me if it's permanent.' Ava reaches for the water and gulps it down.

'How much memory loss do you have?'

'Well, put it this way – my last memory of us together is dancing at the Luna bar after winning the Potesky case, which preceded the worst hangover of my adult life! So, about ten years.'

Sarah lets out a stifled laugh. 'I'm sorry, I don't mean to laugh, but the Luna bar? Jesus Christ, that really is another life…' she trails off.

'How are you, anyway? How's Nick?' Ava asks.

'Oh, Nick and I broke up years ago.' Sarah waves a hand like this is no big deal.

'No! Really? But we were just planning your wedding…' Ava loses her words mid-sentence.

'We didn't get married,' Sarah clarifies. 'It kind of fell apart and we knew it wasn't right. He ended up marrying someone else, they've got a couple of kids. He's happy, I believe.'

'You're not in touch then?'

'No, it got a bit ugly in the end. It's okay, we've both moved on. I got married too… then got divorced three years later. Happily single now.'

'Kids?'

'No, not for me. Nick was better off without me. We would never have gotten over that hurdle. I'm happy he found someone who wanted kids.' She's matter of fact about this but Ava wonders if there's more to it. She senses a sore spot but doesn't press it.

'You probably know I have a little boy, Noah. I wouldn't have pictured it either.'

'I'm glad it worked out for you.' Sarah smiles, but it's forced.

Ava's not sure if anything has worked out for her at all, entrenched in a life that she didn't get to create as she is. An actor cast in a role in someone else's movie. Surely her friend knows this isn't her.

'Do you know what happened? To Seb and me? Why I cheated on him?' Ava's cheeks go warm, ashamed of that version of herself.

'I wasn't around when it happened.' Sarah shrugs. 'I'd already started my new job in Sydney. I was back sporadically, trying to make it work long distance with Nick, but that wasn't going well. I was distracted. I don't think it was intentional though, it just kind of happened.'

'I was sad to hear we lost touch.' Ava lowers her eyes to her napkin.

'That was probably laziness on my part. I'm sorry. I got so caught up in my new job and lost touch with all my Melbourne friends after the move. I was selfish back then.' She looks remorseful as she speaks.

'Well, I'm glad you're here now.' Ava reaches across the table and pats Sarah's hand – a gentle reassurance that she isn't a burnt bridge.

'Me too. Actually, I have a proposition for you.' Sarah's ocean-blue eyes sparkle behind her glasses.

'Oh?' Ava takes her hand back and sits up straight in her chair.

'I'm starting a new firm here in Melbourne. You want to get back in the game?'

~

Ava is buoyant as she walks back home, high on the fumes of her old life comingling with her new one. Two potential job offers in one day. She wonders if she can make this work and reclaim something from the life she remembers. Not paying full attention to where she's going, she nearly collides with Steve as he's lugging a bag of mulch out of his ute.

'Sorry, Ava, I didn't see you there!' He drops his mulch and stops to check she's alright.

'Totally my fault, Steve. My mind was somewhere else.'

He raises an eyebrow at her with a nervous smile and says, 'See, ordinarily I would make a joke about that, but I worry it's too soon for memory loss gags.'

Ava laughs, relieved that someone else in her life is starting to treat her more normally.

'Please feel free to joke, Steve. I definitely need a laugh.'

'Will do.' He flashes her a warm grin. 'I'm about to finish up with the veggie patch, let me know if there's anything else you need before I go.'

'Actually, I did want to talk to you about a fairy garden, but let's do that next week.' She waves a casual hand in the air as if it's an afterthought any mother would have.

Steve laughs, 'You're definitely feeling better if you've got your creative juices flowing again. I might have to do my research to get a head start!'

'Am I a high maintenance client?' Ava winces at him.

'You keep me on my toes. Plus, ever since you got me onto Instagram, I need the content. I have a few thousand followers thanks to you. I even did an ad on it for Bunnings last month!'

Ava laughs, pleased that he doesn't think she's a pain in the arse. A car horn beeps behind her and she turns to see Freya pulling into the driveway with the kids in the backseat, home from swimming. Steve excuses himself while she helps Freya unbuckle them. Noah offloads all the details from kinder and swimming in a constant stream of words as they make their way to the front door. She tries her best to show the appropriate amount of enthusiasm by animating her face at various intervals, as she's learnt it's best to let him get it all out without interrupting.

Ava ushers them inside, insisting Freya and Pip stay for dinner. The kids run straight outside to the trampoline and Ava seizes the quiet. She gestures for Freya to sit down at the dining table, where she's laid out the paperwork to wind up Freya's testamentary trust. She exercised an early clause, giving Freya full access to her share of their mother's estate and the independence that she couldn't trust her with years ago. Freya stays quiet, digesting this, and Ava sits down across from her and babbles to fill the silence.

'There's a set of financials in there detailing what assets you have. There's the country house in Daylesford and a generous managed fund, which seems to have performed well over the past few years, giving you lots of options. Rachel has an old colleague she recommends for financial planning advice too, which is probably a good idea to get it set it up how you want it.'

'Why are you doing this now? The trust was due to wind up next year, what spurred this on?' Freya's tone is low as she keeps her eyes on the papers in front of her.

Ava doesn't want to tell her it was guilt, because deep down she still believes that she did the right thing.

'I guess I figured you were ready to get on with things. You're settled, you have Pip to look after. I didn't think you needed a trustee anymore.'

'I asked you to do this three years ago, when I found out I was pregnant with Pip. You refused.'

Ava lets out a dejected sigh, 'I obviously can't remember that... I'm sorry if I wasn't there when you needed me.'

'Oh, you were *there*. You were there controlling me – or rather, Mum was controlling me from the grave and you helped her.' Freya's voice is that of a wounded child.

'That's bullshit, Freya, and you know it.' Tom's voice startles them both from behind.

'Is it, Tom? Is it?' Freya glares at him.

'You were barely six months clean when you got pregnant. She was protecting you.'

'"Six months clean." You say that like I was lying in a gutter with a needle hanging from my arm. I smoked a bit of weed, let's ease up on the theatrics.' Freya rolls her eyes, slumping back in her chair and folding her arms.

'A bit of weed?' Tom scoffs. 'And the admission to hospital when you'd slipped unconscious at the warehouse rave, when Ava had to go and sit by your bed until you woke up? Then had to arrange a month in rehab and forever worry her little sister was going to accidentally kill herself one day?'

'Freya?' Ava looks at her sister, her eyes dripping with disappointment.

'He's being dramatic, I took one dodgy pill...' Freya rolls her eyes.

'I do facts, Freya. Drama is your specialty.' Tom cuts her off with an edge to his voice, taking Ava by surprise.

'Well, everything's obviously not "water under the bridge" is it, Tom? Good to know how you really feel about me,' Freya spits back.

Tom sighs, the same way one would when talking to an errant child. 'Freya, don't manipulate the situation. You were trying to make her feel guilty for not handing you a load of money when you were barely getting your life together. The you of today is significantly different to who you were three years ago. So cut the shit.' Tom holds himself tall and authoritative.

Freya gets up and walks to the back door, calling Pip back inside, then gathers up the papers on the table.

'I'll give these to my lawyer. Thanks,' Freya deadpans.

Ava hates the thought of parting like this, Freya hot with rage and betrayal. She begs her to stay for dinner.

'I seem to have lost my appetite,' she bites. Freya doesn't look back as she walks out, leaving Ava and Tom alone in their kitchen.

Flooded with adrenaline, Ava turns to face him, now cagey about what else he's not telling her.

'Why didn't you tell me about all that stuff?' she shoots at him.

'Because it didn't seem important. You and Freya had been getting on the best you had in years and I didn't want to upset that.'

His nonchalance is irritating and she's peeved that he gets to be the arbiter of her memories.

'Is that why you didn't want me to wind up the trust? You knew it would blow up?'

He shrugs and sits on the edge of the dining table.

'Do you think I did the wrong thing?' The tone in her voice suggests there's only one right answer.

'You always do what you think is best for Freya, even if she's too pigheaded to see it.' He rubs his temple.

It's hard to look at him as she simmers under the surface. The anger about the missed interview has bubbled in her gut all afternoon. Did he lie to keep her subdued in this domestic life? To make sure she was there to cook dinners and handle all the kid-related logistics?

Gardening as a serious hobby? Does he believe that's enough for her? There's a chance that she didn't tell him about the interview, but if that's the case then how well does he know her and who is he to tell her who she really is?

'Are there other things you're keeping from me, Tom?' She looks him in the eyes and sees him flinch a little, but he gives her a baffled expression. He's such an obvious lawyer, not conceding information until he sees her hand.

'The day of my accident, where was I going?' She holds herself taller than her petite frame.

He drops his eyes to his hands before looking back up at her, still refusing to say it. So he *did* know.

'You lied to me.'

'I didn't lie to you.' He's emphatic, which only irritates her more.

'You kept telling me how happy I was without my career and you fail to tell me that I was trying to resurrect it?'

He scoffs. 'Hardly. It was one meeting with some mid-tier guy you met at a stiff work function. You were being polite.' His dismissal hurts. She doesn't believe him for a second; she wouldn't have bothered if she wasn't interested. Why waste her time? He's distorting the narrative. *Her* narrative.

'Why did you lie to me, Tom?' She holds firm.

He shakes his head as if she's the one who's being unreasonable.

'You just got out of hospital with a major brain injury. I didn't think it was something you needed to worry about.' He throws his hands up like he's being made to apologise for doing her a massive favour.

'What else have you lied to me about, Tom?' She delivers it like a threat.

He looks at her for a moment as if he doesn't know who she is, then gets up, shaking his head. He walks out, wordless, and she can hear him putting his stuff back into the guest room.

THIRTEEN

UNABLE to sleep for most of the night, Ava gives up trying at about 5am. She grabs some stretchy pants and a T-shirt that she'd left on the chaise lounge near the door yesterday and creeps past the closed doors of Noah's room and the guest room. Annoyingly, Tom was right about the yoga pants: they are ridiculously comfortable. It makes sense that this is supposedly her outfit of choice. Maybe she took up yoga as a hobby just to wear the clothes. Comfort appeals to her. The last couple of days have been an assault on her mind and it's making her short of breath. Hopefully an early morning walk will clear her head.
The cold air whips around her face as she leaves the house and walks the few blocks to the beach. The suburb is still asleep and the quiet is welcome. Walking along the sandy beach as the sun rises over the still bay should provide the recipe for some kind of peace, but her mind is still swirling. She jolts between Tom's dismissive tone, Freya's rage and missing Seb, caught in the middle and it's selfish to feel anything but sorry. She's hurt them, even if she doesn't remember doing it. A need to shoulder the blame permeates her stiff body.

Rekindling her friendship with Sarah is only deepening the guilt. The offer to partner at her new firm is alluring but she knows Tom's going to be disappointed if she entertains it. This was her dream ten years ago and now it's within reach. And to do it with her best friend adds another layer of joy. Despite Tom being supportive thus far, she suspects that he wants her around for Noah, not working eighty-hour weeks. How can she learn to be a mother and have her career too? Taking the job would hurt both Noah and Tom, and not taking it would be self-torture.

Sinking her body onto the sand to sit, she looks at the mesmerising waves as they hit the shore. She's aching to talk to her mother. Luci would be able to tell her what she needed to hear. Ava closes her eyes and tries to hear Luci's voice inside her head, but her inner monologue drowns it out. *I miss you I miss you* plays in her mind on a loop, and a few salty tears roll down her cheeks.

Taking her phone out of her pocket, she does what she thinks Luci would tell her to do. Focus on what's important first. After three rings, Freya's groggy voice crackles through the phone.

'What time is it?'

'Nearly six. Sorry if I woke you.'

'What's wrong?'

'Fighting with you is making me feel sick. I need to make this better,' Ava blurts out.

'We're not fighting, I was just... blowing off steam. Probably more at Mum than you, which I obviously know isn't fair.'

With Freya talking to her, Ava feels like she can breathe again and lets out a sigh.

'Frey, I would never want to hurt you and I'm sorry you think I abused my power in some way. But... I'm not sorry for protecting you.'

Freya lets out a sigh of her own. 'It kills me to admit, but you did the right thing. Tom was right. I was an asshole back then. Actually, maybe I still am...'

'Yeah, well Tom's being a bit of an asshole himself at the moment. I wouldn't take it to heart.' She kicks at the sand in front of her.

It's a relief to say that out loud. Tom has been lauded as *the good guy* since the accident; maybe underneath it all, he's just *a* guy.

'I'll come over later and bring two tubs of ice cream. Okay?' Freya's foolproof solution to anything is food.

'Buy the good stuff.'

'Yeah, yeah, I know. You live in *Briiiiighton.* Nothing but the best!'

They laugh, and despite the cool breeze blowing across the water, Ava thaws with the love of her little sister wrapped around her. She doesn't have to pretend to be anyone other than herself with Freya. They fight, they forgive, they love. They belong to each other.

~

After an hour in her second Bliss Body class, Ava can't deny that her body feels better. The gentle contortions seem to awaken her muscles and give her a new ease of movement, and she's glad she agreed to come again. On a whim, she decides to sign up for an eight-week yin yoga course and make use of the forty pairs of Lycra pants that are sitting in her wardrobe. Resisting so much of what is new has proven exhausting and she concedes that it's worth trusting New Ava a little bit. Also, top physical condition is imperative if she's going back to work any time soon.

After leaving Bliss Body, Ava and Rachel walk to the kindergarten to pick up the boys. They go the long way, winding through the public gardens, taking advantage of the light as the warm breeze gives strong nods to spring. Rachel seems different today and Ava feels comfortable enough to ask her if she's okay.

'Jeff and I had a bit of a fight,' she divulges, flipping her loose hair over her shoulder and fidgeting with her tortoiseshell sunglasses.

'Nothing serious, I hope?'

'I'm sick of him being so lazy, you know? He expects me to do everything, plus I'm trying to take on a new client to build up my portfolio. I know it'll get easier next year when Harry's at school but I need him to pick up the slack a bit in the meantime. It's like he pretends to care about my career until it impacts his in any way,' Rachel vents.

Ava nods in solidarity. 'I get it. They're like, three-quarter feminists. Super supportive and encouraging as long as we do most of the childcare and cook dinner. That's obviously why I had to stop work – as some kind of sacrifice to motherhood.'

Rachel tilts her head for a moment. 'If we hadn't been sleep-deprived and emotional, I wonder if we would have given up our corporate jobs. We told ourselves it was what we wanted, but I'm not sure now.' She gives a shrug of resignation.

Ava wonders if she isn't an aberration after all. Maybe all women feel trapped between the old and new versions of themselves.

'I've been offered to buy into a partnership with an old colleague,' Ava confides.

'Really? Congratulations!' Rachel's smile is broad and generous.

'Tom will hate the idea. I haven't told him.' Ava has been trying to work out the best way to broach it with him.

'If you want it bad enough, he'll come round.'

Ava hasn't been game to think about what she wants anymore. Trying to be who people keep telling her she is has monopolised her energy. She's been caught in a bizarre limbo, perpetually waiting for a kettle to boil; waiting for things to happen to her.

'Does anyone know what they really want?' Ava muses, not expecting Rachel to answer, but she straight away offers an emphatic 'No', followed by a small, forced laugh.

'Sometimes I want *more* than all the wife and mum stuff, but I don't know what the *more* is. Does that make sense?' Rachel asks, a bit bereft.

Ava nods but isn't sure she's allowed to want more yet. She's too busy trying to want what she already has.

'I think I need to do a better job of all the mum stuff before I get to want anything,' Ava says. She blinks hard as truth stings her eyes.

Rachel puts a gentle hand on Ava's arm, and they stop walking to look at each other. Rachel says, 'You're doing a great job being a mum.'

Even though she's not totally sure that's true, Ava's eyes well up with gratitude for her friend's kindness. She hasn't been game to ask Tom if he thinks she's doing a good job with Noah, afraid that he thinks she isn't. The unsolicited positive feedback is a relief.

When they start walking again, Rachel says, 'And let's face it, it can be a brutal, thankless, relentless job, no thanks to our selfish, faux-feminist, fancy corporate lawyer husbands!' which makes them both laugh in agreement.

As they continue to stroll along, Ava tries to resolve that she can do this. That she can be a mother *and* be a lawyer and they don't have to come at the expense of one another. She just has to find a way to convince Tom. Her accident has given her the gift of a second chance and she's not prepared to waste it.

~

'Just one more bite,' Ava coaxes Noah, holding a spoon to his face. He shakes his head, covering his mouth with his hands, unmoved by her pleas for him to eat. Defeated, she lets the spoon drop back into the half-eaten, slightly limp tuna casserole. She'd reheated it as per Jane's instructions taped to the lid, but despite her best efforts, Noah still gave up on it in five bites, saying it was 'too wet'. Over the past week, she's observed he often finds food too cold, too hot, too sticky, too chewy, too dry, and now she mentally adds 'too wet' to her list. There are, of course, outliers like ice cream that seem to straddle many of these categories yet remain firm favourites. Irrational aversions must come with the territory of being a kid. Victorious, Noah leaves the table to resume his puzzle while Ava finishes her own plate before poking in what's left of Noah's.

A quick glance at her watch reveals it's already seven o'clock. Tom's late, which is unusual, given his recent consistency with getting home early. She hasn't done the evening routine without him yet and isn't sure she wants to. The bath and bed fiasco can be akin to extreme sports if Noah gets fired up. Last night, they had a pyjama soccer tournament in the hallway as if it was a normal thing. Given she knows he's meant to be in bed in half an hour, she decides to give it a go.

After shepherding Noah into the bathroom and making the mistake of letting him add the bubble bath soap himself, she can barely see him amongst the mountain of foam. She peppers him with instructions of what places to wash, which he ignores in favour of a secret submarine mission that involves him rising out of and ducking under the water with impressive vigour. Her T-shirt is now soaked and slick to her body as she tries to at least wash his face when he comes up for air. After fifteen minutes of negotiating, she gets him to release the plug, before helping him out, covered in suds. She turns to get his towel off the rail and finds him gone. A trail of small footprints and bubbles reveals he's left the bathroom, and soon she hears giggles of abandon from down the hall. 'Fuck,' she says under her breath, traipsing after him with towel in hand. The bubbles lead all the way down the wooden staircase, and before she can warn him of the dangers of running around like a soaking wet lunatic, he stumbles, smashing his leg onto the edge of the bottom step. He's howling and clutching his knee when she reaches him, and she drapes the towel around him, scooping him into her lap as they sit crumpled together on the floor. A slick red ooze of blood is slipping down his leg, and she realises she has no idea where the band-aids are kept.

In between Noah's throaty sobs, she hears the thud of the front door and Tom appears next to them, then disappears and comes back with the first aid kit. He props open a three-tiered, well-appointed kit complete with the paraphernalia of a small pharmacy. Plasters and bandages in multiple sizes, creams, anti-septic sprays, ointments, waterproof dressings, steri-strips, scissors, tweezers and alcohol wipes are poised for an array of emergencies. Tom blots at Noah's knee with the towel, turning it from white to red, and reveals a small cut that, mercifully, doesn't look too deep. He gives it a quick spray with antiseptic before deftly applying a Superman plaster, which is enough to stem Noah's tears. Tom carries him upstairs to get him dressed for bed, leaving Ava to mop up the trail of suds on the stairs.

Once Noah is tucked in and kissed goodnight, and the drama of his injury dulled, Tom flops onto the couch next to Ava with a bowl of the reheated casserole resting on his lap. The atmosphere between them is still tense from last night, both of them trying to perch on the moral high ground. Was that why Tom came home late tonight? Skipping bath time to make her crack under pressure? She hates it when she isn't good at something and she's sure he knows this.

'Are you enjoying this?' She prods him.

'This? Mum's casserole?' He looks down at his sloppy plate and shrugs. 'Not especially.'

She shakes her head, miffed that he's being deliberately thick.

'Not the food, Tom. Does it please you to watch me doing all this badly?'

He sighs and abandons his dinner to the coffee table.

'You're not doing it badly,' he concedes. 'Four-year-olds are hard work. You should have seen this place when you were in hospital. I've had to, ah, *upskill* of late.' He looks embarrassed.

Ava's sort of relieved to see that his confident parenting display is inflated by necessity. Even still, she hates being the novice.

'Why were you late? You're still mad?' She refuses to articulate it fully, wanting to hang on to her own anger.

He turns to look at her and she can't read his expression, but it doesn't look like irritation. More like hurt.

'I'm sorry for not telling you about the interview, okay? You're right, you should have had all the information. But it would be hypocritical of you to punish *me* for not telling *you* something…' He raises an eyebrow in challenge.

Can he read her thoughts? Does he know she's been thinking about Seb? It's too risky to divulge anything yet, so she remains silent.

'I know about Sarah's partnership offer. Why didn't you tell me?' His eyes plead with hers and she closes her eyes to break his gaze.

'Because…' her voice is soft, 'I don't know how to tell you I want to take it.'

Tom nods his head in a knowing acceptance, but he seems disappointed, like he hoped he'd been wrong.

'How did you find out?' She's a bit annoyed that word got out, even though she's aware Sarah is tapping into several people from their old network.

Tom's mouth goes tight at the edges as his eyes slide over to meet hers again.

'Seb. We were in court together today.'

The mention of Seb's name renders her conspicuous and she tries not to react in front of Tom. Seb knows, and he either cares enough to repeat it or he's trying to ruffle Tom in court. Both could be true. Both could mean he still feels something for her.

'I didn't know you were up against him.' She keeps her voice even.

'A lingering case the DPP is thrashing to death.'

'Seb's at the DPP? Didn't think he was that altruistic.' The surprise registers on her face.

'He isn't. He's preening himself for inflated offers when he decides to jump ship.' Tom lifts his leg up on the coffee table and leans back into the sofa.

The irony of Seb and Tom still facing off after all these years floats in the air, unspoken, a smoky haze they both pretend not to smell.

'Have you signed with Sarah?' Tom asks, keeping his gaze straight ahead.

'I told her I need time to decide. And to recover,' Ava adds in haste, but she knows Tom can tell if she's disingenuous.

He shifts his body to face her and runs his hand over the back of his neck. She notices hints of hair at the top of his shirt where he's loosened his tie. She hasn't looked at him properly since their "date" the other night, scared to rouse any feelings. Scared of what she might allow herself to do. Scared of betraying Seb again.

In an effort to quell the heat in her breath, she steers the conversation back to Noah. She tells Tom she can't make any work decisions right now until she herself can "upskill". She's got a steep learning curve when it comes to being a mother and hates that she isn't good at it. Whenever she needed to learn a new skill, her solution was always practise. When she learnt to play tennis, she would practise until her body hurt. So that's what she'll do now. Before she can be anything else, she's going to learn how to be Noah's mother. The lawyer in her will have to wait. So will the wife.

FOURTEEN

A few weeks go by in a thrum of domestic routine. In an attempt to prove to Tom that she can handle being more than just a mother, she throws herself into the task. It's not only for him, though. Her overwhelming urge is to prove it to herself. She may have been cast in the role of mother without conscious acceptance, but it was always a possibility at the back of her mind. Time was on her side back then, making the concept abstract and far away, but she can't pretend that Noah isn't real. And she doesn't want to.

As she parents, she regains her lost independence, chipping away at living in this day-to-day. She learns Noah's routine, beyond logistics and down to the minutiae. She learns he has a penchant for chicken nuggets, which she serves alongside steamed veggies despite his predilection to push them around on the plate until succumbing to a couple of mouthfuls, the remainder cast off to the compost bin. After incorrectly cutting his sandwich into squares, she learns that he prefers them crustless and cut into triangles. She practises playing with him, which she had no idea could suck up hours at a time with no sign of fatigue on his part. They construct LEGO scenes and Noah follows instructions with the same rigour that she employs when following a recipe. They get messy on the big outside table with paint and Play-Doh, where she deduces that much of parenting seems to involve an array of cleaning supplies for the inevitable aftermath. She has to run him around a park for at least two hours a day in order to maintain their collective sanity. It reminds her of the golden Labrador, Blondie, they had when she and Freya were children, who would get antsy if she wasn't walked by lunchtime. She begins to carry snacks in her handbag to fend off any unanticipated hunger meltdowns, which she finds to be surprisingly common.

She starts driving again. Small, tentative trips at first to rebuild confidence, but her trepidation is swiftly overridden by the freedom that the car affords her. She starts doing the grocery shopping again. It's a task she'd never given that much thought to, given she and Seb would eat out most of the time, but shopping for a family seems to involve a solid hour of her attention, armed with a list and an armful of reusable shopping bags, which she'd found in the boot of her car. Not to mention the time spent deciding what three people will eat all week in order to construct the list in the first place. At first, she'd attempted to do the weekly shop with Noah as her companion, but quickly realised he came with a significant bump to the time taken and the cost involved. She eventually had to restrain him in the trolley seat and let him hold a lollypop to halt the flow of 'Mum, can I have… (insert frivolous item here)'. Tom had mentioned that he sometimes did the food shop on the weekends, though she's yet to see any tangible evidence of that.

She devotes hours to trawling cookbooks for things that look easy enough to master and that Noah might agree to eat. It's surprising to find that she didn't hate her evening cooking routine, even finding it meditative after long days. And if she allows Noah to help her, he's more likely to eat a few extra mouthfuls.

She throws herself into yoga and, after a month of classes, acquires a newfound smoothness to her movements. Despite no visible effect, her belly feels tighter and she regains a structural sturdiness that had been lacking since the accident. Strength edges back into her body, which in turn, galvanises her mind.

Noah asks so many questions that her Google history looks like the spattered thoughts of a mad scientist. *What makes lightning? How much blood is in the human body? Do eels sleep? What happens if you put metal in the microwave? Will I die if I eat Play-Doh?* Some questions, however, were ungoogleable – those are the ones that belong to Ava herself. *Is it normal to find motherhood tedious? If I can't remember things, are they still real?*

What happens if I don't love my husband? Where do lost memories go? Will they ever come back?

Tom is still sleeping in the guest room, neither of them game to mention it one way or another. She's made significant progress and she doubts he wants to rock the boat.

Sitting in Kelly Anderson's waiting room, she's quietly smug as she tallies up the hours of devotion she's thrown into her family over the past month. She's shown them she can do it. She can handle things. Even the other mothers at Noah's kindergarten had started to include her in their school-gate banter. It was mainly banal and centred around who was the most sleep deprived or underappreciated, but she was included nonetheless.

Kelly appears from behind the glossy white doorway, ushering her into her office, and as Ava takes up her position on the couch, her smugness dissipates. She can't lie to herself in here. The permanent box of tissues sits on the small table in front of her. She can't decide if they're an invitation or a threat. After weeks circling the same issues – loss, grief, confusion, anger – she feels like she's wasting Kelly's time. And her own.

Kelly leads with the usual questions about her physical health and Noah. Ava gushes, relaying their trip to Science Works, where they spent hours soaking in exhibitions and left with an overpriced bag of goodies from the gift shop. Ava feels like a parody of herself. *Look at me! I'm a mother! I foster educational activities with my child and overindulge him because of my overbearing love. See?*

'And Tom? How's the relationship going?' Kelly hones in on Ava's weak spot.

Ava fidgets in her chair, trying to get comfortable, and clasps her hands together to recompose herself. Her fingers absently trace her foreign wedding rings.

'I mean, it's fine. We spend lots of time together once Noah's in bed. I never knew middle-aged people watched so much *Grand Designs* though.' Ava attempts to distract Kelly with a joke.

She had thought Tom was joking when he'd flicked on the

episode, but it has since prevailed as an initiation of sorts. The seven-thirty Saturday night episode, watching hapless renovators traipse around muddy worksites, all overenthusiastic and chronically underbudgeted, is now a ritual. Bunnings trips and *Grand Designs*. Marriage is weird.

'And what about intimacy?' Kelly asks, impervious.

Non-existent. 'Slowly coming along,' Ava lies, though unsure why.

'In what way?' Kelly chirps back.

In no way. 'I'm not sure we're ready.' I'm not sure *I'm* ready, she thinks.

'Do you want to progress your relationship in that way?' Kelly looks up from her notebook.

No. Yes. Maybe. Depends on the week, the day, the moment.

Ava shrugs.

'What about some homework?' Kelly prefaces with a too-wide smile. 'Something small, like a hug?'

'You want me to hug Tom?' Ava tilts her chin. She objects to being patronised.

'This isn't about what *I* want. If you want to explore intimacy with Tom, then small gestures are a good way to start,' Kelly clarifies.

Ava is a bit put out by the pedestrian advice. Tom has hugged her, they've held hands, they've been close enough to feel each other's breath. But that was weeks ago. Lately it's been very *polite* between them. The initial desire he had for her seems to have been shelved, in the same way she's attempted to shelve her desire for Seb, or anyone at all. She wishes she could feel sexy in this foreign body – even though it made her drip with guilt, Tom *did* make her feel desired. She agrees to Kelly's assignment in the hope she can reawaken what's gone dormant.

~

Ava's black, sequined dress sticks to her skin as sweat beads down her chest. The music is nineties retro and every song seems to speak to her soul. The four cocktails she's devoured might also account for her sudden ability to find profound meaning in a Britney Spears lyric.

Sarah was the one who suggested a girls' night out, and Ava was more than happy to comply, roping in Rachel and Freya to come too. A night off from *Grand Designs* and the awkward dance between her and Tom also appealed. Freya initially groaned when they walked into the nightclub, hearing what she dubbed "tragic nineties music", but the booze had worked for her too, and she was now grinding her body up and down against Ava's to Shania Twain's *That Don't Impress Me Much*.

After a solid performance on the dance floor, Ava excuses herself to go to the bathroom. Sarah goes with her while the others head off in search of more drinks. Ava examines herself in the mirror and pushes back the sweaty strands of hair that cling around her face. To salvage her melting makeup, she reapplies some red lipstick, rubbing her lips together, semi-satisfied with the result. Sarah stumbles across to her, draping her arm over Ava's shoulder, and they look at each other in their mirrored reflections.

'I've missed you,' Sarah slurs through a floppy smile, and Ava hugs her wet body against her own. Sarah pushes her back an arm's length to look at her.

'You look hot! Lemme take a photo.' Sarah gets her phone out of her clutch bag and makes Ava do sexy poses in front of the toilet cubicle doors, then holds the camera at arm's length and snaps them in a selfie.

Returning to the crowd of pulsating bodies, they find Rachel and Freya have secured a booth at the back of the club as well as a bottle of champagne, which luxuriates in a bucket of ice. Sarah pours everyone drinks and they raise their glasses.

'What should we toast to?' Ava asks.

'To having you back.' Sarah meets her eye across the table and Freya and Rachel push their glasses forward in an enthusiastic clink.

They slump back against the plush velvet booth and Rachel lets out a large exhale.

'Man is it good to be out of the house. Harry pushed all my buttons today, topping it off by drawing on the leather sofa with a sharpie.' She takes a gulp of champagne to punctuate her point as

Freya nods along in agreement.

'I had a nightmare day too. Pip did a giant poo in the supermarket and it started oozing out of her nappy. I had to abandon the trolley mid-shop and go home to clean her up. We still have no food and I'll have to do it all again tomorrow.' Freya shakes her head at the thought.

'Gross.' Ava makes a disgusted face.

'You're lucky you can't remember all the toddler shit explosions.' Freya raises her glass as if to congratulate her, but Ava's heart pangs with the void of lost memories – even the literal shitty ones – and she doesn't feel lucky at all.

'Geez, is there anything good about having kids?' Sarah blurts out and both Freya and Rachel flinch a little but don't respond.

Noah had clung to her leg as she was leaving to go out. Tom had prised him off and given him a cuddle and it surprised her that it was hard to leave him. Her edges have softened in an unconscious unfurl, and it's been a sort of relief. Love flows easily from Noah and it's begun to flow out of Ava in the same way; a current of emotion that runs without bias or condition. It occurs to Ava that nobody has ever loved her like Noah does.

'Love,' Ava counters at Sarah, and Rachel's lips curl up in a knowing smile.

'I don't need a kid for that. I'm pretty sure I'm going to get it later from that tall guy over there by the bar.' Sarah gestures to the group of men gathered in their eyeline, immediately getting up and strutting over to them.

Ava laughs, watching her friend on the prowl, but doesn't miss the urge to partake.

'I know she thinks we're tragic mothers, but I kind of hate that she gets to sleep in tomorrow.' Freya raises her eyebrow in jest.

'You can't have it all. At least not all at once,' Rachel mutters, finishing her drink.

'When do I...' Ava slurs, trying to find her words. 'When will I be back to normal, do you think?'

Freya gives Rachel a concerned look.

'You mean physically normal?' Rachel clarifies.

'Like *normal* normal. Like myself. Not just like a mother. Not just somebody who exists for someone else? When does that feeling come back?' Ava is tipsy and needy as she looks at her sister and her friend, expectant.

Freya and Rachel share another glance and Freya shrugs in a kind of defeat.

'Never.' Rachel pats her hand. 'This is who we are now. You can't uncook an egg.' Rachel spouts wisdom like some kind of mother guru and Ava is her eager student.

Ava nods as if she knew that was the answer and her head wobbles a bit in a champagne haze. The more time she spends in this life, the less sure she is of who she's trying to get back to. Maybe she's been driving away from herself the whole time. After all, she was the one who left Seb in the first place. As if thinking about him has conjured him, Ava sees Seb walking through the crowd.

'Seb?' Ava cocks her head up, shaking off her thoughts.

Freya whips her head around, clocking him, muttering something under her breath as he saunters over to where they're sitting.

'Ladies,' Seb purrs at them.

'What are you doing here?' Freya barks back.

'Nice to see you too, Freya,' he says, ignoring her question.

Ava props herself up to stand next to him but stumbles and he grabs hold of her arm to steady her. His fingers are warm against her skin, and goosebumps run up her arm under his touch.

'Are you alright?' He asks, his breath hot against her neck.

She nods in an elongated fashion to assure him that she still has her faculties, which likely has the opposite effect, and he reaches across the table for the water jug, filling a glass and handing it to her. The water tastes of cold nothingness after the tantalising cocktails but she's grateful for his concern. Music beats in her ears, drowning out her thoughts, and the room starts to spin a little bit, making her wobble again.

'I'm going to put her in a cab,' Seb yells to Freya, causing her to get up and push him out of the way.

'I'll handle it. She's not *your* wife anymore, Seb.' Freya glares at him and he backs away with his hands up, walking off. He looks back over his shoulder to see Ava still watching him as he disappears into the crowd, and she wonders if he was even here at all.

~

The Uber drive home sobers them up a little, and Rachel insists on dropping her off first and helping her all the way to the front door. Ava hugs her goodbye, effusive with "I love you"s and hollow promises to see her at yoga tomorrow.

The house is dark and silent like it's already been put to bed. Attempting silence as the oak door slowly swings closed, she still startles herself with the click as it locks into place. Kicking off her heels gives her toes instant relief, and her feet enjoy the cool timber floor while clumsily navigating her way through the house and up the stairs.

There's a dull ringing in her ears, the remnants of a good time, and the sweat on her body hasn't dried yet; she's still warm from the alcohol. Her body stops still at Tom's closed bedroom door. The therapist's advice replays in her head. *Hug your husband.* Without considering anything but the thrum in her body, she enters Tom's room and walks over to the bed where he's crumpled up in sleep.

Her hand runs over his bare shoulder and he rubs his eyes as he opens them, squinting to focus on her.

'What time is it?' His eyes are bleary as he sits up.

'Shh, don't talk,' she soothes in a too-loud attempt at whispering, before lifting her leg to sit straddled on top of him, their bodies separated by the lumpy doona.

'Ava, wait, what...' Tom mutters before she lowers her lips to his and kisses him with such force his head bangs into the rattan headboard behind him.

He pushes her shoulders back, forcing their mouths apart, before holding her upright. Even with her wobbly head she can see his bewildered expression.

'I thought... you wanted...' she stops short of finishing the sentence with *me*. A wave of embarrassment engulfs her and she gets off him, slipping down to the floor to hold her head in her hands.

Wordless, he bends down beside her and picks her up, laying her down on the bed still fully-clothed. He pulls the covers up and tucks his body in behind hers. He strokes her hair as the sweat on her neck leaves the pillow damp. The night has been a confusing collision of her lives. Seb flashes in her mind before the alcohol numbs her thoughts to sleep.

FIFTEEN

THE city is alive with morning commuters, replete with the constant hum of heaving traffic. Ava soaks it all in, arriving at the slick city office block ten minutes prior to her meeting with Sarah. The reception area is white and sparse but for a gigantic fiddle leaf fig in an oversized pot, which annoys her as she's never been able to keep one alive. The city view framed by the large windows serves as art. The receptionist, a tall, slim, brunette woman, who couldn't be more than twenty-five, sits behind the huge marble desk. She stands to greet Ava, looking immaculate in a pinstripe skirt suit, ushering her over to a sleek, uncomfortable-looking white sofa next to the window to wait. From the towered view, she can see people below weaving through the busy city streets and laneways, triggering a pang of longing.

Sarah soon appears from behind a heavy wooden door, looking glamorous in tailored black pants and a navy silk shirt, topped off with black patent leather pumps. Following as Sarah guides her down the hallway towards her office, Ava glances a critical eye down at her own outfit. All her old corporate clothes were too tight and the best she could find in her wardrobe was a cream shift dress paired with a grey houndstooth blazer. Despite the four-hundred-dollar label that had been still attached to the jacket, she feels not quite good enough walking behind Sarah.

Ava tries to shrug off her inferiority as she sits in the plush armchair in Sarah's well-appointed office.

'How was your hangover yesterday?' Sarah asks, taking her own seat behind her large, oak desk.

'Diabolical. How was the hot, tall guy?' Ava grins.

Sarah furrows her brow, conjuring the memory, and they both laugh at her forgettable sex. *Better than no sex*, Ava thinks to herself, reliving her pathetic fumble in the dark with Tom.

'I love that painting,' Ava comments, looking at the geometrical masterpiece on the opposite wall to distract herself.

'Amazing, isn't it? Mondrian inspired, with a less hefty price tag. When I saw it I had to have it.'

Sarah was an insatiable consumer in a way that Ava thought confident, but for anyone else would have been plain reckless.

'I know you're not here to admire my décor. I wanted to run a little proposition by you. I know you need more time to decide about the partnership, so what do you think about a little trial run? To dip your toes back in?' Sarah offers.

'What do you have in mind?' Ava replies, intrigue spreading through her.

'I've got a small fraud case. Family business, ripped off by their son-in-law who's been skimming the pot. Semi-high profile so they'd prefer to settle quietly, ideally no court. I want you to strongarm the son-in-law into as small a settlement as possible in exchange for his shares in the business.' Sarah hands her the brief in a crisp manila folder.

This case is comfortably inside her wheelhouse, which Sarah would be well aware of. This is not a test. This is a slam-dunk to whet her legal appetite again, ensuring that she won't be able to refuse the partnership deal.

'I assume this is a murky family case and the wife of the thief also has shares in the business?' Ava clarifies.

'Correct.'

'No wonder you wanted to handball this one.' Ava smiles and flicks her eyebrows up.

'Bill your hours directly to me at a grand an hour. You'll also get a kickback on any settlement amount under three million, fifteen percent on the shortfall.'

'Generous.' Ava's eyes widen. 'They must really want this kept quiet.'

'They do. So, you'll do it.' Sarah omits an inflection, making this more of a command.

Ava nods, hopeful this will be a good compromise for everyone. She can help Sarah and prove to Tom that she can handle working again.

'Also, I hear your husband annihilated Seb in court this morning. Got the case dropped. Any inside details?' Sarah leans forward, eager for information.

Ava tries to conceal her surprise. Tom had given her vague snippets about his case against Seb but she hadn't pried, not wanting to seem too interested. He failed to mention they were facing off today. She brushes off Sarah's questions with a casual laugh, saying she could never betray Tom's confidence. Inside, however, she's bruised that he didn't confide in her.

She shelves her hurt and tries to focus on the case at hand. Sarah has confidence in her, and Ava wants to prove her right. Despite her initial reservations about not being good enough, Ava walks onto the street below Sarah's office with new buoyancy. With a quick glance at her watch, she notes that she still has two hours before she needs to collect Noah from kindergarten. Coins clink into the meter beside her Range Rover as she tops up her parking and struts in the direction of her favourite shopping strip. It's time to up her game.

~

Ava waits for Noah with her back gently resting against the big oak tree outside the kindergarten gates. The day has shed its morning chill and she's enjoying a gentle bath of afternoon warmth. Her phone vibrates from inside her handbag and interrupts her calm. It's been weird between them since Tom rebuffed her attempt at seduction the other night. Avoiding each other seemed to be easier than the humiliation of discussing it, so she's surprised he's calling her.

'Hi,' she answers, trying too hard to be cool.

'Hey, quick question, did you just spend about eight grand on the credit card? They called me to report unusual activity.' Tom's tone is clipped.

'Er, yes actually. I needed some clothes for work. Sarah gave me a case as kind of a trial run.'

'You need eight grand worth of clothes for one case?'

'Well, I'm planning on more than one. I thought you said we weren't weird about money?'

'We're not, but you don't generally go on *Pretty-Woman*-style shopping sprees that send up red flags to the credit card fraud team.'

'You bought a new Audi R8 a few weeks ago, and I didn't give you the third degree.'

'That's a lease through work, Ava.' His tone is that of an exasperated parent; therefore, trying to spar with him is a bad idea.

'Oh, don't panic. I'll probably bill at least twice what I spent, plus bonus.'

'So you're taking the job, then?' he bristles.

'I haven't decided yet.' Her tone betrays her and he can probably hear the lie, but before he can call her out, she deflects with having to pick up Noah and hangs up.

Tom's refusal to embrace her career plans and his audit of her credit card still has her stewing when Rachel appears next to her.

'Hey there, dancing queen.' Rachel gives her a friendly nudge.

Ava's face turns crimson at the memory of her drunken antics. 'I was such a dick.'

'Don't be ridiculous, you were fine. It was fun.' Rachel smiles.

'Tom didn't think so…' Ava trails off and Rachel's questioning eyes implore her to elaborate.

'I kind of… threw myself at him, and he didn't… we didn't… it was mortifying.' Ava covers her face with her hands.

Picturing herself astride Tom as he fended off her drunken advances makes her body hot with regret.

'He probably just thought you were too drunk. Didn't want *you* to regret it,' Rachel offers.

Ava's head nods on autopilot but her stomach still carries bricks of shame.

'And Seb being there was… weird.' Ava tries not to sound too invested in Seb.

'Maybe he's stalking you? Sarah kept tagging us all in photos on Instagram.' Rachel shrugs.

Stalking seems incredibly efficient now with the advent of location-based technology. Seamless and also terrifying. It's not really Seb's style though.

'Sarah went home with the hot tall dude.' Ava moves the conversation off Seb.

'Ah, kids today and their one-night stands,' Rachel jokes with a faux wistful expression. 'Jeff was asleep on the couch when I got home, next to half-empty bags of UberEats. I ate his cold chips,' Rachel laughs.

'I have news. I'm officially back to work. I've just picked up a case for Sarah.' Ava knows at least Rachel will be happy for her.

'Does she want to see if you're up for the challenge?' Rachel asks.

'No. She wants me to be hungry again so I can't say no to her offer.'

'Are you hungry?' Rachel raises her eyebrows.

Ava pauses, taking a breath, before answering. 'Starving.' In every sense of the word.

They exchange a knowing glance and Ava remembers for a brief second how it felt to be hungry all the time. Her mind sobers as a gaggle of thundering four-year-olds run out of the gate, pelting themselves at their parents. Noah flings himself into her legs, smearing dirty fingers across her cream skirt, and she finds herself not minding. Noah provides the cantilever to her new existence. She takes his grubby little hand into hers and they stroll home.

~

The next morning Ava is sitting across from her new clients, Eliza and Rafe Montgomery, in the drawing room of their ample Toorak mansion. If she'd had any second thoughts about her little shopping adventure yesterday, they were immediately justified when she drove through the double gates of their riverside estate. She and Tom have a nice home by regular standards but this is next level, like walking into a painting. Looking the part is imperative today.

After rifling through the sordid details of their family business, Ava gets the impression that Eliza and Rafe are nice people. They wanted to help their daughter by bringing her husband into the business. Though they never explicitly say it, she gets the impression that Baxter Barrett had never been quite good enough for their only daughter, but they had to trust him to keep her close. Or, more likely, they kept him close because they didn't trust him.

'I think I have all of the particulars in order, apart from what you want to happen with your daughter's shares. Are you intending for her to hold her stake?' Ava asks.

'Yes,' Rafe is quick to jump in, 'she'll retain the equity, but she'll no longer have a seat on the board. Our youngest son turns twenty-one next month, he will be given access to his shares and take the board seat.' Rafe fiddles with the cufflink on his shirt and Ava can sense his ill ease.

'Mr Montgomery, I only mention this to be thorough, but are you sure you want to remove her voting rights? From the records I've been provided, it looks like Laura has worked hard for your family business since graduating. She denied any knowledge of her husband's alleged fraud.'

'She's staying with him,' Eliza says as a complete sentence, her thin lips tight at the edges, and Ava gets the message.

'We're trying to protect her.' Rafe's eyes soften and Ava can see that they're all hurting. Money brings out the worst in families and it was always Ava's least favourite part of her job. Her body shifts awkwardly in the high-backed, Victorian armchair.

'Might I suggest that you don't suspend her voting rights, at least not yet? I think it's more important to repurchase Mr Barrett's shares at this point. Laura's shares in the company are protected within her trust; no court will touch them in the event that she and Mr Barrett did part ways. You'll still have voting majority with your shares and those of your sons. This is about your family. Removing her from the board isn't a financial decision, but it *will* hurt her.'

Ava observes Eliza and Rafe hold each other's gaze, weighing up her words and mirroring each other's struggle. Eliza eventually breaks the silence, looking at Ava.

'We don't want to hurt her.'

'I know you don't, Mrs Montgomery. I understand this is difficult. I would want to protect my son too.'

'Oh, you have a son?' her eyes light up. 'What's his name?'

'Noah. He's four.'

'Such a delightful age. It's funny, you think it's the hardest thing in the world when they're little…' Eliza trails off.

'He's got lots of energy, that's for sure, and I'm learning more about dinosaurs than I ever thought possible.' Ava lets herself smile and alleviates the tension a little.

'We'll leave the board seat for now. Thank you, Ava,' Rafe says, in a soft voice.

Ava nods and wraps up their meeting, agreeing to draw up all the details for the impending mediation. As she leaves the estate, the huge iron gates close behind her; the finality of the movement is prison-like. Looking behind the veil of that kind of privilege leaves her hollow and unsettled.

~

That evening, Freya is sprawled out on the couch while Ava attempts to peel open a packet of ravioli, finally resorting to stabbing the plastic film with a kitchen knife.

'You know, you could help me!' Ava shouts.

'Why? You look like you've got it under control.'

'Have you forgotten that I've got a brain injury?'

'Oh please, not that again,' Freya jokes, walking over to the bench. 'I remind you that you knew how to open store-bought pasta before you smashed your brain up.'

Freya pulls a large pot out of the cupboard and fills it with water before flicking the gas on and putting it on the stove, narrating her process in a slow monotone as she goes.

'And that's how you boil water,' she finishes.

'You're an asshole.' Ava smiles sweetly.

'What's an *asshole?*' Noah says, appearing out of nowhere.

'Oh, nothing, sweetheart. It's a bad word, I shouldn't have said that.' Ava kicks herself at her untamed potty mouth. A good mother probably never swears.

'What *is* it?' He cocks his head to the side, imploring an explanation.

'It means bum hole,' Freya interjects, matter of fact.

Noah throws his head back laughing in delight at the mention of the word "bum", and runs off yelling 'bum hole, bum hole' on repeat. Freya laughs from behind a tea towel and Ava rolls her eyes.

'Ideal. I'm supposed to be showing Tom I can handle things around here.' Ava gives Freya a playful whack on the leg with her wooden spoon.

'Oh relax. Tom knows you're human. He's not a bum hole.' Freya laughs at her own joke. 'What's he doing in Sydney anyway?'

'He had to go up for a few meetings. He'll be home tomorrow.'

'Are you nervous with him gone?' Freya asks, chewing on a carrot stick.

'Not really. It's nice to have a bit of space at the moment.' Ava regrets letting that slip out.

'Are you fighting?' Freya's interest piques.

'Not exactly. He's not happy I'm working.' She doesn't tell Freya about her embarrassing sex attempt, knowing she'd never let her live it down.

'One case is barely working.' Freya makes a face.

'I want to buy into the partnership. He doesn't like the idea.'

'Well, he saw you when you were miserable. He's trying to protect you.'

'That was different. This is a completely new firm, with my friend. No stupid office politics, it's a clean slate. I'm not the person he remembers.' Ava throws the ravioli into the boiling pot, splashing a bit on her hands.

'Cut him some slack. He thought you were going to die, and then you kind of did die. The Ava he married is dead.'

'Yeah but the Ava *I* remember is dead too. How long do I have to be the living dead person? Whose memory gets to be saved?'

'Well, from where I sit, probably neither. You can't change what you remember, and neither can he. You have to rebuild somehow.' Freya sounds unusually wise.

Ava lets out a big sigh and slumps on the stool next to Freya.

'I'm trying.'

'Are you?'

'What are you saying?'

'I'm saying,' Freya puts her arm around her sister, 'don't be a bum hole.'

A giggle escapes her mouth, and she gives Freya a quick hug.

'You're annoying when you're right,' Ava says.

'I must annoy you constantly.'

'You do,' Ava says, flashing an overly sweet smile, and Freya digs her in the ribs before changing the subject.

'Want to come couch shopping with me tomorrow? I need to pick one for Daylesford and given *your* annoying trait is impeccable taste, I could use your help.'

'Sure, but it will have to be after ten. The real estate agent on my flat called today, tenants have vacated and I'm doing an inspection before it goes back on the market.'

Freya agrees to drive Ava to the flat and she's secretly glad of the offer. She's not sure what state she'll find her old home in and some moral support will be nice. Not that she can admit it out loud, but she's been missing her cozy flat. The prompt from the real estate agent gave her the perfect reason to stroll through her memories and she hopes it will reignite something that's lost.

~

'You okay?' Freya asks.

'I think I'm in shock. It's like I've been robbed,' Ava responds, eyes wide, looking around.

They're standing in her old lounge room surveying the scene. On a superficial level, the flat looks pretty good. There are scuffmarks on the floorboards and some peeling paint, but nothing a good clean and some minor repairs won't fix. The reality of standing in her old home, however, is a different beast. She's not quite sure what she expected, but it wasn't this. Knowing on a rational level it wasn't going to look like what she remembered, but the experience is like standing in the dregs of her own personal warzone. The emptiness is haunting and indicative of the otherness of change.

Freya steps across the room and holds Ava's hand while she takes it all in.

The agent had been clinical, handing Ava a checklist of maintenance she should undertake before they advertise it again. Oblivious to her turmoil and ready to move on to his next appointment, he suggested they lock up themselves once they'd finished the inspection. Ava made a mental note to switch agents once it was ready for market again.

'I don't know what I thought would happen,' Ava muses, 'maybe I was expecting some kind of epiphany.'

She walks over to the balcony door and pauses, running her hand along a small dint in the frame. Seb left that mark. He fell into it, drunk, at one of their New Year's Eve parties. Her lip curls up into a half smile at the memory. She'd helped him and his bleeding elbow into the bathroom and covered it up with band-aids as best she could. He'd kissed her slowly at first, then more frantically as he pushed her up against the bathroom wall, and she pulled open the buckle on his pants. The raging party in their house no deterrent for their greedy bodies. That's what it had been like with Seb. Frenzied passion punctuated by crushing lows. Their hunger for one another would prevail, and they'd find their way back to each other. Though it's not a stretch to imagine that the desire would dull eventually, and she's not sure who they would have been without the flame.

Outside, she stands on the balcony, expectant. She tries to imagine kissing Tom out here for the first time, attempting to recall a flicker of something. Anything. All she can conjure are thoughts of Seb. He would cook summer barbeques out here and sit on the deck chair to read the weekend newspaper. The engulfment of Seb hurts against the nothingness of Tom. In her heart of hearts, she's betraying both of them.

SIXTEEN

EXPECTING an empty house, Ava is surprised to find Tom in his study when she returns home from furniture scouting with Freya. He turns to smile at her in the doorway, but it doesn't reach all the way to his eyes and he looks spent.

'Plane was delayed. I thought I'd skip the office and finish up here for the afternoon. Where's Noah?' He asks.

'He's having a play date with Harry, I'll pick him up in an hour.'

She walks to the small sofa opposite Tom's desk and flops on to it.

'Big morning?' he asks.

'Yeah. I went to inspect the flat now that the tenants have moved out, then shopping for couches with Freya.'

'How was that?'

'Exhausting, she's a painful shopper.' Ava rolls her eyes.

'I meant the flat. Was it weird to see the flat?'

She pauses, watching him watching her. He has the upper hand on reading her so she can't avoid the truth.

'It was harder than I thought it would be.'

He slides his office chair over beside her on the sofa and takes her hand, waiting.

'I was hoping for...' she chokes a little searching for the words.

'I know,' he says, pulling her head into his chest and letting her stray tears fall wet onto his shirt.

Her pain runs into him and confusion swells. She feels warm here. Safe. Loved. The heat of his body runs through her chest and she can feel his heart beating. The unevenness of their exchange niggles at her, but she pushes it down until Tom's even breathing quiets her thoughts.

'It needs a bit of work, some paint and minor fixing. I think it will be fun, actually. Freya is going to help me.' She wipes her eyes as she pulls her head up.

'Great. Should fetch a higher rent when you relist, the market's pretty inflated at the moment.'

'Actually, I wanted to talk to you about that. Freya's decided to move to Mum's Daylesford house. She even thanked me for not selling it and looking after it for her. But she asked if she could use the flat when she's in town. She's going to commute for work until the end of the school year. I thought I could make it a short-term rental the rest of the time.'

'You don't need my permission.' She sees something in his eyes but isn't sure exactly what.

'I know. I *care* about what you think.' She softens her voice.

'I think it's fine if you want to short-term let. You're right. You'll probably make double what you would in a traditional lease. We've talked about it before but never got around to it. A bit more of a hassle with cleaning and furnishing.'

'Freya has a friend who manages them, I'm going to chat to her about it. I know I won't have time to do it myself.'

'Because of the partnership?'

'Yes.' She keeps her voice quiet and lets it land on him.

Tom sighs again and gives her a gentle nod, which looks like defeat.

'I've got the mediation tomorrow morning, but it could go well into the afternoon if they play hardball. I've asked Jane to pick Noah up in case I'm not back in time. I have to be in the city by nine, can you do the drop off?'

'Yeah,' he acquiesces, then mutters about having to get back to work, and she takes the cue to leave. The weight of the unsaid words is heavy.

~

Churning nerves make Ava rise early the next morning, her gut twisting with fear and excitement. She barely slept for the last few days thinking about the case. She wants to prove to herself, and everyone else, that she can do this. This is her stage, and she intends to perform.

It takes time selecting an outfit because she second-guesses herself as she goes. Wearing a skirt suit would appear more feminine and disarm the room. Or are trousers a better choice to show strength and control from the outset? Is a plain shirt best or is a pattern better to give her more personality, keep them guessing? She's aware she's overthinking it but knows this stuff matters. A man walks into the room and nobody questions his ability, yet the first thing people notice about a woman is what she looks like. Curating a deliberate image is part of the job.

Tom pokes his head into her wardrobe, as she's standing there in her underwear, paralysed by choice.

'It won't matter if you wear black shoes or red shoes when you kick them in the dick.' He winks.

Ava laughs, grateful for the morning banter. They didn't speak much last night and the mood was edgy. He leaves her to make her final decision and it's encouraging that he's making an effort, even though she knows he's not totally on board with all the change.

She decides on black pencil skirt suit with a green-and-white printed Gorman shirt, which is sleeveless with a high neckline. Her arms are toned from all the yoga and she wants to capitalise on the bits of her body that she actually likes at the moment. The skirt pushes her arse into a shape that she can tolerate and she tops it off with black Louboutins with the trademark red heel. She figures she can wear black *and* red shoes when she kicks Baxter Barrett in his metaphorical dick.

The boys are mid-way through breakfast when she joins them for a quick bite before her Uber arrives. Tom looks up as he butters Noah's toast and stops to stare at her.

'What? No good?' She looks down at her clothes, brushing her hands over her hips.

'Amazing. It's just been a while since I've seen you look like that.' His lips curl up at the edges.

'Well, it's certainly more comfortable in yoga pants,' she muses, sitting down at the bench and pouring her cereal into a bowl.

Tom's still looking at her, which is unnerving. After saying no to her mere days ago, is he having regrets?

'Can you pick up Noah's allergy medication? The kinder teacher emailed saying he's been rubbing his eyes again.' Maybe she's imagining it, but he says it as though she's the one who should have noticed.

'Well, what do I have to get?'

'I don't know the name of it. Just ask the chemist.' His tone makes her sure she's not imagining it. She clenches her jaw and decides to ask Freya about it, not wanting to concede to Tom's petulance. Is he punishing her for the other night?

Noah counters the tension by launching into a speech about the wingspan of the pterodactyl and asks if she knows that they have ninety teeth or that a baby pterodactyl is called a flapling. This softens Tom and he smiles across the bench at her. Despite herself, the cocoon of family still surprises her.

After finishing their breakfast, she ruffles Noah's hair as she picks up her bag to leave. 'Goodbye my little flapling. Mummy's off to work.'

~

The conference room in Sarah's Burke Street office is generous and well-appointed. Ava and Mr and Mrs Montgomery sit on one side of the large mahogany table, ready to battle the other side. Her face is neutral, presenting a calm front to assuage any nerves and put them at ease. Calm is better for everyone today.

Baxter and Laura Barrett arrive on time with their lawyer, Andrew Saunders, who Ava knows casually but whom she's never appeared against. Andrew is slick and looks exactly how one would imagine a lawyer. He's sporting an expensive tailored suit on his lanky frame, capped off with a fancy watch and a smug smirk.

'Ava. Long time no see.' Andrew offers his hand for her to shake. Like a typical man, he doesn't squeeze her hand hard enough. Limp handshakes from male colleagues irk her. Does he think she'll break?

'Andrew, good to see you. Please, take a seat, everyone.' Ava gestures with a sweeping arm, retaking her own seat next to Eliza and Rafe.

Laura can't even make eye contact with her parents as she sits next to her husband, cold and guarded. Baxter Barrett is an annoying homage to inflated confidence. He's decked out in a navy Hugo Boss suit with his brown mop of hair slicked back like a private high-school boy. He looks slippery and Ava treads with caution.

'We all know why we're here today. I don't think it would be advantageous for any of us to end up in court. Let's have a discussion, shall we?' Ava opens.

Baxter scoffs a little under his breath and she dislikes him more. She wants to make him as sorry as possible, which, for someone like him, usually comes down to money.

The morning proceeds with cool hostility and denial from both sides of the table. Ava and Andrew do their best to guide their clients towards resolution but their rigidity is prevailing. Nobody wants to budge. They hit the five-hour mark and Ava decides she's going to have to play dirty to get this finished.

'Mr Barrett, 2.2 million is a fair offer for your equity, given you were stealing from my clients for over 18 months...'

'Allegedly, counsellor,' Andrew interjects, but she ignores him and continues.

'My clients have yet to press criminal charges against Mr Barrett. Would he like to roll the dice with a police investigation and potential jail time?'

'Oh please, it was a clerical error,' Baxter scoffs, 'and they won't want that kind of press, right Rafe?'

Ava holds up her hand to implore Rafe not to bite back, indicating she'll deal with him herself.

'It makes me wonder what kind of press *you* want, Mr Barrett?'

He gives her a dopey look, raising an eyebrow.

'Can we have the room? Eliza, Rafe, Laura, would you mind stepping out?' Ava meets eyes with Eliza and Rafe, willing them to trust her.

Baxter leans back in his chair and nods permission to Laura. They close the door behind them and even Andrew looks intrigued by her tactics.

'What's going on, Ava?' Andrew asks.

'I'm simply pointing out to Mr Barrett that perhaps he doesn't want to expose all his skeletons. Perhaps it's in his best interest to remember that he can't blow up my clients without blowing himself up in the process. 2.2 is more than generous for an *alleged* criminal.'

'The shares are worth double and you know it,' Baxter pipes up.

'Okay, for fun, let's do a little math. Criminal case, legal fees, three, maybe, four hundred grand. Potential civil case, legal fees plus damages, could add up to multiple millions. Not to mention the possibility of prison,' she rattles off.

'You're reaching, Ava. You know they'll never go to court,' Andrew responds in an exasperated tone.

'You both seem very sure about that. It's cute.' Ava sits back in her chair and folds her arms as both men bristle at being called *cute*.

'What do you have?' Andrew seems to sense there's a reason for her smugness.

'Former employee, willing to go on record describing Mr Barrett's fraudulent activities. Has evidence in writing, including a generous payoff from your client to keep her mouth shut. Lisa Wellsley. Ring any bells, Mr Barrett?'

Lisa is her trump card, and she watches the blood drain from Baxter Barrett's face as she smells his fear. What she can't mention in front of the independent mediator, of course, is her knowledge that Baxter had a long-standing affair with Lisa, who herself is out for revenge. The *written* evidence is loose, but she makes a convincing bluff. Judging by Baxter's expression, Ava deduces that Laura is in the dark about his extracurricular activities, which is exactly what she was counting on.

Baxter's face tells her that he knows that she knows, and that he's lost.

'We'll need a minute,' Andrew says, through gritted teeth.

'Of course.' Ava gives them a forced smile as she exits the room.

~

After everyone has left, Ava borrows Sarah's empty office to finalise the paperwork for the Montgomerys. She can't be sure exactly how long she's been there when Sarah enters the room.

'Hey, you're still here. How'd it go?'

'Yeah, I thought I'd get a jump on the contracts. It was great. Baxter settled for 2.2, plus an NDA. Rafe and Eliza were happy and Laura retains equity and a board seat.'

'What? How did you get him down that low?' Sarah looks impressed.

'I went down an online rabbit-hole stalking his social media and found a former colleague that was happy to tell me who Baxter really was. Gave me some leverage.'

'That must have been *some* leverage.'

'Scorned lovers have loose lips.'

'Gotcha. Want to get a drink to celebrate?' Sarah asks.

'Sure, what time is it? My phone died and I was distracted getting this done.'

'Four thirty, perfectly acceptable hour to start drinking.' Sarah fishes a mobile phone charger out of her drawer and hands it to her.

Ava plugs in her phone intending to give Tom a quick call when her phone starts pinging with message after message. Tom, Jane, Freya, thirty missed calls, multiple messages.

'Oh no...' Ava flicks through the messages on her phone.

'Something wrong?'

'I don't know. I need to call Tom.' Ava clicks on his name as she speaks.

It goes straight to voicemail and her gut sinks. She dials Freya next.

'Where the hell have you been?' Freya hisses down the phone at her.

'I'm at work, my phone died, what's going on?'

'Noah. He's at the children's hospital. He's okay but you need to get there. He's broken his wrist and they're taking him into surgery now. Tom's with him.'

The blood drains from her face as she processes what she's missed.

She turns to Sarah. 'Noah's in the hospital, I've got to get there.'

'My car's out front. I'll drive you.'

They get out of the building as fast as Ava's feet can move in her stupid high heeled shoes; all the while she's trying not to vomit as bile taunts her throat. The success of the day is obliterated and all she wants is to be with Noah.

~

Tom looks up as her shoes click on the linoleum floor towards him. He's sitting alone, slumped in the middle of a row of blue plastic chairs attached to the wall. He doesn't get up as she approaches him.

'What happened? Is he okay?' She sits next to him, dumping her bags on the floor.

'Clean break of his wrist falling off the play equipment. They're operating now to reset it.' Tom doesn't look at her and his voice is tight.

'Oh Christ, I'm sorry I wasn't there.' She holds her head in her hands.

'The kindergarten called you, why didn't you answer? They ended up getting an ambulance and Mum had to meet him at the hospital, he was terrified.'

'My phone died in the mediation, I didn't realise.' Ava shakes her head, mad at herself.

'I knew this would happen, Noah comes second now.'

'Hang on, that's unfair. And where the hell were you? Why didn't you pick up?' She's defensive, the inequity of the partnership suddenly on display.

'I was in court. I didn't see the messages until I got out.' Tom says, without a trace of irony.

'Oh, well that's okay then, is it? You can be unavailable at work but I can't?' She's baffled by the implied double standard.

'Yes. Okay. Yes. *Someone* has to be around, okay! And yes, we decided, *together*, I might add, that you were going to be that someone. You wanted it that way!' He shouts and throws his arms in the air.

'I'm not *her* anymore!' Ava's release is guttural.

'Then who *are* you, Ava?' Tom matches her fury.

A middle-aged nurse comes out of the swinging doors looking tired and put out. Ava and Tom stand up, self-conscious, and wait for her to speak.

'Noah is in recovery; the surgery went well. I'll bring you in to see him. But you need to keep your voices down.'

They nod like scolded children and follow wordlessly behind her into the recovery ward. Noah is lying on a bed with the rails up on both sides. He looks tiny under the thick white covers and his little face is obscured with an oxygen mask. His arm hangs out one side, encased in a huge blue cast. Ava's heart hurts seeing him so fragile and small.

She walks over to one side of the bed and pulls the chair over, sitting next to him to hold his free hand. Tom mirrors her move, sitting on the other side of the bed. The smell of the hospital is triggering, the potent mix of disinfectant combined with a general aroma of sickness. Her heart gains unpleasant momentum. Her own trauma still fresh, she realises she hasn't tried to deal with it, not properly. Half-baked attempts at therapy and burying it with work likely isn't the answer and she realises she isn't okay. The room blurs around Noah's drug-woozy body and panic rises like a tide within her. Her head starts to swirl and she's vaguely aware of Tom moving toward her and wrapping his arms around her shoulders.

'It's okay, he's going to be okay and so are you. Breathe, baby, breathe.' Tom's voice encourages calm and she makes herself aware of her chest rising and falling until the panic recedes.

Noah garbles incoherently underneath his oxygen mask and Ava shifts her focus back to him. A nearby nurse comes and removes the mask, giving him a brief check then moving on. He moans with his eyes still half closed before his gaze steadies on her.

'Mummy,' he squeezes out in a raspy voice.

'Hi, Noah.' She fights tears as he looks at her.

'You were gone,' he mumbles and closes his eyes again.

Guilt engulfs her and it breaks her heart that he's right. She is gone. She needs to work out a way to come home to Noah. She hopes there's a way to preserve his memories without torching her own.

SEVENTEEN

DULL fluorescent light filters under the doorway as Ava adjusts her bleary eyes. Her shoulder is contorted underneath her cramped body, and it takes her a minute to realise where she is. Sitting up in the small fold-out bed in Noah's hospital room, the springs creak through the thin mattress. Noah's asleep in the adjacent bed and she watches his little chest go up and down with the gentle motion of breath. A quick glance at her phone next to her tells her it's 3am. Tom left at midnight after they told them only one parent was allowed to stay overnight. He didn't argue when she said she wanted to stay; perhaps he was relieved something maternal was kicking in.

She wonders if it's okay to call him; he might be awake. She pauses as she's about to dial his number, not sure exactly what she wants to say. She does it anyway, thinking maybe that's exactly the point.

'Hello?' He's groggy and it's obvious she's woken him.

'Sorry,' she chokes.

'It's okay. Is he okay?'

'Yes he's fine. But I don't mean sorry for waking you. I mean sorry for... all of it.' Flashes of her failures as his wife ripple through her mind.

Tom lets out a sigh, which mostly sounds sad.

'Babe, don't be sorry. *I'm* sorry. I know I haven't been fair.'

'I know your heart's broken, Tom. I know I'm not the same.'

There's a pause, providing space for the words to land rather than making her uncomfortable.

'I just miss you,' he says through a breaking voice.

With his pain on display it hurts that she can't reciprocate in the same way. It's not him she misses. Her heart doesn't know him and she doesn't even know if she wishes she felt differently. Seb is still rattling around in her head and she can't see past him.

Talking to Tom over the phone is making her braver with the truth, and although she knows it's the coward's choice, she decides to do it anyway.

'I'm going to move into the flat for a little while. I'm sorry.'

His muffled sobs echo through the phone and her own eyes drip soft tears. After they hang up she cradles her phone, lying awake and staring at the ceiling. There will be no reward of sleep after what she's just done.

~

Noah is sitting up, bright-eyed, having toast and orange juice, when Tom appears in the doorway with a big teddy that has a bandage on its arm. He looks terrible and she can tell he didn't get any sleep either. She walks towards him, intending to give him a hug but he moves past her and goes to Noah, whose face lights up at the teddy bear.

'Look, Mum! He's got a broken arm like me,' Noah beams.

'You'll have to take good care of him then and make sure he rests a lot. What will you call him?' Ava asks.

'Bruce,' Noah responds without pause.

Noah busies himself tucking Bruce under the covers next to him and offering him some toast, and Ava takes the opportunity to talk to Tom.

'Are you okay?' she whispers.

He looks at her, stunned, and she feels stupid for asking.

'Let's just get through today,' he says, looking away from her.

An officious nurse comes into the room to discharge Noah and runs them through his pain medication and care plan for the next few weeks. Ava is trying to listen, but she's relieved when the nurse hands her a printout with everything written down. It's not long until they're all bundled into the car, ready to head home. Tom's in the driver's seat and he turns to look at her coldly.

'Shall we drop you off at the flat on the way home?'

'What? Tom...' Ava's bereft at his coolness.

'It's what you want, isn't it?' He's curt.

'I don't have anything packed. It doesn't have furniture yet...' She panics.

He raises an eyebrow, which seems to suggest that he doesn't consider any of this to be his problem.

'Can we please get Noah home and then talk about this in private?' she whispers, invoking Noah, trying to get him to soften.

'No. I dropped your stuff there this morning on my way here. I left you a camping mattress, it will do until you get what you need.' He keeps his eyes straight ahead.

'Tom. Jesus. Why are you doing this?' Her pulse rockets as time swirls.

'I'm protecting Noah,' he hisses through gritted teeth, peering into the backseat at Noah, who is distracted by a dinosaur book, Bruce tucked under his arm.

'You can't drop in and out of his life whenever you want, he's been through enough.'

'You think banishing me is better for him? I want to work something out for all of us. I'm not disappearing.'

'You've already disappeared.' His words cut her.

With that, he starts the car and heads in the opposite direction of home as yet more loss pulses through her.

~

Joni Mitchell croons in the background with the odd crackle from the low-budget portable speaker. The lyrics *I really don't know love at all* float through the air, piercing Ava's heart as she contemplates her shambolic marriages.

'He left me crying by the side of the road, Freya,' Ava sobs into a glass of red wine.

'Stop talking, you'll ruin the effect,' Freya replies through a closed mouth like a ventriloquist.

Freya had rushed over to the flat with some essentials, which, in addition to the portable speaker, included wine glasses, red wine, a box of mix-matched cutlery, chocolate, and something called a 'sheet mask'.

'How long do I have to leave this thing on for?'

'Until you feel rejuvenated,' Freya mumbles through the mouth-hole of her own mask.

Ava peels the wet mask off her face, discarding it on the floor where she is sitting on a cushion. It leaves behind an oily residue that smells like lavender and will evidently remove years off her face. *If only*, she thinks.

'Hey! You'll ruin the magic serum skin-fixing properties!' Freya says while removing her own mask with the same care usually reserved for newborn babies.

'I know you got a baby-sitter so you could drop everything and come and scoop me out of my hole, but this isn't helping.' Ava cradles her serum-wet face in her hands and Freya shuffles over on the floor to put her arm around her.

'Okay. What do you need?' Freya shifts gear.

'You have to talk to Tom for me. Get him to be reasonable. I have to see Noah.'

'Tom isn't going to stop you seeing Noah. He's probably just upset.'

'You didn't see his face when he left. He basically said to call him when I had myself sorted to work out a custody arrangement. He talked to me like a lawyer, which is fucking annoying on top of everything else.'

Tom's face was maddening as he spat words at her through the half-open car window. He wouldn't look at her or negotiate at all. He said if she wanted life to be this way then she'd have to work it out without him, but in the meantime he was shielding Noah from her trauma.

'He's hurt. You left him.' Freya shrugs her shoulders and takes a gulp of her wine.

'I haven't *left* him. I just need space to breathe again.' She lies to herself to soften the ramifications.

'Ava, you said you wanted to move out. How did you expect him to react?'

'I don't know. Okay, so tell me what to do now.'

'Well, you need to get this place sorted. Furniture, a room for Noah, make it look like a home. You want to live here, so *live here*.' Freya says the words as if they're simple, and Ava isn't convinced.

Ava has never lived here alone. Even though she'd bought it by herself years ago, Seb had moved in pretty much straight away. She's not sure if she knows how to be in this place by herself. Every crevice of the flat has memories of the two of them together and she bathes in them to keep the memories real. It's an exercise in exquisite torture but she can't stop.

Freya gets up and walks around the various rooms making a verbal list of things Ava needs. Ava isn't paying full attention but the odd word registers in her mind, like *IKEA* and *tomorrow*. She groans and lies down on the floorboards, balancing her wine glass on top of her stomach.

'Are you even listening to me?' Freya is standing above, hands on her hips.

'No,' Ava moans with her eyes closed.

Freya sighs and sits down next to her.

'Do you remember when I got busted for smoking pot and the cops called you?' Freya asks.

'Was that the same night you were skinny dipping in the fountain in the community gardens?' Ava rubs her temple, digging for the memory.

'Different night, similar vibe though. Anyway, Mum was away for work, you were nineteen, they let you take me home as my guardian. You somehow managed to talk the cops out of charging me, saving us all the humiliation of court.'

'Dave Farraway,' Ava mumbles.

'What?' Freya jerks her head up, confused.

'Dave Farraway was the cop who arrested you. He was three years above me at school and I'd let him fondle my boobs at a party a couple of years earlier. He was a rank kisser, like a real octopus tongue, you know? Gross.' Ava pretends to gag at the memory.

'He let me go because he had the hots for you? Well, what do you know. I just assumed you were a natural legal genius.'

'I was. Knowing how to work a cop is very useful. And happily, it doesn't usually require groping.'

'Jesus, okay, that was a tangent. Anyway…' Freya gets back on track, 'do you remember what you said to me that night as I was crying in your car?'

'Stop being a fucking idiot?' Ava guesses.

'Well, probably, but no. You said, "You can choose what happens in your life."'

'Well that was bullshit. Obviously…' Ava sweeps her arm around the room to illustrate her point.

'Ava, you need to choose what happens next. You've never had a problem making decisions, so it's time to make some. For your sake, and for Noah's.'

Thinking about Noah makes her throat thick with sadness. Freya's right, though; she needs to make choices for both of them now.

~

It's eight o'clock when Ava knocks on his door in the dark. It's weird to knock when she has a key but caution is imperative now. Knowing the rules to this game somehow makes it worse, and she'd give anything for some blissful ignorance.

Tom opens the door but doesn't say anything.

'You're not answering my calls,' Ava says, making her voice small.

'I'm angry.'

She's relieved he's being honest with her and she allows a little hope to creep in.

'Can I come in?' she asks.

He pauses, moving aside, letting the oversized front door engulf her, and he gestures for her to sit in the "good room".

'I thought this was only for visitors?' She attempts banter.

'You are a visitor.'

This shift in him is bruising but she doesn't have time to be sad about that now. She came here for Noah.

'I want to see Noah, you can't keep him from me.' She sits down on the immaculate couch as he sits down opposite, with the glass coffee table providing a buffer.

'And how do you intend to do that with your hectic schedule?'

'Well, I guess I'll manage it the same as any other working single parent. How do *you* intend to manage it?'

'You're a single parent now? Is that what this is?' Tom looks pained as he avoids her question with his own.

'Tom, I just wanted some space. Some time. You're the one who's forced my hand on this.' Her shoulders fall, resigned.

Tom lowers his gaze and shakes his head to himself in what she hopes is defeat. She doesn't *not* love him, and she knows he loves her. Surely throwing barbs at each other isn't sustainable.

'Okay. What do you propose?' he asks.

'Well, I think we should talk to him about it, but I'd like a fifty-fifty split during the week. Maybe two nights on, two nights off, with weekends and Sunday nights alternating?'

'Jesus, you really have thought about this.' Tom looks crestfallen.

'Tom, I know you and I are in a weird grey area, but Noah is part of me. I don't need memories to feel that connection. It's... primal somehow.' She felt the tug between her and Noah since he first walked into her hospital room. However unnatural motherhood feels, the space between her and Noah was genuine from the outset.

Tom half smiles and a tear rolls down one cheek. 'You said a similar thing when he was born. That you felt like you already knew him.' Tom's own eyes shine with the memory.

'I love him. And I'm even starting to like dinosaurs.' She smiles and he mirrors her.

'Bloody dinosaurs. I still misspell pterodactyl every time I have to google it,' Tom says with faux irritation.

She lets out a soft chuckle and waits for him to speak again, letting him take the lead.

'Okay. You want to start tomorrow? You don't even have furniture.' Tom raises an eyebrow.

'I went shopping today. I've got everything except a couch, which is on order. I think Noah will be fine with the dinosaur beanbag I got for now anyway.'

'What do we tell him?' Tom balls his hands up on his knees.

'The truth. Mummy is having a hard time remembering things and needs to live in her old house for a while to help her feel better. He will come for sleepovers and have lots of time with both of us.'

'*Is* that the truth?' He keeps his eyes on the floor.

'Yes, Tom. I'm drowning. People keep telling me who I am and I need some space to work out who's right. It's not that I don't have feelings for you, I do. I just need to...' Ava searches for the word until she realises she doesn't know what it is.

'Okay.' He nods. 'Is it okay if we talk? Can I call you?' His tone slips a little into desperation.

'Of course.' She moves to the opposite couch, sitting next to him to wrap her arms around him. He smells like woody aftershave and his salty tears make her cheek wet as it's pressed up against his. He folds his arms around her back but it's not the same, as though he's lost permission to touch her like he used to. The shift sits uncomfortably in her chest and she misses him, even though he's right here.

~

After spending most of the next day assembling minimalist furniture with complicated instructions and tiny tools, Ava is relieved to pick up Noah from kinder and bring him back to the flat. He busts through the door and runs to find his new room, which looks like the remnants of a dinosaur explosion. Ava watches him gasp at the discovery of the dinosaur doona cover, framed prints on the wall and a basket of toy dinosaurs in the corner. She knows that she made the correct choice with the theme and his excitement gives her some joy amidst the uncertainty of their new situation.

'Is Daddy coming over too so I can show him?' Noah asks, expectant.

'Not tonight. Daddy will pick you up tomorrow though and we can show him then.' She flashes him a smile of reassurance and he goes back to playing, seeming unperturbed.

The afternoon passes quicker than Ava would have liked and she realises time with Noah now has a sense of urgency. Knowing that he's going home tomorrow creates a pressure to soak in every small moment with him. She's more attentive than usual and plays all the games he suggests until they are both exhausted, flopped on beanbags watching *Bluey* before dinner.

Even though Rachel had dropped off a homemade chicken pie for their dinner, Noah asked if they could have pizza and she agreed. Saying yes to takeaway was a small concession in the midst of all the change. The doorbell rings and she rushes to answer it, expecting to find their pizza delivery on the other side. She's startled to find that it isn't that at all.

'What are you doing here?' She asks when she sees Seb standing in her doorway.

'I wanted to see it for myself,' he slurs back at her.

'You're drunk, you can't be here. Noah's here,' she adds, suddenly protective.

He seems not to hear her and leans in against the doorframe. His breath reeks of bourbon, making her reel back.

'You know, I always knew you'd end up back here, knew it wouldn't last.' His eyes are half closed and her irritation is growing. Being sober when Seb is drunk has never been fun.

'How'd you even know I was here?'

'You have your spies and I have mine.' He tries to tap his nose but ends up poking his own eye.

'For the last time, Seb, *what do you want?*'

'I wanted to see you hit rock bottom.' The venom in his voice jars. Maybe he still hates her underneath it all.

'*Me* hit rock bottom? Take a look at yourself,' she hisses at him.

'Yeah, well that's your husband's fault, isn't it? He fucked my career, now nobody wants to touch me, I'll rot in the public service...'

'I don't think one lost case is career-ending.' She doesn't indulge his theatrics.

'I don't know what to do.' He crumbles to the floor as he starts to cry.

Ava looks at him in a heap on her doorstep and can't pinpoint her emotion, but it's swirling around pity and annoyance. The annoyance is squarely at herself because she can't stop caring about him.

'Hello,' Noah pipes up as he appears by her side, staring at Seb.

'Hello Noah, I'm Seb.' Seb looks up at him and attempts to hold his head up and smile.

'Why are you sad? Did you hurt yourself?' Noah asks.

'Yep, mate, I sure did. Hurt myself badly.' Seb nods.

'I broke my arm, see?' Noah holds up his cast to show him.

'Okay, I think Seb needs to go home now to rest and feel better.' Ava cuts off any potential burgeoning friendship and ushers Noah back inside, before turning back to Seb.

'Don't come here again,' she says through gritted teeth, shutting the door on him.

Noah is still watching her, looking confused.

'Is he your friend, Mummy?' he asks.

'No, darling. Let's go finish our show.' She guides him back into the living room with a gentle arm. Friend is not the right word for Seb, so it's not technically a lie.

As she watches a family of blue heelers frolicking across her TV screen, she can only think of Seb slumped against her front door. The guilt is corrosive and she knows he's a mess she has to clean up. For tonight, though, she brings her mind back to Noah. He doesn't deserve to pay the price for her baggage. Though it makes it hard when her baggage is literally on her doorstep.

EIGHTEEN

THE morning has an unusual chill as Ava waits for Tom in the almost-full car park. He's ten minutes late, which is typical for the Tom that she remembers, though less so for *new Tom*. Shifting from one foot to another, she rubs her hands together, trying to heat up. She'd agonised about what to wear today, not sure exactly what impression she should be giving, eventually deciding on high-waist jeans and sensible Gucci sneakers, in so far as *Gucci* can be considered a sensible choice. It was baffling to find seven pairs of jeans in her wardrobe, all high waisted like a seventy's diva. The low-slung jeans of her past, apparently relegated in favour of what Rachel told her were *Mum jeans*. However, her saggy tummy is grateful for the movement. Her favourite YSL leather jacket topped off the outfit; it had almost made her weep when she found it packed away in a box a few weeks ago. Stroking the soft leather on each arm provides some comfort in the familiar, and she's grateful that jackets are more forgiving on her post-childbearing body. Rachel had commented on how cool she looked when she passed her at the morning kinder drop off, which initially gave her confidence a boost. Anxiety then kicked in on the drive here, worrying that cool was the wrong vibe and wondering why she had stopped dressing like this at all. Why was she happy floating in the abyss of active wear?

Tom appears from behind a bank of cars and approaches with a quick stride. He looks good, wearing a light-grey tailored suit that hugs his muscular frame.

'Sorry I'm late. Traffic.' He gazes at her for a few seconds longer than would be considered normal but then switches back into action.

'We better go in, it's meant to start in five.' He pushes his dark aviators back down over his eyes.

They make polite small talk as they walk across the car park but it's stiff and unfamiliar, leaving a bad taste in her mouth. She follows him through the enormous gates of the exclusive boys' grammar school, which leads them through vast, resplendent grounds up to an array of buildings not dissimilar to a castle. Apparently, Ava had booked this school tour months ago to help them decide where to send Noah next year, but she wonders why she chose this one. The whole place is intimidating and a far cry from the small state primary school she'd attended as a child. Tom doesn't seem fazed at all, sauntering into the giant reception area and greeting the vice principal with an easy handshake. A myriad of staircases go off in several directions and the walls are lined with portraits, all of which are old, white men. They mill around a trestle table finding their name tags, before being ushered into a grand hall to take their seats for the opening presentation. People shuffle around into their seats, causing reverberating echoes around the vast space.

'Are you sure about this place?' Ava whispers close to Tom's ear, pausing a little to breathe in his scent.

'You picked it.' He shrugs. 'I'm happy for him to go to the local primary.'

She tries to be open-minded listening to the principal's address as he espouses the benefits of the school, but her thoughts keep wandering. Looking around at the other prospective parents she notices a definite theme. The men are almost all dressed in suits and swirl around in a sea of navy and pinstripe. The women vary between corporate chic and expensive casual. Almost all of them are white and the lack of diversity is stark. Looking down at herself she realises she fits this elite mould, leaving her disappointed. The twenty-one-year-old version of herself that backpacked around the world, drinking in culture as if it were life's elixir, would hate this.

A round of tepid clapping interrupts her thoughts, bringing her back to the present, and she and Tom shuffle out of the hall to join in with smaller tour groups. They inspect classrooms, sport facilities and

STEAM labs, which are allegedly the bedrock of child genius these days. Everything is state-of-the-art and a world away from her '90s education. Blackboards don't seem to exist anymore and it's all electronic whiteboards that automatically download to students' devices. She's still learning how to operate the iPad and most of the information that is meant to impress her leaves her more confused.

They return to the lobby for some "light refreshments", which include a huge array of pastries, finger sandwiches and an exotic fruit platter. A barista at the mobile coffee cart is making swift work of the caffeine orders which she's grateful for. Without a coffee machine at the flat, she only had a cup of instant before leaving the house. Her sad morning drop has been leaving a pang for Tom and she misses their morning ritual.

She's about to ask Tom how long they have to stay here when a voice booms from behind them, 'Thomas! As I live and breathe…'

She swings around to see Nick approaching them with the same broad smile that she remembers, but with far less hair, what is left flecked with grey. She hasn't seen him since his and Sarah's engagement party another lifetime ago.

'Ava! Oh my god, long time!' Nick gives her a warm embrace, going on to shake Tom's hand and give him a friendly slap on the back.

'It's good to see a familiar face,' Ava replies.

'Yeah, I heard about your accident, glad to see you're alright.'

Ava nods, but *alright* is not quite the right word for how she is.

'Do you have a boy coming here next year?' Tom asks, moving the conversation along.

'Max will start next year, and Harrison the year after. I'm an old boy so it's kind of a rite of passage in our family. My wife's over there, interrogating the principal anyway though. How about you two? I knew you got married but didn't realise you had kids.'

'Noah, he's four. We're just doing the rounds, weighing up the options,' Tom says.

'I heard you settled a big case last week, Ava. My firm offers occasional in-house legal services to the Montgomerys. Rafe was impressed, and it's pretty hard to impress him.' Nick gives her a gentle congratulatory elbow.

'Yeah, it was my first one back. I'm actually joining a partnership, with ah… Sarah.' Ava flushes red at the mention of Sarah.

'Really?' Nick's eyes pop a little and Ava feels stupid that she's brought her up.

'I was shocked to hear that you two, you know…' Ava fumbles with her words.

'Ah, yeah. Geez it really has been a while, Ava.' Nick's eyes flash a little sadness and Ava regrets making it awkward.

'Nick!' A small blonde woman calls from across the room, interrupting their reunion, and Nick excuses himself after mutual promising to catch up properly soon.

'Well that wasn't awkward at all,' Tom says, taking a sip from his coffee.

'Oh god, I wish I hadn't said that. Do you think I upset him?'

'Nobody likes discussing their exes.' Tom shrugs.

'I still can't believe they broke up. They were my golden couple.' Ava finishes her paper cup coffee.

'Yeah, oh well, ancient history I suppose. Want to get out of here now?'

As they walk back to the car park they exchange some notes on what they've seen at the school but agree to shelve any decisions for a few more weeks. Ava hates that their conversations have lost their ease and are threaded together with formality instead of their usual banter. It hurts more than she'd like, but it's too cruel to confide in Tom given she's the cause of it all. She decides to extend a small olive branch though, in the hope of some repair.

'Noah wants to show you his dinosaur room, do you want to have dinner with us Thursday night when he comes over?'

'Are you cooking?' He crinkles his forehead.

'Takeaway. Obviously.'

'Phew.' Tom wipes his brow in a show of exaggerated relief.

They part ways and she's more optimistic that maybe she hasn't ruined their chances at some kind of family after all. As she walks back to her car, her phone vibrates in her bag. She looks down, thinking Tom has sent her a funny message, but it isn't him.

Seb: *See you tonight.*

~

'This is a mistake,' Freya says as she shovels stuffed toys into a moving box and gestures for Ava to hand her the tape. Ava's regretting helping Freya pack up her flat and telling her about her dinner with Seb.

'Yeah, well, you're probably right.' Ava pulls out a huge piece of tape, using her teeth to release it then handing it to Freya.

'Definitely. I'm *definitely* right.' Freya shakes her head like she's disappointed.

'Well it's too late, I already said I'd come over,' Ava says, knowing full well she doesn't want to cancel anyway.

'He's a train wreck. You can't fix him. Trust me, unfixable dickheads are *my* specialty.'

Freya doesn't understand that he's not the one she wants to fix.

'I can't stop thinking about him, and it's not fair to Tom if I can't find a way to move past him somehow.'

'I don't think Tom wants you to go over to his house for dinner either,' Freya deadpans.

Guilt sinks in her stomach and it's annoying how well Freya can call her on her bullshit. After his little episode on her doorstep, she told Seb they needed to talk properly, once and for all, and he offered to make her dinner. Apparently, he knows how to cook now too, which may be the most impossible fact of all for her to accept.

'He's going to make moussaka, which I need to see to believe, okay?'

Freya knits her brow and glares at her.

'I just... I need to put this to bed.' Ava sighs.

'Yeah, that's what I'm worried about. Don't pretend it hasn't crossed your mind.' Freya jabs her in the ribs.

Ava would be lying if she said she hadn't thought about sleeping with Seb. Even though there is lingering tension with Tom, the ache for the familiar is strong. She buries her face in her hands and groans.

'Freya, I need to know why. Didn't I ever tell you what happened? Didn't I talk about him?'

'No. You hate him. You look very uncomfortable if his name is ever mentioned. He's like Voldemort.'

'Who?' Ava raises her eyebrows at another pop culture reference that's passed her by.

'Oh, for fuck's sake,' Freya mutters under her breath. 'Doesn't matter. I was away when it all went down, but you seemed more than happy moving on with Tom. I didn't pry.'

'How very unlike you.' Ava flicks her eyebrows up.

'Yeah, well, I was pretty stoned back then.' Freya smiles.

'Mum would know these answers. I really miss her.' Tears begin to well behind her eyes.

'I know.' Freya softens and puts her arms around her sister, for which Ava is grateful, but it's not enough to stem the pain. She's sick of being overwhelmed by sadness, sick of being on the back foot for everything.

'I'm okay, let's keep packing. Take my mind off things.' Ava wipes her eyes on the back of her sleeve and starts assembling another box.

It's impressive that Freya has had the gumption to organise her move so quickly. Once she'd decided to live in their mother's old house it's been like a fuse lit underneath her, and there was no stopping her. Tradesmen were organised with the precision of a German train timetable and she even rolled up her own sleeves to repaint the interior. The garden was apparently so dilapidated she needed special machinery brought in to clear around the house. Ava had recommended her gardener, Steve, to help her out and he seemed to have all the right connections to get the job done at Freya's required breakneck speed.

Packing boxes was all Ava could sign up for, still too anxious to go back to the house yet. Helping Freya get ready for moving day was also meant to provide a distraction from her problems, but now she's not sure it's working. Freya managed to line up a new job and childcare, so she won't be commuting back and forth to the city after all. Ava's been pretending that it isn't happening because it means two things. Firstly, that she won't have her sister close by, but also that she's going to have to go back to her mother's house at some point. Both things elicit raw hurt that she's not ready to face.

~

The street around her is dead quiet as Ava sits inside her car in a state of semi-paralysis. She can't get out of the car and she can't drive away. Her phone vibrates in her handbag and when she digs it out, two text messages sit unread.

Seb: *Dinner ready in 20. Where are you?*

She sighs, knowing she can't stop herself from going in even if she'd wanted to. She flicks down to the second message.

Freya: *Don't sleep with him*

Followed by two emojis. An eggplant and a big red cross.

She laughs a little, which relaxes her somewhat. As she walks to his front door she repeats Freya's mantra in her head: *don't sleep with him, don't sleep with him, don't sleep with him.*

Seb's house is in Fitzroy, where trendy people like artists and musicians call home. Due to the hefty inner-city price tags, middle-aged lawyers who like to think they're still cool also take up a chunk of the offerings. The gate of the detached Victorian creaks loudly as she pushes it open and she notices the decrepit state of the small front garden. It's mostly half-dead English Box edging with a lonesome Japanese maple tree in the middle, dappled with about half as many leaves as it should have this time of year. The front door opens while she's still surveying the scene and she looks over to see Seb standing there barefoot in distressed jeans and a white Calvin Klein t-shirt.

'You should water your garden.' She waves her arm over the valley of death.

'I have a guy who mows and takes care of it.' He shrugs, indifferent.

'Well you should fire him.'

'Since when do you know anything about plants?' Seb asks, gesturing for her to enter.

'I've been learning how to garden. Apparently I'm into that sort of thing now.' She wishes she hadn't said that, not wanting to offer him any information about her new self. Afraid of what it could mean.

The narrow hallway leads them into a sleek, open-plan back room housing a combined kitchen, dining and lounge area. It's fitted out with a bulky timber dining table with black chairs and an oversized charcoal couch. Monochrome art lines the walls and the white kitchen provides perfect juxtaposition, making the room feel bigger than it is. It's masculine without embellishment, whilst still relaxed and unpretentious. It's not what she would have picked but she likes it. It's hard to picture a child in here, though. Noah wouldn't last five minutes without smearing something on the clean surfaces.

'Dinner's nearly ready, drink?' He offers, holding a wine bottle aloft.

'Sure.' She takes the glass of red wine from him.

She looks around the room without trying to pretend that she isn't. There's no point pretending anything with Seb. An acoustic guitar is propped up on a stand in the corner making her smile. Seb fancied himself as Jeff Buckley whenever he played a few chords, never letting a lack of talent dampen his ego.

'Like it?' he asks.

'Yeah, it's nice. It's what I imagine you'd want for a bachelor pad.'

She throws out the word *bachelor* as a kind of bait, wanting to test if it's true.

'Yeah, no compromises here, which actually made it hard to decide.' He furrows his brow as if he's realising this for the first time.

'You never did see the value in compromise.' Her tone is even and she's not trying to poke him.

'You're right. I got used to getting my own way.' Seb offers up a rare moment of honesty and it rattles her. If he's trying to disarm her, it's working.

'Do you live here alone?' She makes deliberate eye contact, which makes her heart race.

He pauses for a moment, a small smirk on his lips, before simply saying, 'Yes.'

She doesn't ask for any more facts. If he had somebody worth mentioning, then he would have.

'When did you learn to cook?' She walks past the bench, examining a salad, and looking through the oven window to see the moussaka bubbling away, the aroma of which is impressive.

'Oh you know, old dog, new tricks, that's all. This is pretty much the extent of my repertoire though. I figured if I could do one dish really well then that would be enough.'

She chuckles, relieved that he hasn't changed as much as she thought. Then on second thought decides that's probably a very good reason to keep her guard up.

'Why am I here, Seb?' She's not sure if she's asking him or herself.

'You're the one who wanted to talk?'

Typical, Seb. Always deflecting.

'You showed up on my doorstep, wasted and blaming me for your life. Why?' Her eyes are soft, imploring him to be honest.

'I was angry. You were right, though. It's my fault, it's all my fault...' He rubs his temple.

'What do you mean?'

He looks away for a brief moment and sighs as if searching for words.

'I only have myself to blame. Screwing up that case, losing you, it was all me. Seeing you again is just really fucking with me. Seeing the *old* you I mean.' He comes closer to her and she can smell him. His light, peppery cologne wafts over her. It's exactly as she remembers, making her inhale sharply. 'Seeing the you who loves me,' he finishes, and hovers his face near hers. Any sense of reason she walked in with dissolves.

His lips are familiar and she lets him kiss her. Wrapping his arms around her waist, he pulls her close to him. He's hard against her leg and her heart is pounding. His tongue is urgent in her mouth as his hands paw over her body and she's not sure if it's guilt or that she prefers the way Tom touches her, but something feels wrong.

'Stop.' She pushes him away and steps back, leaving them both panting.

'Did I do the wrong thing?' He looks hurt.

'No, I just... can't. I have to go.' She leaves him standing in his kitchen with his erection and home-cooked meal. She doesn't even feel bad about it. Something stopped her tonight, not Freya, not a memory, but something in her bones knew this was a bad idea. If only she knew why.

NINETEEN

AS Ava glides through the last downward facing dog of her morning yoga class, the tension from last night melts out of her. Seb obviously finished off the wine on his own because she got a few incoherent texts as it edged closer to midnight. She'd turned her phone off in the end in order to get some sleep and when she woke up this morning her head was lighter. Maybe she can trust new Ava's judgement after all.

Whilst she's supine in *shavasana*, Rachel turns to her from the neighbouring mat and whispers, 'Coffee?' Ava nods, grateful for both the promise of caffeine and the opportunity to debrief. They roll up their mats and make their way to their now-regular post-yoga coffee shop, choosing a table in the sun. The morning is warm, prompting them both to slip off their jackets to soak it in.

'What did you do last night?' Rachel asks as the waiter deposits their hot chai lattes in front of them.

'Had dinner with my ex-husband.' Ava fakes nonchalance.

'What?' Rachel splutters her first sip.

'Well, technically that's not true. I left before dinner.'

'I thought you were washing your hands of him after the "drunk on the doorstep" episode?'

'I was, but he was persistent and impossible to ignore.'

'Like thrush?' Rachel quips and it's Ava's turn to splutter her drink as she laughs.

'Anyway, I think I'm done. I get it now. He is the same as he always was, and I'm... not.'

The reality hit her as she left Seb's house. He's the same guy.

Uncompromising, hot headed, selfish and, annoyingly, still incredibly good-looking. She doesn't want to go back to being who she was when she was with him. Being Noah's mother has changed those priorities. It was subtle at first, but now it's pervasive. Seb always made sure he came first, in all ways that matter, and she doesn't have the appetite to sustain that kind of love. Not anymore.

'Did you... you know?' Rachel nudges.

Ava flushes and knows there's no point lying to her.

'He kissed me. But it was weird. I stopped him. Well, first I kissed him back, but then I stopped him. Ugh, I'm a terrible person. Should I tell Tom?'

Rachel pauses, considering her answer. 'No. It's over. Why hurt him more?'

'Yeah, I've already hurt him enough.' The truth sits heavy on her chest.

'I didn't mean it like that.' Rachel puts her hand on top of Ava's.

'I know, I know. But it's true.'

They sit in the silence of the truth for a few moments and Ava appreciates the non-judgmental space, though she's not convinced she deserves it.

'He's coming over tonight for dinner. I'm going to try and make an effort. Try to like, date him a bit.' It's weird to say that aloud and she shakes her head, wishing her words would come together better.

'I think he'll like that.' Rachel gives her a smile of encouragement.

'Is he okay? Has he said anything to Jeff?'

'Jeff never tells me specifics, but they've had a few boozy sessions lately. I think he's lonely.'

'I miss him. I'm surprised at how quickly I missed him.' She felt it the moment he drove away from her and it's lingered in her bones ever since.

'I think that's a good sign. Kissing Seb feels wrong. Missing Tom feels right. Good, no?'

Ava shrugs and drains her latte. Trusting her feelings has been hit-and-miss as of late, which is making her afraid to fully lean in to any one emotion. Unwilling to take up all the verbal real estate of their catch up, Ava changes the subject and gives Rachel room to unload about her latest drama at work. Rachel relaxes as she vents, prompting a swell of guilt in Ava about her lack of reciprocity amidst her own flailing messes. She makes a silent vow to herself to stop using Rachel as a one-way life raft and be a better friend.

Ava leaves the café feeling good and strengthened by the sisterhood. Then she remembers that Tom is coming over for dinner tonight and butterflies resume dancing in her gut. In order to recalibrate herself, she dials Freya's number.

'Whazzup?' Freya delivers the line like a '90s rapper.

'What's Tom's favourite food?'

'I dunno, meat?' Freya guesses.

'Unhelpful. Be more helpful.'

'Er... steak?'

'Something *I* can cook, or preferably, buy already cooked.'

'Just order in and call it a day.'

'That won't impress him.' Ava is getting exasperated.

'Ava, calm down. You don't need to impress him. He doesn't care what you feed him, he only cares about you coming home.'

'Have you talked to him?' Ava bristles into an accusatory tone.

'Not lately,' Freya snipes back.

'Then how do you know that for sure?'

'Um, because it's obvious. Why are you being a dickhead?'

She doesn't know. Taking out her nervous energy on Freya is reflexive and selfish in a way that's specially reserved for sisters.

'Sorry, I know, you're right. I'm stressed about him coming over.'

'Get a grip. Go and have a facial or something. You don't need to win him over, you've already done that.'

'Yeah, but I'm worried I've blown it all up.' The truth hurts her throat as it comes out.

'You haven't. Trust me, okay? Now I have to go and pack another forty thousand boxes before tomorrow, but call me if you fall over the edge again.'

They hang up and Ava feels better and worse. Everyone is telling her the right things, but he is the only person she wants to hear it from and she's not convinced he's going to say it. Googling *facials near me*, she decides to take Freya's advice and check out for the afternoon in a last-ditch effort to put her best self forward, once and for all.

~

There's what could only be described as a mild flood in Ava's tiny bathroom as Noah thrashes around with his battleship, which is apparently on a super-secret mission. Luckily, they opted for the waterproof cast on his arm. She doesn't want to scold him for making a mess, worried that the moments with him are too precious now that they are fewer. Plus, who cares anyway? It's just water. As she procures a stack of towels from the linen cupboard, anticipating the cleanup, the doorbell rings, causing her stomach to somersault.

Ava swings open the door to reveal a smiling Tom. He's dressed in faded jeans and trainers with a simple black T-shirt showing off his broad chest. She's gotten used to seeing him in suits lately and appreciates the more natural version.

'You look good.' She grins at him.

'You too.' He nods at her floaty knee-length dress. It's black floral with a plunging v-neck that shows a hint of her lacy bra underneath. Colour flushes to her cheeks, knowing full well that it wasn't accidental.

'Noah's in the bath, come on in.' She switches back into mum-mode.

Tom follows her through to the bathroom, the floor of which seems to have gotten wetter, though she's unsure how that's possible.

'Hey, mate! Whoa, what's going on in here?' Tom looks around at the water carnage.

'I'm on a secwet mission!' Noah beams at him through a face of bubbles.

'Well I think it's time to keep some water *inside* the bath, okay?'

Tom grabs a towel and starts mopping up the excess water, then halts to look at Ava.

'Sorry, is this okay? I didn't mean to take over...' He lowers his eyes and appears unsure if he's overstepped.

'Not at all.' She grabs another towel to join in the cleanup. 'I didn't want to rain on his parade, although rain seems like the right word for it.' She laughs, keeping the mood light.

The doorbell signals the arrival of their dinner and Tom offers to finish up bath duty. They've slipped back into being a team again. Maybe she hasn't blown it all up after all.

Tom emerges with a damp-haired Noah, clad in fresh pyjamas, as she's setting the table with plates and napkins around the pizza centrepiece. They all sit down and Noah goes quiet as he chews on his first piece.

'I had lunch with Nick today. He's actually on the board of the school, I suspect he was trying to shore up the intake.' Tom takes a big bite of pizza.

'Geez, that was cheeky of him.'

'Don't worry, I remained non-committal.'

'You're not sold on the school?' Ava poses it as a question, but is ultimately relieved.

'Nah. I think the local is better for primary school. It's walking distance and lets him be a bit more normal. Less pressure. The place was a bit Stepford for my taste.'

'Tom, *you* went to an exclusive private school.' Her forehead crinkles.

'Which is how I *know* it's wrong.' He winks.

'Good. It felt wrong for me too. Let's enrol him at the other one. What else did Nick have to say?' Ava asks.

'He didn't say much. Just asked how you were and a bit about the case you had. Not in a nosy way though, I think word got out about it because Rafe is such a tough client. He must be singing your praises around town.'

'Well that's good, I guess.' Knowing her work is still a sore spot, she does her best to be humble.

'Do you have more work on?' Tom seems genuinely interested.

'Not yet. I asked Sarah to let me have a couple more weeks to decide on the partnership, while I work out my… life.' Ava waves her arm over the room.

'It used to be *our* life.' Tom's words are soft but they hit hard.

'I didn't mean it like that.' Her fingers move reflexively to touch his hand but he shifts it out of reach, shaking his head as if to indicate *not now.*

'How's that pizza, buddy?' Tom changes the subject.

'Gweat,' Noah says with a full mouth, which should be gross but they both laugh.

'Have you had any friends over yet to play in your special room?' Tom asks him.

'Mummy's fwiend came over, but he hurt himself and had to go home. He was cwying.'

Tom scrunches up his face and Ava's heart sinks.

'I'll tell you later,' Ava says, but panic surges knowing she'll have to explain Seb's antics. And the rest of it.

Dinner carries on with a perceptible shift in Tom. He's frosty, like he's preparing for the worst, and so is she by extension. After stories and cuddles, Noah is happy to drift off underneath his dinosaur covers, and her buffer for the evening is now gone.

When she returns, Tom is sitting on the couch with one leg hitched up on his knee, taking up space as he leans back into the soft sofa, but still looks uncomfortable. Without speaking she sinks down next to him. The room is quiet but for the hum of the TV and the air is thick with the unspoken. He cocks an eyebrow at her and waits.

'Yes, he came here. Drunk and pathetic. Moaning about the case he lost. I didn't let him in.' Ava decides to stick to facts at this point.

'Why didn't you tell me?'

'There was nothing to tell. I told him to leave, he left.'

Tom is quiet again but he looks pained, like he can't decide whether or not to dive farther into Pandora's box. The guilt rises and she won't continue to lie to him by omission.

'I saw him yesterday too. I needed to get some closure. I won't be seeing him again though, I'm done.' She keeps her head high and shoulders back in a show of certainty.

Tom looks up at her and she hopes she's pulling off a convincing display.

'Where'd you see him?' He asks.

She shifts, uncomfortable like a schoolgirl caught red-handed with cigarettes.

'His place. He cooked dinner.' She's careful not to add, *and he fondled my arse.*

Tom looks unsettled but doesn't speak for a few moments, as though he's weighing up his options.

'Do you...' Tom pauses with a slow inhale, 'do you still love him?'

Letting herself pause, she thinks about her answer. Does she love him? Her world used to begin and end with Seb. Since the accident, she's wanted to go back to when things were just the two of them and be who she was before. Was it really about Seb, or did she just want to look at a version of herself that she recognised?

'I'll probably always love him. But not in the way you mean. Not anymore.' She knew when he kissed her that something was different. Something visceral and permanent.

Tom exhales and she lets him take his time without filling the silence. It's obvious to both of them what he's not asking her.

'Okay,' he says finally.

She inches closer to him until they're touching and she picks up his hand in hers. There's a flicker of gloom in his eyes.

'Do you want to ask me?' she whispers, then immediately regrets it.

'I'm scared of the answer.' He hangs his head and closes his eyes.

'I'm sorry,' she manages to squeeze out, making him look down at her with sad eyes.

'You slept with him?' Tom's eyes shine with the slick of threatening tears.

'He kissed me, but it feels just as bad.' Her eyes fall to her lap, not wanting to look at him as she says it.

'Did you want him to kiss you?'

'Yes. But then it felt wrong and I realised that it was mostly because it wasn't you.'

He pauses again and she's struggling to read him. He's calm but still looks injured.

'I'm going to go...' He stands up and panic swarms her body.

'Do you hate me?' The need in her voice surprises her.

'No. But I'm going to need a bit of time. We're both muddling our way through this. I don't want to rush the next steps.' His voice stays soft.

'Because you don't trust me?'

'Well, were you going to tell me any of this if Noah hadn't brought him up?' His eyes show her that he can see inside her, unmasking all the hidden elements.

She looks to the floor with an almost imperceptible shake of the head.

'I just need some time,' he repeats under his breath.

She can't watch as he leaves, and she remains on the couch as gentle sobs come out in endless supply. Her heart's been in her throat most of the evening and now it's pouring out of her eyeballs. She transfers her body to her bed in order to lie down and wallow in her misery. The mattress is still on the floor because the frame was too heavy to put together by herself. She was going to ask Tom to help her after dinner, thinking it could serve as possible foreplay with some banter over the Allen keys. Given that's been thwarted by her self-sabotage, she's forced to survey the grim scene of her single-mum bedroom. There's the sad state of the bed, artless walls and a bland beige rug that isn't quite big enough for the room. The crappy IKEA clothes rack in the corner, heaving with her wardrobe overflow, solidifies the failure of the room. Her Chanel bag is cheapened, slung over one end of the rack, adding to the abyss in which she finds herself. She couldn't see herself in her life until she left it, but now it's the only life that makes sense. This is hurt. This is heartbreak. Seb's love never ran deep enough to hurt her like this. Nobody's love has hurt her like this. Now she understands and now it might be too late. She underestimated Tom. She didn't think he had the capacity to hurt her. In the end it is his absence that's the knife to her heart.

Fumbling for her phone, she shoots off a couple of text messages, knowing exactly who she needs now.

~

'He just walked out... couldn't even look at me,' she mumbles into the wine that Sarah brought over after receiving an SOS text. Ava put the call out to Rachel too, knowing she needed both of her best friends to help plug the hole in her heart.

'He'll be back.' Rachel pats Ava's knee and fills up her glass as if it's somehow medicinal.

'Maybe. But maybe you should think about what you want. You? Remember you?' Sarah offers, jolting her a little.

'What do you mean? You don't think I want him?' Her glass teeters a little on the coffee table as she puts it down.

'Maybe not, maybe you got sucked into this suburban life and now you're bored?' Sarah muses, kicking off her boots to the floor and tucking her legs underneath herself.

'That's not really how Ava and Tom are. They're actually pretty great together,' Rachel interjects with a protective edge to her voice.

'Well, you never saw her with Seb.' Sarah shrugs, sipping her pinot gris.

'Maybe you're both right,' Ava placates. 'Seb and I had a different relationship for sure, but I don't think that lessens what I seem to have with Tom. I hate being pulled in both directions and I wish I could remember...' Ava crumples against the couch, making her wine-heavy head fuzzy.

'That's what I mean! Why do you need to be pulled? Why not decide what *you* actually want,' Sarah says.

'You say it like it's simple,' Ava responds, still slumped.

'It is. Decide what you want.' Sarah drains her drink. She was never one to overanalyse. Things came easily for her.

'I think having a child makes this a bit more complicated. They're a family,' Rachel chimes in.

'Seb was her family too,' Sarah counters, ever the lawyer and loving having the final word.

Rachel scoffs under her breath but doesn't respond, and Ava labours herself upright and tries to quell the tension.

'None of this is in dispute. I loved Seb and we had a life together. But that's over and I have a whole other life with Tom and Noah. They're not a competition.'

'Aren't they?' Sarah stays firm, causing Ava to wobble.

'All I know,' Ava begins, 'is that I felt sick when Tom walked out the door tonight in a way that I didn't when I walked out Seb's door.'

She flashes back to last night when she left Seb's house. Relief had engulfed her as she closed the door behind her. He didn't try to follow her either. And she didn't look back as she got into her car and drove away.

'Well that sounds like you've made your choice.' Rachel smiles, giving her hand a little squeeze.

'Tom's the easier choice.' Sarah stays combative.

'That's unfair.' Rachel's defence is immediate and Ava's starting to think she would have made a good lawyer too.

'No, she's right,' Ava says, causing them both to whip around and look at her, imploring her to continue. 'Tom *is* the easier choice. Being loved by him is easier. Seb always came with… caveats…' Ava slurs.

'Okay, I think it's time for bed. Waking up with a clear head will help.' Rachel removes the wine glass from Ava's swaying hand and she nods in tacit compliance.

Rachel's arm is warm underneath her fingers as she's led to bed, where she collapses under herself. The pain of the evening is now numb from the wine and once Ava closes her eyes to sleep, the choices evaporate, for tonight at least.

TWENTY

THE aroma of coffee nudges Ava into consciousness and she wakes up to Rachel bringing her a hot mug in bed, together with two Panadol and some buttered toast. Her tongue has the consistency of sandpaper and the shame throbs almost as bad as her head.

'Oh god, I don't deserve you,' Ava moans, sitting up in bed and reaching for the Panadol first.

'I thought I'd better crash on the couch just in case. Noah's had brekky and he's watching cartoons.' Rachel perches on the side of the bed.

'I was a train wreck last night.' Ava's remorse swirls. How infantile to need a friend to babysit her, not to mention Noah. Some mother she is.

'What are friends for?' Rachel smiles.

'Sorry about Sarah. She can be a bit… opinionated.' Ava grimaces in apology, knowing that Sarah's not everyone's cup of tea.

'She was trying to protect you. She doesn't know the Tom that I know.' Rachel shrugs but lowers her eyes.

'She used to. It's been a while I guess.' Ava sips the coffee, eliciting a grateful sigh.

'I've got to go if I'm going to make it to yoga today, you want to come?' Rachel tilts her head.

'There's something I've got to do today. But I'll call you later.'

Rachel gives her a proper hug before making her exit, leaving Ava to curl up on the couch with Noah to watch cartoons. His intermittent laugh keeps her thoughts from straying too far from the moment and her headache abates while they soak up the remainder of their morning together.

After weeks of anxiety, Ava knows what she needs to do today and she's finally got the guts to do it. Escaping all the drama she's created adds to the appeal and she resolves to drive to the country and spend the night with Freya. Tom was probably right: time and space is what they both need. She drops Noah off at home first, and seeing Tom standing in the doorway in his torn jeans and faded Nirvana T-shirt makes her ache even more. As he sweeps Noah into his arms she's reminded that his affection doesn't belong to her right now, and how she took it for granted when it did. He gives her a weak smile as she walks back to the car, mumbling about getting on the road to beat traffic although they're both aware that Saturday morning freeways are anything but hectic.

Once she's back in the driver's seat she pauses for several elongated breaths to calm down, while watching Tom and Noah disappear behind the front door. Her loneliness hurts so much more having the people she loves within reach.

Once she's cruising down the freeway, the twist in her gut becomes even more apparent and the drama with Tom recedes, as today doesn't belong to him. The wrench in her heart is for her mother and she's been trying not to think about it from the second she told Freya that she was coming. It's been the festering band-aid that she knew would have to come off eventually, but with the day upon her she questions if she's ready, knowing deep down that she'll never be. Grief and love, the two intertwined bedfellows, tug at her heart. She can't ignore the reality of Luci's death forever and avoiding the house is merely a tactic to stay in a sad purgatory. But she wants to do this for Freya and support her in this new adventure. That resolve wanes as she peels off at the Daylesford exit and has to fight the urge to turn the car around.

Driving through town, she's relieved to find the quaintness has remained and it's still as charming as she remembers. There are cottages in abundance and fruit trees pepper the lush front lawns behind white picket fences. It's a place where dreams are bundled up and sold to strung out city folk under the labels of *wellness* and *rejuvenation*.

Her mother's house is a few minutes out of town, away from the main thoroughfare of village life. The front gate is an open greeting, beckoning her down the kilometre-long driveway. The cypress trees that line the drive allow light shards to stream through at intervals, bathing the road in streaky beams. Part of her wishes she could believe her mother was looking down on her so she could soak her up like sunlight. The afterlife is too much of a stretch for her fact-ruled mind and wanting to believe isn't enough for her. Her mother is everywhere and nowhere in a painful illustration of the great dichotomy of death.

As she rounds the last curve of the driveway the house appears, sparkling in the morning sun. The white cottage stands proud with its wraparound veranda and robust tin roof. It presents as a picture from a storybook, exactly how she remembers it. A flowering wisteria twines itself through the wrought-iron lacework, offering up its dappled purple beauty across the porch. The front garden beds are bare, and reflect the only small change in the entire vignette. She turns off the car engine and sits to look at it for a few moments. It's not yet as painful as she thought it might be and she exits the car with cautious optimism.

Freya and Pip rush out to greet her, and an excited Pip flings herself at Ava, who grabs her and swings her around a few times, then squishes a few kisses into her chubby cheek. Ava has learnt that toddlers are excellent at cutting through tension, due to their unbridled glee at the simplest of things. It's been the most refreshing discovery she's made about children, whom in her previous life she mostly found at best disinteresting and at worst, terrifying. Freya steps forward to embrace her and it's good to be close to her again.

'I've missed you,' Ava mutters into Freya's shoulder.

'I've been gone two days.'

'I know,' Ava replies, with no trace of irony.

Ava releases Freya from the hug and holds her back to look at her in an exaggerated way. She's dressed in a kitsch floral pinafore with black tights, topped off with yellow wellingtons. On anyone else it would look like an oversized toddler outfit but on Freya it's perfect. Her light auburn curls are freely bouncing around her shoulders and she looks happy.

'We're still working on the garden, obviously.' Freya sweeps her arm over the empty beds.

'It looks pretty much as I remember. This place has always felt like that though,' Ava trails off.

'Like a time warp, right? It transports me back to childhood too.' Freya nods her agreement.

Ava walks up the steps of the wide porch, ready to face the front door. Freya must sense the unease because she sidles up next to Ava, taking her hand in hers as Pip runs in ahead of them. They walk inside together and Ava inhales sharply as she stands in the hallway. Her whole life floods back over her and she wonders if she was too cocky to think this might be anything but difficult. Piercing the moment, Pip screams for Freya from the back of the house and Ava is left alone. She peeks her head into the front sitting room, which, but for a new sofa, looks like her memories. Two bookshelves straddle the central fireplace, which is perfectly stacked and ready to light. The bookshelves used to heave with books when she was a child but are now barren. A couple of boxes sit unpacked on the floor and Ava deduces that Freya is yet to get around to them. Even still, the room is inviting and she can remember rainy days by the fire, roasting marshmallows and playing scrabble. Freya would end up in tears, being the inevitable loser, and though it's a bit sadistic, the memory makes her smile. Freya calls out from the kitchen and Ava wanders down the hallway, following the smell of something baking.

The kitchen and living room have had the biggest facelift. The paint is fresh and what was once a decrepit peach colour is now a soft sage green. The kitchen cabinets have also been painted a crisp white, which is a big improvement on their previous mission-brown.

'This looks amazing. And you've stripped the floors back too!

How have you done all this?' Ava is shocked at Freya's gumption on this project.

'Yeah I've been pretty busy, it's taken a few hard weekends. Scone?'

'You baked? Who are you?'

'It's *your* recipe.' Freya laughs as Ava takes a warm scone off the bench and slathers it with butter and jam.

Freya leads her out into the back garden carrying a tray of more scones and a fresh pot of tea, and Ava continues to be amazed at the transformation as she surveys the scene. The bluestone paving has been pressure washed and restored to its former glory, illuminating a pathway through the apple trees. A huge plot has been dug beside the house with uniform rows of freshly planted vegetable seedlings, and there are half a dozen chickens in the chook shed. It's a forager's heaven and she can't believe her wild little sister now belongs here.

'*How* have you done all this?' Ava sits down to grab another scone as Freya pours the tea.

'Well, I've had some help. Steve did most of the garden.'

'Oh yeah, I'm glad that worked out, he's great.' Ava smiles.

'Yeah.' Freya looks down. 'He's more than that actually.' Freya looks up at Ava who stares back, now confused.

'We've been seeing each other.' Freya swallows hard delivering her news.

The shock registers on Ava's face followed by immediate guilt that she's been oblivious to her sister's new relationship.

'Oh Frey, why didn't you tell me?'

'I was waiting to see where it was going, plus you've kind of had a bit on lately.' Freya shrugs.

'I'm sorry. I've been a mess. You know you can always tell me stuff though, I love when you tell me stuff.' Ava reaches over and squeezes her hand. She hates herself for being so selfish and unavailable.

'I like him. He's normal and reliable and not a lazy scumbag. Plus he's really hot.' Freya's cheeks go red and she breaks into a wide grin.

'I did notice his muscles when he was carting bags of compost for me. Good for you Frey, I'm glad you're with someone you like, who's not a dickhead.' Ava raises her teacup in a toast.

'I keep waiting for the bubble to burst.'

'It doesn't have to.'

Freya wrinkles her nose and seems unconvinced.

'He must be pretty keen if he's coming all the way up here to see you all the time. Plus doing all this…' Ava waves her arm over the garden.

'He's coming up later to have dinner with us, you can grill him then,' Freya says and changes the subject. 'You going to tell me about your fight with Tom?'

Ava lets out a big exhale at the mention of Tom.

'It wasn't exactly a fight, but he knows about Seb.'

'Bloody Seb. I told you not to go there.' Freya takes the rare opportunity to remind Ava that she was right.

'Yeah well, I don't know what to do now. He can't even look at me.'

Tom's dismissal last night was cold and final in a way that she didn't like. She's been replaying it over and over in her head like some kind of emotional self-flagellation.

'Give him time to cleanse the revolting Seb pash from his head. It's not the end, he's made of stronger stuff, I promise. Now let's go and collect some eggs so we can make some custard for dessert later.'

Ava gets up, shaking her head, unable to get used to this domesticated version of her sister. As she follows Freya and Pip through the garden a quick breeze blows gently past, making the daisies ahead of her wobble. Even though she knows it's not true, she feels Luci. Everywhere and nowhere.

~

The pot-bellied fireplace radiates a dazzling heat and the flames dance behind Ava, who's doing her best impression of an elephant. Pip copies her and flails her little arm around like a trunk before sitting back down in her lap, waiting for the next page of *Who lives at the Zoo?*

When they've finished, Pip waddles around the room collecting her myriad of stuffed animals to re-enact the story with props.

'It's beautiful watching you spend time with Pip like this.' Freya's eyes are glassy as she watches from the couch.

'What do you mean? Do I not normally play with her?' Ava is baffled.

'It's just...' Freya pauses, 'you found it hard to be around her when she was born. It was only six months after Violet died and... it hurt too much.'

Without the memory, she can't mirror Freya's pain but can see the open wound between them and knows she's responsible for it.

'I'm sorry if I wasn't there, like *properly* there.' Ava goes over to sit beside Freya and gives her arm a squeeze.

'You don't need to be sorry, I never blamed you. We were all devastated, of course, but *you* were in hell.' Freya wipes the escaped tears with the back of her sleeve.

'It's the one thing I'm glad I can't remember.'

Though not remembering her daughter's death is a reprieve of sorts, the lost memories of Noah continue to haunt her. Not remembering how it felt to have him roll around inside her belly or to hold his tiny baby body in her arms is the cruellest of blows.

They sit and watch Pip for a few moments as she talks to her toys and lines them up, counting them as she goes. Her sweet little niece, looking the epitome of a little girl. Is this what Violet would have been like?

'I'm glad I'm here now, *really* glad.' Ava smiles solemnly at Freya, hoping that fresh memories can expunge the stale, bad ones.

'Wine?' Steve calls out from the kitchen where he's been holed up working on his famous roast lamb.

'Yes,' the sisters call back in unison before laughing and lightening the moment.

Freya excuses herself to wrangle Pip into bed while Ava keeps Steve company, offering no practical help beyond pouring the wine.

'Thank you for making Freya the happiest I've seen her in ages,'

Ava says, before taking a sip of her merlot.

'I'm the one who should thank *you*. I'd never have met her if it weren't for you. If I'm being honest, I've had a bit of a crush on her for ages.' Steve winks.

'Oh, by the way,' Steve continues, 'I found a supplier that has fairy gardens if you still want me to build one for Noah? Freya wants one for Pip too so it's no trouble.' He whisks the homemade gravy with a delicate arm over the stove, as her thoughts drift back to her old home with Tom.

'Um, I'm not sure I should be making gardening decisions right now, given the circumstances with Tom.' Ava blushes acknowledging it out loud.

'Oh I don't think Tom would mind. I've been working for you both for a long time. He's always deferred to you with design decisions.'

'Okay, then yes please, I'd love you to make him one. I think he'd love it.' She nods her appreciation, though doubts the gesture will aid in any reparation.

'Kids love a bit of magic, don't they? I'm still learning but Pip can't get enough of my famous *I've got your nose* trick.' Steve flashes her a broad smile.

Talking about kids makes Ava's heart pang for Noah, so she excuses herself to FaceTime him before bed. The leap in technology during her memory lapse is amazing and she loves that she can see his squishy little face pressed up against the camera. He fills her in on his day, which seems to centre around a trip to Zephyr's house for a play date, culminating in an ice-cream after dinner. Tom pops on the phone at the end and she decides to take out her jealousy on him.

'You went to Meredith's house for lunch?' she grills him.

'Yeah. We've been flooded with play date offers lately. All the kinder mums seem to think I'm incapable of solo parenting. They keep dropping off casseroles too.' He sounds evasive, though she can't tell if it's on purpose or not.

Ava's offended that none of the yummy mummy brigade, with

the exception of Rachel, have even sent her a text to see how she's coping, let alone drop off a casserole. Irritated, Ava clips the conversation short and promises to pick Noah up by the following afternoon. Though he doesn't say anything, she got the distinct impression that Tom was enjoying her discomfort. She'll text Rachel later to thrash out what a meddling bitch Meredith is. For now, though, she follows the aroma of dinner back to the table and shelves Tom, wanting to give Freya and Steve an evening free from her emotional drama.

After too much eating and drinking, Ava is grateful to retire to the guest bedroom. This used to be her room as a child, which Freya has gently resuscitated after years of passive neglect. The walls have been painted a dusty grey, which is almost blue depending on the light, offset by crisp white picture rails and ceiling. The original moulded ceiling remains and a blush-coloured glass light fitting has replaced the tired frosted pendant that she remembers. The side tables are a rustic timber with a simple built-in shelf, which she suspects Steve had a hand in. The room is perfumed by freshly cut hydrangeas in a vase by her bed, which is made up in gorgeous linen sheets, providing a perfect completion of the space.

Lying on the bed, she's grateful that her memories are still alive in here. The rainy days when she and Freya would build a cubby house with the bed covers and giggle, eating stolen biscuits and making up ghost stories. The balmy summer nights when she would leave the window open to inhale the breeze and watch the stars, only to be woken up at first light by the cacophony of birdsong. The nights with Seb, where they would curl around each other in the small double bed and sleep intertwined. The intrusion of Seb makes her wish that Tom was here now, so she could burrow into his warm body. Noah would love it up here too. Her thoughts swirl around her boys until sleep overtakes, offering sweet respite from reality.

~

In her dreaming, Ava's mother is still alive. They're sitting on a rocking chair and Luci is humming a lullaby and stroking eight-year-old Ava's hair in a soft rhythm. As she tries to recall the exact tune the memory starts to recede. She's floating away as she watches her child self and mother intertwined while the tune gets louder, but she still can't decipher it. She's shaking her head trying to place what she's hearing when she jolts herself awake and realises the noise is her phone screaming at her from the bedside table.

 Disappointment at reality swirls within her as she gets her bearings, wondering who would be calling at this hour on a Sunday. She answers the unknown number with a groggy 'hello,' and the manic caller on the other end jolts her into action. He's not who she expected to hear from and his disaster is about to become hers.

TWENTY-ONE

ADRENALINE courses through Ava's body as she drives back into the city. Freya shoved a couple of blueberry muffins into her bag as she raced out the door, three-quarters dressed and frazzled, the crumbs of which are now littered across her lap. She weighs up if it's too early to call Sarah, given the enormity of what she needs to tell her. Deciding she has no choice, she asks Siri to dial the number, marvelling that you can command your phone and car to cooperate on a conference call.

'Ava?' Sarah's groggy voice comes down the line.

'Sarah, sorry to wake you. I have news. Rafe Montgomery called me this morning. Baxter Barrett has filed for divorce and he wants me to represent Laura in what is sure to be vindictive and unpleasant.' The information spills out of her at speed.

'Jesus.' Sarah sounds more alert. 'Andrew Saunders representing him?'

'Er, no. There's an extra layer of drama. Seb's representing him. He's left the DPP and gone out on his own.' Seb must have known about this when he kissed her the other night, making her feel dirty.

'Jesus. Conflict of interest for you?' Sarah asks.

'I made Rafe aware, said it wasn't a problem for me if it wasn't a problem for him. He also wants to freeze the share agreement, which thankfully contained a clause to cover this kind of stunt. I need to dig deeper into that fraud stuff now.'

'Does this mean you'll sign the partnership deal?' Sarah's eagerness purrs down the line.

Something inside her still can't say yes to Sarah. Not yet. Not until this case has been properly put to bed and she's proved to herself she can still do this. The self-doubt won't let her take the risk of disappointing yet another person in her life.

'I promise to make a decision soon. I need to take this slowly so I don't screw another thing in my life up.'

'What have you screwed up? Tom?' Sarah's tone softens.

'Everything,' Ava answers, distracted.

The world blurs around her as she flies along the stark freeway and tallies up all the ways in which she's hurt him.

'Want to have dinner later? I can bring over some food and we can thrash out a plan for this case,' Sarah offers.

'That sounds great, actually. As long as you don't bill me, I can't afford a partner's rate.'

Sarah laughs and it sounds warm and more like the friendship that she remembers. With Sarah onside she relaxes, now able to focus on how she's going to tackle this case. Given Seb is her opponent, it's going to take all she's got.

~

Tom and Noah are kicking a football on the front lawn as she enters the driveway, halting their play when she steps out of the car. Noah drops the ball and bolts towards her as she bends down to grab him up in a bear hug. His rosy cheek is squished against hers and a flood of warmth rushes through her. Noah feels like home, regardless of location, the realisation of which makes her aware that nobody has ever given her that before. Tom strides towards them looking better than he should, with his bed-ruffled hair and scruffy gym shorts.

'You're early,' he notes, confused but not seeming disappointed.

'Yeah, sorry. I was actually hoping we could talk, I need some advice?'

'Sure. Coffee?'

She nods, grateful for the offer given she flew out Freya's door without even a lowly cup of instant.

Once they're seated in the kitchen and Tom slides over her barista-quality coffee, she settles a little, yet she's still aware she doesn't live here right now.

'I feel like a visitor.' She lowers her sad eyes so she doesn't have to look at him.

'It's not what I wanted.' Tom's voice is soft but devoid of desperation.

'I'm sorry about the other night. I'm sorry I didn't tell you about Seb and I'm sorry it happened at all. Really, really sorry.'

'I know.' He lets out a big sigh and she senses that he still can't talk about it with her. 'What did you want to ask me about?' He moves the conversation along.

'The Montgomery case has blown up and is entering divorce proceedings. I need concrete proof that prick stole from the family business and get some proper leverage over him. I had to bluff a little last time, but it's not going to cut it now given I'm up against...' She stops short of saying Seb's name out loud again, knowing that every time she does it chips away at Tom.

'Seb?' he guesses, wide-eyed.

'Yes.' She shakes her head. 'He must have got pushed out by the DPP after losing that case.'

'Motherfucker.' Tom lets the uncharacteristic slur out under his breath.

'I know he's going to make this as painful as he possibly can. I can't have this dragging on in court, plus making him suffer would be a bonus.'

Tom smiles and she shoots him a quizzical look imploring him to explain.

'You've started to talk about him the way you used to, when we first got together. Cool disdain. I like it.' He grins.

She reaches over and takes his hand in hers to squeeze it.

'He's my *ex*-husband, Tom.' She holds his gaze as his tentative fingers slowly glide over the top of her hand in a tiny gesture that feels huge.

The doorbell rings, interrupting their moment, and Noah races down the stairs shouting like a lunatic.

'Zephyr's here!'

'Zephyr? Again?' She raises an eyebrow at Tom.

God-damned Meredith.

'Noah insisted he come over, they had fun yesterday.' He shrugs.

It annoys her that Tom has slotted into the play date scene without effort and the jealousy bubbles watching him do this better than her. The fact that Meredith grates on her may also explain her thumping inner rage.

Meredith's sing-song voice floats down the hallway in a constant flow of verbal diarrhoea, until she claps eyes on Ava sitting at the bench and is unable to hide her surprise. Ava notes Meredith's wispy dress with a plunging neckline. It's much too minimal an outfit for the cool morning and Ava decides it isn't an accident. Tucking her wayward hair behind her ears, she's acutely aware of her frumpy sweatpants and cardigan that she threw on in the dark.

'Ava! Hi! I wasn't expecting to see you here,' Meredith blurts out, flicking her long, bleached hair behind her shoulder.

'Really? Why not?' Ava enjoys her discomfort and Tom's mouth curls into a knowing smirk from behind Meredith's head.

'Er, of course, ridiculous, of course you'd be here. How are you, sweetheart? How are you feeling?' She angles her head into a patronising tilt.

'I feel great, thank you, Meredith. I actually have a few errands to run so I better get on with it.' She moves over to Noah to hug him goodbye 'I'll see you later tonight, buddy.' She kisses the top of his head and leaves Meredith alone in the kitchen while Tom follows her out.

'Ah, about your case.' Tom clears his throat, 'Rachel has an old colleague, he's a forensic accountant. I've used him before. If there's something to find, he'll find it for you.'

'Thanks, I'll call her. Enjoy your play date.' She walks out the door before he can reply. When she gets back in the car, she sees him still watching her from the doorway.

~

'He's not sleeping with Meredith.' Rachel's tone is calm as she passes Ava an oversized mug of herbal tea.

She fled to Rachel and Jeff's house under the guise of her case, but mostly for moral support after her morning with Tom.

'She's hotter than me. Bet she hasn't touched a carbohydrate in a decade.' Ava sips her tea, burning her tongue, before grabbing a croissant off the platter Rachel laid out.

'She's not sexy,' Jeff chimes in, brushing pastry crumbs from his mouth as Rachel whips her head around to glare at him.

'What? She's not. She's like a manic chipmunk. A conversation with her makes me want to day drink,' he clarifies, with an exaggerated shudder.

Ava laughs, removing some tension, but she's still annoyed.

'He probably didn't know how to get out of it, Meredith is relentless,' Rachel offers.

'Middle age is bullshit. Tom isn't really single, yet women are flocking around him with casseroles and play dates while I'm left with rogue kilos I don't even remember eating and grey regrowth.' She takes another bite of her croissant.

'Tom isn't trying to be single, he's lonely. He misses you,' Jeff says, before adding, 'and I bet he'll miss you even more after a couple of hours with the chipmunk.'

She laughs, despite feeling like a bit of a bitch for trying to make Meredith the bad guy, knowing in her heart that she herself carries that mantle.

'Okay, thank you for the pep talk, but I actually need to talk shop. Tom said you know a forensic accountant that may be able to help me dig up a paper trail for the thieving scumbag I'm trying to annihilate.'

'Fred. He's the best. Not cheap, but if he can't find it, then nobody can.' Rachel's voice is confident.

'If I can prove there's fraud, he'll be looking at jail time.'

'A handy incentive for him to settle out of court. What about Seb? How do you intend to punish him?' Rachel asks.

Sipping her tea, now temperature perfect, her cheeks flush with the promise of justice.

'Slowly.'

~

The lounge room floor is covered in a sea of scattered papers hiding the floorboards beneath. Ava spread them out in an effort to make sense of it all. Her apartment-sized dining table had quickly proved incompetent for the task, but she's now in an overwhelming pit as the enormity of the case engulfs her. If she can't link Baxter Barrett to the *alleged* fraud, then Seb could tie them up in court for years fighting over the myriad of trust structures that encompasses the Montgomery estate. She wouldn't object to stringing out years of legal fees – she couldn't in good conscience pretend to be above that – but the thought of facing off with Seb for years leaves her blood cold.

Her doorbell rings and looking at the clock she can't believe it's four o'clock already. She's been at this for three hours. Not that she has much to show for it. Her limbs stiffen as she drags herself off the floor to the front door, jerking it open to find Tom delivering a grinning Noah for their night together.

'Hi Mum! I've got a dinosaur backpack!' Noah jumps up to hug her.

'I love it! Oh, I missed you,' she says into his little shoulder, pushing her cheek into the softness of his neck.

He runs inside to play in his room, which is still proving to be a novelty. Tom follows her inside and notices the papers strewn all over the floor and half of the couch.

'Christ,' he mutters, leaning against the doorway.

'I know right? I'm screwed if I can't find any dirt. These trust structures are a complicated nightmare.'

'I can help you,' he says before adding, 'if you need.'

'Thanks. Sarah's coming over later to help me, but I'll definitely pick your brain at some stage.'

Tom clears his throat. 'About today…'

'It's fine, you don't have to explain,' she cuts him off and keeps talking to fend off her embarrassment. 'Actually, can you take a look at this discretionary trust for me? The Trust Deed is complicated...'

Tom kneels down on the floor in front of the line of papers as Ava sits next to him, indicating which section she's referring to. His woody cologne wafts over them and her skin prickles with electricity.

'I think you could definitely get the spouse excluded from this one, see this clause here? It's badly worded, but essentially if he hasn't been named as a specific beneficiary then no judge will open this can of worms. And there's nothing going on with me and Meredith, or me and anyone for that matter...' He leaves his eyes on the papers in front of him, waiting for her to respond.

She turns her head slowly and he mirrors her movement until their eyes are locked. They move their heads closer together, lips hovering close enough to feel the other's breath but not touching.

'That's good to know,' she whispers, biting down on her lower lip.

Tom takes a sharp inhale and runs his hand up the side of her leg, making her groin ache. Her eyes close to kiss him when she's startled by Noah's scared voice calling 'Muuuuum!', making them jolt apart and run to his room, finding him in a heap on the floor next to the bed.

'What happened?' Ava drops to the floor next to him, scooping him into her lap.

'I fell off the bed being a stegasawus. My arm hurts,' he whimpers.

'Should we go to the hospital?' Ava looks up at Tom, her face pale and searching.

'Have you got some kids' paracetamol?' he asks.

'Yeah, all the painkillers from the hospital list are still in the kitchen cupboard.'

'Let's try a bit of that and a rest first and see how he goes after that.' Tom's voice is measured and there's safety in one of them knowing what they're doing.

Once Noah is ensconced on the couch, sated with painkillers and cozy in a blanket, Ava begins to relax. After a plate of chicken nuggets, he nods off to sleep watching TV and Tom manoeuvres him into his bed without even a flicker of his eyelids. Logically, she knows that parents have to deal with all kinds of intermittent, unpredictable chaos, but she's still out of her depth. Tom remains the rock and she's still quicksand.

'Are you always this good in a crisis?' She flops on the couch next to Tom.

'Well I've had some practice of late, but usually it's me following your lead. This is unchartered waters for both of us.' He rubs his hand over the back of his neck.

'I've texted Sarah not to come tonight. I want to look after Noah without the distraction.'

'I can take him home if you're worried and want to get some work done?'

Ava doesn't answer but inches closer to where Tom is sitting and picks up his hand in hers.

'Actually, I was hoping you might stay here tonight too…' She pauses with her heart in her throat.

'So you can take advantage of my tax knowledge for your case?' he jokes and twists his fingers through hers.

'Yes, but I'd also like to take advantage of you in other ways.'

He smiles but is clearly holding back. He puts her hand down and angles himself in her direction and her gut sinks.

'I can't do the dance anymore, Ava. You can't come and go as you please. It's not fair on Noah. Or me. If we do this, you have to mean it.'

This is more than fair and she doesn't want to hurt either of them. Does she want Tom because she's jealous or lonely or selfish? The gravity of the moment makes her hesitate and he gets up from the couch.

'I think you should think about it.' He grabs his jacket off the back of the couch and heads towards the door as she follows behind, crestfallen.

The closer he gets to the door the more her heart sinks. She can't have him walk out the door again. That's not how this ends.

As he pulls the door ajar she presses her body against his back and reaches her hand around him, pushing the door until she hears the soft click of the lock. He hangs his head and she can hear his ragged breathing. Her hand slides up to his chest and she can feel his heart race beneath her fingers. He reaches up and holds her hand in his, before turning to face her, still holding on and waiting for her to speak.

'It was you all along. I'm sorry I've been so terrible at falling in love with you.' She holds his gaze.

'I'm sorry I expected you to.' He brings her hand to his mouth and runs his lips over her fingers.

'You and Noah. It's what I want, I promise,' she vows.

Tom's shoulders descend as he exhales, looking like the weight of the world has dropped off him. His eyes shift and soften, his guard dropped, and she knows he's back. He didn't give up on her.

This is the moment that she can't remember. A reinvention of their history perhaps, but a beginning in its own right. This won't be exactly how it happened the first time, but she knows how it should start.

'I want you to kiss me,' she says in a breathy whisper.

Tom lets his face hover close to hers for a few seconds, and she sees a small curl of a smile as he strokes her bare arm, leaning in close enough that she can feel his breath on her lips. He runs his hand up the side of her neck, then grazes her chin with his thumb as he guides their mouths together, kissing her. His tongue is fervent against hers and rolls through her mouth in delicious, practiced strokes. Her arms drape around his neck as he pulls her in close, awakening her senses as he does. After what could have been seconds or minutes, she's at a loss to know, he stops and pulls back, waiting and gauging her reaction. Their breathing is ragged and she wants more. More of whatever this is. She takes his hand and leads him into her bedroom, pulling him down to her mattress on the floor as they continue grabbing at each other's clothes and kissing like unsupervised teenagers. Tom navigates her fragility with care but it's obvious that her body is a known commodity to him. His hands are soft yet deliberate, knowing exactly where and how she likes to be touched, and she's unable to focus on anything except how good it feels. He slips his fingers underneath her silk underwear and inside her, moaning into her neck as he notices the ease at which her body is responding to him. She arches her back as he plants soft kisses all the way down her neck, unbuttoning her shirt as he goes, before reaching her breasts, nipples stiffening under his touch. He takes one at a time into his mouth as she feels herself getting wetter by the moment.

Her moans intensify as he kisses his way down her belly, before hooking her underwear under his thumbs and dragging them off in an agonisingly slow display. He carries on kissing the inside track of her leg all the way down to her ankle and back up before finding a home for his mouth in between her legs. She arches her back, digging her head into the mattress, as his tongue ripples over her in a steady rhythm. Tom's keen attention has her body escalating to orgasm and when she can't hold it back any longer, pleasure pulses through her as she writhes on the bed, releasing herself to him.

Not fully satisfied, she wants more. Everything. All of him.

'I want you,' she whispers in his ear, giving his earlobe a soft nibble.

To get a better view, she props herself up on her elbows to watch him undo his jeans and discard them to the floor in haste. He stands naked before her and she licks her lips in approval. He lowers himself on top of her, still kissing whatever available flesh he can find, until reaching her mouth again as if it's a homing beacon. She groans as he enters her and moves her hips in sync with his, finally finding the antidote to all the mounting pressure. Tom provides the perfect pace while continuing to kiss and touch her seemingly everywhere. Soon she's overcome again with sensory bliss and peaks at one of the most intense orgasms that she's ever had; only then does Tom let himself go too.

Their sweat-drenched bodies lie entwined, panting, each catching their breath. After a few minutes, Ava decides to speak, sensing that

Tom is once again holding the space for her.

'Wow. That was, yeah, wow. Is that, um... usual?'

'Well, I'd love to say I bring my A game every time, but ah, broadly speaking, it's always been pretty great for us.'

'Lucky us.' She smiles, excited to repeat the experience.

Tom props his head on his elbow, turning to face her as she strokes the stubble on the side of his face.

'I, er...' Tom clears his throat. 'I wasn't sure that was ever going to happen again.'

She pulls his face down to hers, kissing him deeply, enjoying the taste of his salty lips. Her body remembers him even if she can't. Their lips release and Tom curls his body around hers, pulling the covers over their naked bodies. She's finally home.

TWENTY-TWO

'NOTHING? How is that possible?' Ava is bereft.

'He's either very clever or he's innocent. I need a bit more time to work out which one.' Fred shrugs his shoulders.

The swivel chair crunches a bit beneath her as she slumps backwards. High hopes of concrete proof of Baxter Barrett's fraud from the forensic accountant, now dashed. All she and Tom have managed to come up with are minimal loop holes in the family trust and she was counting on this to help nail the case.

Fred's office is as depressing as her current mood. It's a soulless square room inside a mission-brown suburban office block. Aside from his desk and two office chairs, the room is barren but for a wastepaper basket and several boxes stacked by the door. A small, narrow window sits just below ceiling height and lets in streaks of light and a weak breeze. Fred himself is tall with broad shoulders and a full head of dark hair. His bright blue eyes glow against his caramel skin and he looks out of place in this boxy shit hole.

'I need some more leads. Associates, lovers, obscure relatives. Anyone that he might use to hide assets.' Fred says.

'Okay.' She nods, and with an aimless swivel of her chair she rams into a box, giving her a jolt in the back.

'Sorry.' Fred reaches to move it for her, 'This office is temporary.'

'Oh, it's not so bad.'

'It's a dump,' Fred smiles, before elaborating, 'but the partnership I was consulting for was wound up so I'm going out on my own. I'm only here until I find a permanent office.'

'I'll keep digging and get you more to go on. The wife is holding out on me, but I can't work out why.'

'Well, in my experience there are only two reasons. Money or money.'

He's probably right, which gives her an idea on how to get Laura Montgomery talking. She leaves Fred in his hovel and walks back out into the open air, taking in an extra breath of the spring warmth.

~

Ava checks her watch again, noting it's quarter past twelve, giving her plenty of time to get from Toorak back to Brighton to pick up Noah. That's if Laura Montgomery would finally show up. She's fifteen minutes late but that could all be part of the game. She strikes Ava as somebody who is rarely held to account, which might actually work in her favour.

Her phone vibrates and she jumps on it, hoping it's Fred with a fresh lead, but she's confused to find it's from Nick instead.

Nick: Hey Ava, give me a call when you can. Cheers, Nick.

He must be really keen to get them to send Noah to that posh school next year. She's about to call him when she spots Laura strolling into the restaurant, easing her oversized Balenciaga sunglasses onto her head as she scans the space. Her platinum-blonde hair is slicked back into a perfect ponytail and she's dressed in a fitted black dress that looks immaculate and expensive as it hugs her slim frame. She thrusts her camel trench coat at the Maitre De, without offering any gratitude, and saunters over to Ava's table by the window.

'Laura, thanks for meeting me.' Ava stands to greet her with a handshake. Laura provides a limp, half-hearted shake, reeking of haughty arrogance.

'How's the case going?' Laura asks, perusing the menu.

'Coming along nicely. I wanted to discuss the family business, actually. We need you to take a step back, just while proceedings are underway.'

'What?' Laura lowers her menu, flicking up an eyebrow as far as her botoxed face will allow.

'It's important that the court see you as a separate entity so that

Baxter doesn't try and take your company shares. Your father's agreed to suspend your voting rights for now.' Ava stays as nonchalant as possible.

'Yeah, I'm sure you had to twist his arm,' Laura scoffs, taking the bait.

'I'm confused?' Ava plays dumb.

'Daddy would love to squeeze me out. Bax has been telling me that for years.' Laura drains her water glass as her demeanour cracks.

'What exactly *has* your husband been telling you, Laura?'

Laura gives her a suspicious look and it seems clear their interests are at odds despite appearances.

'You're protecting him, aren't you? Why?' Ava prods.

'I have no idea what you mean,' Laura shoots back. She's a terrible liar.

'I think you do. This isn't about divorce, is it? This is about getting your *fair share*. Right?'

Laura glares at her but stays silent.

A wave of pity washes over Ava. Baxter has clearly set her up for this, but she's too out of her depth to pull it off. If Ava has learnt anything over the years it's that wronged spouses are always out for blood, especially when millions of dollars are on the line. Fred was wrong. There's more than one reason to hold out in a divorce settlement. Love.

'You still love him?' Ava needles.

Laura shifts in her seat but tightens her jaw, keeping her head tilted up.

'You think that after this settlement you two are going to rebuild? Start fresh? What's he promised you? Eloping to the French Riviera to do it all again?'

Laura scoffs, 'The French Riviera is for Euro trash.'

Ava sits back in her chair, folding her hands in her lap, letting Laura marinate in the discomfort.

'What's in this for you, Laura? This is already yours, why give it to him?'

'Nothing is *mine*,' she spits through gritted teeth.

'And you think *he* is yours?'

'I don't expect you to understand. We're not conventional.'

'That's a nice way to explain a philandering husband. How many have there been?'

Laura pauses then leans across the table, resting her elbows on the table.

'You're asking all the wrong questions. Which is exactly what we're counting on.'

Laura's eyes are icy and with a smug smirk she gets up and walks out of the restaurant, leaving Ava reeling in unchartered waters.

~

Ava's blasting phone interrupts her conversation with the parents in the queue at Noah's pre-school. She's been dreading this conversation since her ill-fated lunch with Laura and walks slightly away from the other parents to answer.

'Sarah, hi.'

'Have you got good news for me on the Montgomery case? Did you smoke Laura out?' Her voice is frantic, like she doesn't have time for any sort of conversation.

'I know the divorce is a sham, but I can't prove it. She's doing this to clean out her father so she and Baxter can sail off into the sunset or whatever.' Ava's shoulders round in defeat.

'What about forensics? Still nothing?'

'Nothing. They're three steps ahead and I can't work out how they're doing it.'

'You know, you might have to concede this one, Ava. Do your best to get a settlement that Rafe and the family can live with. It's obviously going to Laura after all.'

Sarah wants her to roll over? That's not the Sarah she remembers.

'I'm not giving up. I'll string it out with paperwork and hold off on the depositions until next week and see what Fred can find in the meantime.'

Sarah's resigned sigh floats into her ear, before she flies off to her next meeting, leaving Ava perplexed and a bit annoyed that she seems to have lost her appetite to fight. Maybe she only wants to invest time in cases that are a sure thing. Without time to dwell, she sees Meredith skipping towards her, waving, and she fights the urge to roll her eyes.

'Ava, sweetheart, how's it going?'

'Fine thanks, Meredith, you?'

'Hunky dory, darling. Just wondering if you and Noah would like to join us for dinner? I'd hate the two of you to be eating alone.' Meredith adds her trademark head tilt to her invitation, making Ava's blood boil.

Meredith doesn't wait for a reply, but simply launches into another monologue.

'I also hear you're handling the Barrett-Montgomery divorce. I wish you'd been around for my divorce, sounds like you're the go-to girl for fighting tooth and nail.' Meredith winks at her.

'How did you hear that, Meredith?' Ava doesn't bother to veil her annoyance.

'Laura and I go way back. Went to grammar school together. She's my ride or die.' Meredith fixes her eyes on Ava, who is taken aback by this information. Is this meant to be a warning?

'Right, well unfortunately we can't make dinner tonight. Tom's making paella.' Ava waits for the information to land and keeps an unwavering glare on her frenemy.

'Oh, right, you're back home again then? Wonderful! It's lovely you've been able to work it all out,' Meredith says, clapping her hands together in exaggerated joy.

As if to rescue Ava from any more of Meredith's assault, the children are released from the kindergarten gates and Noah hurtles towards her with a handful of artwork and his magnificent grin. After admiring his egg-carton dinosaur she scoops him up, hugging him tight to her chest. This simple joy will never get old.

~

The water in the sink pools and bubbles beneath her gloved hands as she rehashes her long day in her head. Meredith is taking up more mental real estate than she'd like and she can't let it go.

'Are you sure that Meredith didn't come on to you?' Ava is half joking, but this woman has irritated her today.

'If she did then I didn't notice,' Tom says.

'Typical guy.'

'I think she's lonely. Her ex-husband is long gone. Anyway, she told me she's moving back to the UK next year. Wants to be closer to her parents or something. So you won't have to see her at school drop off.'

Shaking Meredith out of her head, she goes back to scrubbing the paella pan, while Tom stacks plates into the dishwasher next to her. Stealing a glance at him, whilst he stacks dishes with no discernible order, a warmth swells inside her. Even though manual labour shouldn't spark joy, right now it does. He looks up and catches her watching him.

'What? You going to give me shit about the way I stack plates?' He grins.

'No,' she shrugs, 'it's just good to be home.'

Her hands resume scrubbing the stubborn pan and Tom's arms slip around her waist. He kisses her neck and breathes her in for a moment before going back to his wayward stacking. Still flushed in the newness of Tom and his ability to disarm her, it's liberating to finally enjoy it.

'You don't have to stop.' She shoots him a coy look.

'We still have to get Noah to bed.' Tom gestures to Noah, who's glued to cartoons and slumped on the couch.

'But,' Tom leans in close to her ear, 'I promise *not* to stop later.' He kisses her as if sealing the contract and her groin pulses with the build up.

'Maybe Mum and Dad sex is better than kid-free sex,' she muses aloud, rinsing suds off her now-clean pan.

'Huh?' Tom jerks his head.

'I mean, I like the anticipation. It's a new concept for me.' She shrugs.

After months of limbo with Tom she'd love to be able to have him whenever and wherever she likes, but the thrill of not being able to is tantalising in a new way. Seb didn't like to wait for anything, so there was rarely any longing unless he was away for work. Longing for someone who isn't around is far less sexy than longing for them when they're literally kissing your neck.

'Whatever works for you, baby.' He winks at her, before leaving the kitchen to go and wrangle Noah into the bath.

Her phone vibrates on the bench with an incoming call. Her gut sinks when she looks at it.

'Yes?' She's curt.

'Sorry for calling after hours,' Seb replies.

'No you're not.'

'You're right, I'm not. I'm calling to inform you that we intend to depose Laura tomorrow. She's apparently heading off to Europe next week, so I need to do it now.' His tone is sharp and matter of fact.

How did she not know about her own client leaving the country in this critical time of her own divorce proceedings! God-damned Laura.

'What time?' Ava asks through gritted teeth.

'9am.'

'Jesus, Seb, that's ridiculous, it's late enough notice as it is.'

'I was only informed an hour ago about your client's intention to travel so it's the best I can offer. I'll text you the location details.' With that, he hangs up, leaving her fuming.

An annoying tactical move by Seb, but her hands are tied if Laura has indeed booked a flight.

'Asshole,' she mutters to herself at the exact moment Tom walks past the kitchen.

'Something I said?' he jokes.

'I've got a deposition for Laura tomorrow at nine. Apparently she's booked a little overseas holiday next week, hence the rush.' She mouths 'fuck' at him so Noah doesn't hear her.

'Stay calm, it's only a deposition. All you have to do is sit there and object when Seb behaves like a prick, which is inevitable,' Tom reassures her, but she's not sure.

'What's his hurry for this? Has he got something on her that I don't know about?'

'Well, if you're right that she and Baxter are in cahoots then she's probably fed him the information,' Tom proffers.

'She's going to blow this up and force a settlement before she buggers off to Paris or wherever.' Ava flops onto the kitchen stool, leaning her head into her hands, while Tom gives her back a gentle stroke in commiseration.

'She said I ask the wrong questions. What are the right ones?' she asks herself out loud.

'Well,' Tom muses, 'you keep saying, "Why would Laura do this?" like there's something in it for her. Maybe you should ask why wouldn't she do this?'

Tom follows Noah up the stairs to the bathroom, leaving her to ponder his suggestion. Maybe he's right. Laura is already unfazed by Baxter's extracurricular activities. There's got to be some other deal breaker for her. Laura needs a reason not to do this; hopefully she can find her one in time.

TWENTY-THREE

IN her trademark fashion, Ava arrives ten minutes early for Laura's deposition in the high-end Collins Street office. The lobby is sleek with dark furniture and looks clean enough to perform open-heart surgery. Seb is either calling in a favour or it's costing him a fortune to rent this office. Laura is sitting alone on the stiff leather couch, looking out the window. She doesn't even shift her gaze as Ava sits down opposite her.

'I'm on your side, Laura,' Ava says.

Laura slowly turns towards her, yet her face remains stiff and unmoved. Maybe nobody has ever been on this woman's side before. At least not without their own overarching agenda. Laura is hardly an aberration, caught up in the dark cloud of money and privilege.

'Good morning, ladies. Right this way,' Seb says, appearing out of nowhere to usher them down another sterile hallway to a window-laden meeting room.

Ava is still miffed at Seb for rushing proceedings and doesn't offer pleasantries, taking a seat next to Laura. The table is big enough for fourteen but is somehow dwarfed with only four people in the room. Baxter isn't here, thankfully, but Seb has an associate to operate the video recording and take notes. He looks young, dressed in a cheap suit, and seems generally nervous.

The initial questioning from Seb is uninspired and probably designed to make Laura tired and irritate her. It's all very theatrical and typical for his style. Seb is constant tactics. He unpacks her history at the family company, her husband's role and their relationship with her parents. Nothing is illuminating, beyond establishing mild familiar tension, and is hardly grounds for divorce. If everyone who hated their in-laws got divorced, the rates would be through the roof. Ava can sense he's building to something and presumes he's enjoying her mounting discomfort, though she's careful not to show any emotion.

'You've sighted "irreconcilable differences" on your divorce application, Mrs Barrett, could you elaborate please?' Seb asks.

'We have differing priorities.' Laura remains cool.

'What are *your* priorities?'

Laura looks confused and Ava starts to wonder how much she really does know. Is Seb setting them both up?

'Let me rephrase.' Seb adjusts his tie and continues, 'Do you want children, Mrs Barrett?'

Laura looks wounded before nodding and letting out a small 'yes.'

'According to my client, it was you who wanted to abandon your fertility treatment, essentially ending the possibility of having children, is that correct?' Seb's smugness at this question reeks of the insensitivity that can only come from a man.

'*Abandon treatment?* I'd had fourteen rounds of IVF in five years. I was broken.' Laura's voice cracks and Ava can see tears well in her eyes.

'Why are my client's private medical decisions relevant, counsellor? Move along.' Ava glares at Seb.

'They're relevant,' he begins in his most patronising tone, 'because *my* client suffered clinical depression after his wife removed the possibility of him having children. Hence, she *caused* the irreconcilable difference that she herself has cited. "Differing priorities" did you call them, Mrs Barrett?'

Laura says nothing, but her eyes shoot daggers of pain as tears fall down her cheeks.

'We require a short break,' Ava says, getting up and leading Laura out of the room and back into the lobby.

Laura breaks down into sobs once out of earshot of Seb and mutters incoherently on Ava's shoulder as she pulls her close to comfort her. The woman isn't a robot after all. Once Laura stops shaking, she speaks again.

'He wasn't supposed to ask any of that stuff,' Laura whispers.

Ava releases her grip, holding Laura out at arm's length, boring her eyes into her.

'What was he *supposed* to ask?' Ava's eyes beg for Laura to drop her guard so she can fix this.

Laura breathes deeply and her shoulders droop with an almost imperceptible shake of her head before capitulating.

'Baxter told me it was a formality. To show my dad as the bad guy, coming between us, forcing Bax out of the business and me by extension. It was supposed to lay the groundwork for me to claim my share of the business after the divorce went through. *That* stuff was private. He knows I wanted a baby more than anything.' Laura seems to loosen a little as she unburdens herself.

Jesus. He's doing this so he can take it all.

'Do you know where the money is, Laura? Where did he hide it?' Ava's voice is stern.

'He never told me. Said it was to protect me.' Laura's eyes are sad and Ava can tell she's telling the truth.

It occurs to her that this was Seb's plan all along. Thwart the case from the outset by keeping Laura onside, then expedite the deposition before Laura knew what was happening. Make Baxter Barrett look like the wronged party before Ava had a chance to get any proof on the little bastard. Without the paper trail on the stolen money, Ava knows she's got nothing. Laura's testimony will just be a bitter wife throwing barbs.

'We'd planned a whole life after this, you know? Try and rebuild after all the baby stuff and friction with my parents. We were going to buy a little cottage in the English countryside and be together. Like we used to...' Laura shakes her head as she relays, what is obvious to both of them now, as more Baxter Barrett bullshit.

'I know what it's like to be married to someone who over-promises,' Ava offers.

Seb was the master of promising wonderful things. More time, more love, more kindness. The promise of more always left her feeling like less. As if on cue, Seb walks out looking smarmy despite his expensive navy suit and perfect hair.

'Can we get back to it now?' He flicks up an irritated eyebrow.

'Actually, we will have to postpone. My client's suddenly not feeling well. She's also postponed her travel plans. You can finish the deposition next week.'

Taking Laura's arm Ava leads her back to the lift before Seb can protest. As she looks back at him she expects to see him fuming but she's more annoyed that he's grinning at her.

~

After missing several of her calls, Ava decides to visit Sarah in person before leaving the city. As she knocks on her office door Sarah jerks her head up from her computer but she doesn't seem pleased to see her.

'Hi Sar, sorry to interrupt, I was a block away and thought I'd debrief in person,' Ava says.

'No worries, come in.' Sarah motions for her to sit down. 'How'd the depo go?'

'Combative, typical Seb, but not detrimental.'

'And the forensic guy? Anything?'

'No.' Ava lowers her eyes, knowing she's a disappointment.

Sarah lets out a sigh.

'Look, Ava. You've been dragging your heels on this partnership thing. I don't think it's something you want. I couldn't wait any longer, I've offered it to someone else.'

The words hit her like she's been punched in the chest.

'Geez, Sarah. You didn't want to tell me first?'

'I've been asking you for weeks. If you wanted it you would have taken it. I don't beg.' Sarah's tone is cool and dissociated.

How can Sarah so easily dismiss her?

'Is this because the case isn't shaping up well? I'm only worth it if I'm winning? I thought we were friends…'

'We are friends, maybe that's the problem. Don't shit where you eat and all that.' Sarah's tone softens a bit, but she doesn't appear to grasp the gravity of the moment.

Unable to stomach anymore, Ava gets up and slings her Chanel bag over her shoulder, then pauses. This exchange confirms her doubts about where her *friend* has been for all these years. Why doesn't she know Noah? Why wasn't she by her bedside after her accident?

'You know what, Sarah? I'm not sure we are friends anymore,' Ava says, and leaves without looking back.

~

The clink of her keys echoes through the empty hallway as Ava dumps them in the marble bowl on the hall table and hangs her bag on the brass hook above. She kicks her heels off as she reaches the lounge room and sinks into the armchair in what is now familiar comfort. With the partnership deal gone and the case in freefall, she's rudderless.

Eventually, after she's bored with her own silent wallowing, she drags her weary body upstairs to have a soak in her ridiculously large bathtub. She missed it when she was in the flat and her muscles still ache when she's on her feet too long. As she eases her way into the steaming water an odd thought comes into her head and there's only one person to ask, so she commands her phone to dial on speaker.

'Yo, yo, homie?' Freya answers.

'Why don't I have pubes?' Ava asks.

'I'm sorry, what the...?' Freya laughs.

'When I was in hospital I figured I must have had a wax, but that's been a couple of months and nothing's grown back, so what gives?' She looks down at her bald nether regions, bobbing underneath the water like a submerged hairless cat.

'I dunno, maybe you had them lasered? You don't generally keep me informed on your muff-maintenance.'

'Fair enough.' Ava laughs. 'What are you doing?'

'I'm turning my compost pile while Pip's napping. Other than your lack of pubes, how are you?'

'Terrible. Seb's dicking with my case and Sarah pulled the

partnership offer.' Ava dips her chin into the hot water.

'Why?'

'Because they're both assholes,' Ava says, even though she's not convinced that it's true. Maybe she's not up to the task and simply too rusty for this life anymore.

'You'll figure out a way to win this thing. You always do.'

Ava appreciates Freya's blind faith in her, but right now it's hollow.

'Want to come up for a visit with Tom and Noah next weekend? Steve's got a new tractor, I think they'd both love to hoon around on it with him.'

'Sounds great. New tractor, hey? That sounds like a serious purchase.' Ava stays breezy, not wanting to frighten a potentially skittish Freya.

'Yeah, well the tractor is a tax write-off, but yes, it is serious. I finally get it now. What it's meant to feel like.' Ava relaxes when she hears the smile in Freya's voice.

'Yeah, me too.' Ava smiles too, warm in the knowledge that they're both in love. Properly, this time.

~

The third city lobby that Ava enters for the day is by far the most impressive of all of them. Glass lines the walls in soaring views across the city skyline from the fiftieth floor. This time though, there's no trepidation on her part. On a whim she decided to dress up and surprise Tom at work and take him out for dinner. The receptionist recognised her and agreed to smuggle her in as a surprise. It was already past six thirty, leaving the office mostly empty as she's ushered to his office door.

'Knock, knock,' she says, tapping on the door, pushing it open.

Looking up from his computer, his initial confusion is quickly replaced with genuine delight as he gets up to greet her with a soft hug.

Tom's office is large with a city view, indicating he must be pretty great at his job. Pride swells together with the tiniest hint of jealousy.

Books are neatly lined up in his shelves and the desk is organised but for a few scattered papers. Photos are on display, visible to him and anyone who comes into his office. One is of Noah as a toddler and the other one is the three of them at Noah's birthday party. The one he'd given her in the hospital. Not by accident, she's wearing the same floral dress from the photo.

'What brings you here, babe?' he says, leaning down to kiss her.

'I thought I'd take you out on a date. Your mum agreed to come over and look after Noah. I was kind of worried she'd hate me after everything.' Ava cringes to herself.

'She doesn't. She was the one who told me to let you have your space. She knew you'd work it out in the end.' He runs his fingers through her loose hair.

'Wise woman. You nearly finished?' She kisses his chin, the light stubble grazing her lips.

'Yep, about to log off now. How was the deposition?' He reluctantly releases her to gather his things.

'Seb railroaded her. But looks like she gets it now, that they're not on her side. Still no leads on the money though. Oh, and Sarah pulled the partnership deal, said I was dragging my heels. So there's that.' Ava shakes her head.

'Christ, what a day!'

'I know. I'm such a loser.' Ava slumps onto the couch opposite Tom's desk in a dramatic display.

'The case is early days, you have plenty of levers to pull yet and it sounds like Sarah's done you a favour. Would you really want to be in business with her? You haven't been proper friends for years.' He neatens the papers in front of him into a stack, leaving his desk clear.

'I can't understand how she did a total one-eighty like that. It was just starting to feel good between us.'

'Well from what I've heard she's been asking everyone we know to buy in. I'd say she's desperate for capital. It probably isn't personal.'

'But *why* isn't it personal? She was my best friend.'

Tom shrugs, implying that trying to unravel the nuances of female friendships is beyond his purview, and Ava sighs in resignation at the whole debacle.

'You look beautiful by the way.' Tom closes his laptop and shrugs his suit jacket on as he walks over to her on the couch.

'I want to make memories in this dress that I can actually remember.' She smiles, standing up again.

He wraps his arms around her waist and breathes into the small of her neck, planting soft kisses all the way to her mouth until they're sinking into each other. Kissing Tom makes time stop and heightens all her senses, making every touch electric. She's beginning to think they won't make it to dinner when her phone starts ringing in her bag, breaking their spell.

'Nooooooo,' Tom mumbles into her mouth.

'It might be Jane.' She gently pushes him back to extricate her phone.

She looks down at the screen and is annoyed to find it's Nick, again. She figures she might as well tell him herself that they're not sending Noah to that school and get it over with.

'Nick, hi?' She answers.

'Hi Ava, sorry to keep calling you,' he begins.

'Yeah, I don't think the school is right for Noah,' she cuts him off.

'Huh? Oh right, cool. That's not why I'm calling though. I've got some information for you, it affects your case, can we meet tomorrow?'

She agrees to meet him in the morning, intrigued and a bit nervous. She's had her fill of surprises and this doesn't feel like a good one.

TWENTY-FOUR

AVA is sitting across from Nick, out the front of a beachside café in the warmth of the November morning sun. The table is wobbly on one side, which is annoying every time she puts her coffee cup back down. She's trying to process what he's saying to her but she's finding it hard to focus as her brain swirls.

'Then you walked into your bedroom and saw them together. Then you walked straight out and called me,' Nick says, his face pained.

'I knew you didn't remember when I saw you at the orientation. I was going to let sleeping dogs lie. God knows I wish I could forget it all. When I realised you were seriously thinking of going into business with her, I knew I had to say something.' Nick gives an audible exhale.

These new facts collide in her head, rubbing up against all the confusion she's had for the last couple of months. Mining the depths of the betrayal that has been lost into the ether of her fogged brain. She plays out what Nick has told her like a movie in her head. An affair. Her husband and her best friend. How original. Trying to make it real in her mind makes it sound more like a prosecutor's opening statements. It was the summer of 2010, Ava had come home early on a Friday afternoon from a work trip. When she'd walked into her flat, there was music playing in the lounge room, which was odd this hour of the day. The initial evidence was on the floor. The black Chanel handbag. The one Ava had coveted. The one Nick had splurged on for Sarah's birthday.

'That's why I could never use my bag...' she mutters to herself as she remembers finding it pristine in its box, shoved in the back of her wardrobe.

The thought of them together sickens her. The ones she'd loved so much didn't love her at all. She'd let Seb touch her. Let him kiss her. He'd exploited her memory loss to claim the mantle of victim. Sarah is worse in some ways. Encouraging her into business, and espousing Seb's virtues. Their names roll around the tip of her tongue like mud.

'Why doesn't Tom know?' Ava asks, still confused.

'We didn't tell anyone. They told us it was one night, one slip. Which of course was bullshit, but at the time we wanted to believe it. They didn't want it to get out because neither of them wanted to be pulled off the case they were on together. It was always success for those two,' Nick says, shaking his head.

Ava remembers being second all the time. Seb prioritised himself. His work, his hobbies, his opinions and, apparently, his affairs. Sarah's betrayal is harder to reconcile. She loved her like a sister. They had each other's backs. They'd cried over missed promotions and spent girls' weekends away together, drinking and talking about everything and nothing into the wee hours.

'You tried to make it work with Seb, for months. You were the one who didn't want to tell anyone, didn't want the judgement for not leaving him. I tried to stay too, but it was clear that she'd checked out. She took a transfer to Sydney, called off the engagement and I got on with my life.' Nick shrugs, matter of fact, though she assumes it was far more traumatic at the time.

'How long until I left?' she asks.

'About four months. You started seeing Tom and left basically straight away. Seb, of course, acted like the wounded party.' Nick rolls his eyes.

'Why did I let him? Why didn't I tell Tom the truth?'

'You told me you wanted it untainted. You didn't want Tom to think he was revenge or a second choice. We kind of lost touch over the years so it wasn't hard to keep my mouth shut.' Nick shrugs.

The Nick she knows is stoic and she can trust that he's kept their secrets. He wouldn't have wanted the pity any more than she would.

'Thank you for telling me now.' Ava reaches across the table and gives Nick's hand a small squeeze.

'I didn't want you joining that partnership without knowing. Especially when I heard Seb had signed on.' Nick takes a casual sip of his coffee.

'Um, what?'

'I thought you knew? He apparently signed yesterday, bringing that juicy divorce case with him that he's telling everyone is "in the bag".' Nick makes air quotes with his hands and rolls his eyes.

It's all clear now. Sarah was using her for information in order to pick the winning horse on the Barrett divorce. Her whole body slumps back in her chair, defeated. Fuck. How long are the lost memories going to continue to torture her?

~

Her eyes fixed on the ornate ceiling rose, Ava is supine on Rachel's couch in a pathetic display. Again.

'I have to tell him, right?' Ava groans.

Rachel scrunches up her face, responding with a non-committal pained noise.

'I can't have this secret. Not now that we're in such a good place. And I'm bloody furious at myself for keeping it quiet all these years.' Ava sits up to drink the tea that Rachel has made for her.

'It was obviously important to you not to tell him,' Rachel says, sipping her own tea.

'Was it? Or did I figure it was too late to bring it up? Was I tortured with it all these years? Did I *wish* that I could tell him? Fuuuuuuckkkkkk.' Ava smashes a cushion into her face in frustration.

'Okay, let's break it down. If you don't tell him, is it going to change anything?' Rachel switches gears.

'Maybe he'll find out one day and hate me.' Ava winces at the thought.

'And if you *do* tell him, will it change anything?'

'He won't have to feel guilty anymore about hurting Seb. Although apparently, Seb and I were trying to make it work, so technically we did betray him.' Ava hears her own words but doesn't know if she believes them. Can you betray someone who's already shat all over you?

'I think it would be good for both of you to drop the guilt for that. You hardly betrayed the scumbag. I think Tom could use the honesty after everything,' Rachel says.

She's right. If the last few months have taught Ava anything it's that she continually underestimates Tom, to her own detriment.

'I'm sorry I didn't tell you either. It could have saved me a lot of heartache over the past few weeks with that Machiavellian bitch.'

'I knew something was off with her, but I was trying to like her even though I was jealous,' Rachel admits, her face reddening.

'Why?'

'I felt like I was losing my *best friend* status.' Rachel drops her gaze, fidgeting with her hands.

'Never.' Ava hugs her friend before adding, 'I'll be lying on your couch spewing all my drama for as long as you'll have me.'

'Well it's good to have you back properly. I need someone to groan in the corner with at Meredith and Zephyr's going away party,' Rachel groans.

'Oh god, that's tomorrow, isn't it? Oh, I'd rather gargle broken glass than go to that but Noah is so excited.'

'Harry too. Apparently there's a jumping castle.'

'Of course there is.' Ava rolls her eyes and Rachel mirrors her.

Being cushioned by Rachel's friendship is stabilising, knowing that in the river of uncertain memories she has someone she can trust.

~

The lounge room is dark but for the lamplight above as Ava sits in her favourite armchair with paperwork across her lap. She's been poring over everything for hours in the vain hope that something will illuminate. It's impossible to focus because she keeps turning over in her mind how to tell Tom about Seb's affair. The question of *if* she should tell him is redundant, as she wants all her secrets to belong to Tom now. Even the dark ones. Tom called to say he was running late, rendering the paperwork a futile distraction from the building knot of anticipation.

She's tortured by the decisions of her former self, which, annoyingly, is hardly original for a middle-aged woman, even one *without* her memory loss. Regrets have a way of rubbing up against your insides like sandpaper until the only antidote is acceptance. Her inability to remember is making her braver in an unexpected way. It's hard to take full responsibility when you can't recall doing bad things. It's akin to behaving like an asshole when drunk, then waking up with a throbbing skull and blissful ignorance. Despite this, she wants, more than anything, to be accountable to Tom.

The clock reads eight-thirty as Tom's keys turn in the lock and she shifts more upright as he approaches. He smiles as he sees her ensconced on the sofa and bends down to kiss her before he flops onto the adjacent couch. He looks at her for a few seconds and she makes no attempt to hide her torment.

'What's wrong? More bad news on the case?' He gestures to the papers on her lap.

She shakes her head as she bundles them up, putting them down on the floor.

'I have to tell you something.' Her involuntary pause allows the gravity of the moment to hang as she searches for more words.

'Seb slept with Sarah, a few months before you and I got together. Apparently I knew all about it.'

Tom's mouth gapes a little as he tries to find his own words and she doesn't rush him.

'Seb tell you this?' There's a flicker of agitation in his eyes.

'Nick.'

Tom nods, letting out a knowing sigh.

'I don't know why I didn't tell you. I feel *sick* that I didn't tell you. Nick said that I didn't want to you to feel second, or like revenge or something, but I...' Ava trails off, frustrated, mostly with herself.

'Seb's such a fucking asshole,' Tom says, getting up to kneel next to her and taking her hands in his. She sinks down next to him on the floor and he scoops her into his arms.

'You're not second,' she says into his chest. 'You were first. I saw you first. That night we all met at the fresher's week beach party. Remember?' She looks up to see him clearly.

He looks down to meet her eyes. She sits up straighter to hold his gaze.

'You were standing in the line for beer and you were wearing a blue Hawaiian shirt and boat shoes. You looked like a man and not like the schoolboys I was used to. I wanted to meet you.'

Tom runs his fingers down the side of her neck like he's trying to commit it to memory before he speaks.

'I saw you dancing, before I met you. You were floating around the dance floor and didn't seem to care who was watching. I saw you first too.' He burrows his head into her neck.

Despite Seb's attempt to exploit her memory loss, her body seemed to remember that she didn't want to belong to him anymore. Tom's love isn't conditional in the way that Seb's was. There's no anxiety intertwined with trying to please him. Loving each other is the only condition. With his arms around her now, she has a kind of peace that she didn't realise she's been chasing her whole life.

~

As predicted, Meredith's going away party is not unlike a small circus crammed into her backyard. There's a jumping castle, a petting zoo, face painting, a clown roaming around making balloon concoctions and even a fairy floss machine.

'Well, that clown is bloody terrifying,' Rachel whispers in her ear as they survey the scene from the drinks table.

'Noah's going to take a week to come down from all this sugar.' Ava groans and takes a sip from her plastic champagne flute.

Even though one of Ava's favourite hobbies is looking for Meredith's flaws, she concedes that the kids are having the time of their lives. It's like watching tiny people getting high at Glastonbury, with less mud, and lollies instead of cocaine.

'Check out this spread!' Tom beams as he and Jeff approach with plates of perfect tiny food.

'How's the case, Ava?' Jeff asks as he shoves a mini quiche into his mouth.

'In the toilet. If I can't get anything soon I'm going to have to settle way above the target, pissing me off, not to mention the client. Cheers!' She gives a fake smile to highlight her plight.

'Damn. I thought Fred would have found something. That guy has hunted many a rat down a drain for me.' Jeff offers a conciliatory head tilt.

'There's still time,' Tom says, squeezing her hand for moral support, though she knows that's all it is.

'It's okay. The partnership deal is dead. I'm not trying to impress anyone. Maybe I'll have to rethink the work stuff. Timing's a bit off.' Ava shrugs, but it hurts to say the words and admit that her career may be a non-starter. Even though she's returned to the roles of wife and mother, she knows it's not enough.

'A client of mine needs some in-house legal for a few months. Maybe you'd consider that after the case wraps?' Rachel asks with her trademark optimism.

A nod of tentative agreement is all Ava can muster, unsure if Rachel is trying to cheer her up. Eyeing off Tom's heaped plate, she excuses herself to hit up the food table. She doesn't want to talk about work. The stench of failure is too permeating. Even though Seb and Sarah lied to her, losing the case is like a punishment for all the truth she couldn't see. Or maybe she didn't want to see it. She's piling up her third mini beef wellington when Meredith appears by her side, wearing a gorgeous silk, floral mini-dress showing off just enough cleavage to be interesting but not slutty. A show of rare restraint for her last hurrah. Her blonde hair is blow-waved to perfection, complementing her flawless makeup. It's not fair to look this good at forty.

'Wonderful of you to come, Ava. Zephy is going to miss Noah so much.' Meredith gives an exaggerated pout but Ava notices that her forehead doesn't move to match the expression.

'Thanks for having us, the kids are loving it,' Ava says.

Ava feels frumpy next to Meredith and grabs a slice of watermelon to counteract all the pastry on her plate.

'When do you leave?' Ava asks.

'Next week. I want to get set up so we can have a proper family Christmas.' Meredith claps her hands together in a show of over-the-top glee.

Thankfully, Meredith gets distracted by another guest and excuses herself so Ava isn't forced to ask her another question. Ava's making her way back to Tom and the others when someone taps her arm. She turns to face Laura Montgomery.

'Hi Ava, didn't think I'd run into you here.' Laura seems genuine in her surprise.

'Laura, hi, of course, I forgot you and Meredith are besties. Our kids are at kinder together,' Ava says.

'Besties is a stretch, but I've known her since school.' Laura gives a casual shrug. Her description is a far cry from Meredith's *ride or die* claim.

'How are you? Nervous about next week? I promise it will go better this time.' Ava touches her arm in gentle reassurance though she's aware she's rambling. She also isn't even sure how she's going to make it better for Laura. Seb's no doubt got more dirty laundry to air.

'I want it over so I can get on with my life. I told Dad everything. He's going to bring me back onto the board once it's all settled. At least I'll get my family back.' Laura's eyes are glassy in a rare glimpse of emotion.

'I'm going to do my absolute best for you, I promise.' Ava tries to sound more competent than she feels. It's enough for surface-level Laura, who nods and moves on to her group of friends.

'Who was that?' Tom asks as she returns.

'Laura Montgomery. Jesus, I hope I can pull a rabbit out of a hat.' Ava puts a mini pie into her mouth, ignoring the watermelon.

'Well if all else fails you can always escape to the English countryside and hang out with Meredith,' Jeff jokes, but Ava is the only one who doesn't laugh.

'Something I said?' Jeff looks confused.

'English countryside,' she monotones. 'I've got to make a call.' Ava leaves them bemused as she finds a quiet corner of the garden, flicking furiously through the numbers in her phone until she finds it.

He answers on the second ring.

'Ava?'

'Hi, sorry, I know it's Saturday. I've got a name. Can you run it?'

'Give me 24 hours.'

She hangs up with cautious smugness, reminding herself that the truth we cannot see is right in front of us.

TWENTY-FIVE

SAFE behind the thick glass of the café window, Ava watches them for a few seconds. Sarah is laughing and Seb is sitting back in his chair looking his usual mix of cool and smug. This is perfect. Neutral territory for their final battleground. Ava smoothes her black jacket, which sits perfectly atop her cream pencil skirt, before strutting inside to interrupt the cosy scene.

The café is largely empty but for a couple of lone corporate men in suits poring over their broadsheets. Dinosaurs, hanging onto the last remnants of paper in the digital age. Seb clocks her first as she walks towards their table in the corner and straightens up, clearing his throat. Sarah follows his lead and fixes her face into a polite smile. Both poised for the wrong fight.

'Well don't you two look like a perfect little partnership. Must be nice to finally be in bed together again.' Ava remains cool as she sits down, gently folding the strap of her Chanel bag before setting it down on the table in front of her. A frosty chill hangs over the table and all are guarded.

'So you remember then?' Seb remains bristly but Sarah drops her gaze to the table.

'I was reliably informed.'

'Ava...' Sarah starts before Ava holds up her hand to stop her.

'Save it. You two deserve each other. I'm here to discuss the case.' Ava reaches into her slim, charcoal leather briefcase and pulls out a stack of paper.

'I don't think we are anywhere near settlement, Ava, but I admire your optimism,' Seb says, returning to his trademark smirk.

'Is that why you took him on, Sarah? Thought he was going to bring in a juicy, drawn-out retainer that would get bogged down in court for two years?' Ava raises her eyebrow at her but Sarah doesn't answer.

'You *both* should have known me better than that.' Ava crosses her arms and sits back in her chair, daring Seb to speak again.

'Whatever you *think* you've got, you don't.' Seb oozes arrogance, which would ordinarily annoy her, but today can't penetrate. Looking at him through clear eyes has loosened his grip on her.

Ava takes her time watching them before she speaks. Sarah seems to become more uncomfortable by the second, which Ava is enjoying. Sarah is smarter than Seb and she knows Ava doesn't have the balls to bluff with this level of conviction.

'I have the paper trail of Barrett's theft from the family company. We found the Cayman Islands account in the name of his illegitimate child, showing the influx of stolen funds matching the exact timeline of the Montgomery's financial records,' Ava enlightens.

'Illegitimate kid?' Seb scoffs.

'You don't know about the kid? Don't feel bad. I didn't either at first. It was a chance encounter at a kids' party, I doubt you get many invitations to those kinds of things.' Ava leans her elbows onto the table in front of her and rests her chin in her hands.

Once Ava connected the dots on Meredith moving to the same location that Laura had casually mentioned the previous week, she had to follow her gut. Fred did the digging on the money in Zephyr's name while Ava went about tying up loose ends. She didn't have to lean on Meredith too hard to get the truth out of her either. A pseudo-sympathetic ear was all she needed to pour her heart out. It seems Meredith was also pretty hooked on Baxter's bullshit from the beginning. She'd left her husband right before Zephyr was born, all because he had promised to leave Laura to be with her. She's been waiting for him ever since. It made Ava almost feel sorry for her. Almost.

'You can't prove it's his kid, and we don't consent to DNA

testing,' Seb counters, spinning his pen around in his hand.

'Yes, that would usually be difficult but for the fact that the mother registered Barrett as the father on the birth certificate, which I don't have to remind you, is public record.' Ava smiles as she drops the clincher on him.

'Well done. What now? You want to revert back to the original settlement offer?' Seb postures.

Ava laughs, causing him to flush, she assumes more in fury than embarrassment, though it's satisfying all the same.

'Oh, you're serious? Cute. Um no, you can consider the original offer redundant. Here's the new one.' Ava pushes the stack of paper across the table to Seb. 'I'll give you the highlights reel,' she begins. 'He gets nothing. My client will, in turn, generously waive their right to prosecution of the fraud, which is now provable beyond reasonable doubt, as long as he never contacts Laura Montgomery again. We are willing to provide him with a one-way ticket to Europe as a parting gift.'

Seb gapes at her like he's seven-years-old and she's just told him Santa isn't real.

'You've got to be kidding me. We were looking at fifteen million for this!' Seb's wrath is on full display while Sarah, still mute, drops her head to her hands.

'You would have got ten,' Ava shrugs, 'but hey, this is better than prison.'

Ava turns to address Sarah, 'I hope losing a multi-million dollar pay cheque hurts as much as you hurt Nick and me.'

Satisfied, Ava gets up and puts her handbag on her shoulder, knowing this is the last time she'll be able to use it.

'You have until close of business today to accept or the police will arrest your client,' Ava arrows at Seb before turning to leave.

'Hey!' Seb yells, making her spin back around as he walks around the table to get face to face with her. He reeks of desperation and too much cologne.

'You're forgetting one thing. Your precious Tom knows nothing about all this. You wanted him unsullied. Did Nick tell you that too? You do this and I'll tell him everything. How he was just revenge to fuck with me.' Seb delivers the words like poisoned darts but they don't hurt anymore. She can't feel him anymore.

'He knows,' Ava whispers, and Seb's face falls as his trump card shreds before his eyes.

She moves closer to him, so her breath is in his ear. 'Tom's everything that you will *never* be. I don't need my memories to know that.'

With that, she leaves Seb and Sarah behind in the cheap café with their cold coffees and stale mistakes.

~

Soft jazz filters through muffled chatter punctuated with the odd clink of cutlery. The restaurant is chic, with heavy linen tablecloths and attentive waiters. Ava beams across the softly lit table as she recounts the story for her eager crowd. Tom looks at her with a proud smile despite hearing it for the second time. He arranged a fancy dinner with Rachel and Jeff to celebrate Ava's win.

'That must have felt amazing, strutting out of there.' Rachel says in awe.

'It was a relief. I'm done with both of them,' Ava replies and Tom squeezes her hand. For the first time, she doesn't question that she really means it.

Ava thought the annihilation of Seb might feel different. Like a validation of sorts. The reality, however, is far better, and she is finally unburdened by the whole ordeal. The parts she can't remember still exist, but she can move forward and trust herself again. Knowing that Seb is firmly in her past makes her lighter. You can't forget what you don't remember, but there are enough sour memories of Seb to know that he was never the right choice.

'Well, it was bloody impressive. You sure you don't want to come and work for me?' Jeff asks, dead serious.

'I'm done working for other people, but thanks for the offer,' Ava says.

With her generous bonus from the Montgomery settlement, and her decision to sell the Prahran flat, it made sense to finally make other plans. In order to be the architect of her life Ava realised she had to take charge herself. Too many things have happened *to* her since waking up from her accident and now is the right time to regain control.

Rachel locks eyes with her from across the table and Ava gives her a small nod.

'There's actually something we'd like to discuss with you both,' Rachel begins, smoothing her hands over the table in front of her.

'Sounds ominous,' Jeff jokes.

'Ava and I have discussed going into business together. A small consulting firm offering both financial and legal services to small to medium businesses. We'll work parallel in the services we offer but there's opportunity to network for each other as well.' Rachel is solid as she pitches their idea.

'We don't want to work for other people anymore but we don't want to give up our careers completely. We want to choose our own clients and hours and have some flexibility for the boys and for ourselves,' Ava adds.

The table falls quiet as the men process what they've heard. Ava notices Jeff look over at Tom, both of them seemingly unsurprised. Both of them know what kind of women they married. That's why they married them.

'I think that is a great idea,' Tom says, meeting Ava's eyes.

'Me too,' Jeff agrees, giving Rachel's shoulder a squeeze.

'Think of all the dinners like this we'll be able to write off,' Rachel jokes and they all raise their glasses and toast their enterprise.

Ava is buoyant as they drive home and steals glances at Tom, feeling lucky that he's by her side. Tom pulls into the driveway and turns off the car before he says what he apparently couldn't at the table.

'I hope you didn't think you needed my permission for going into business with Rachel?' He fumbles with the keys in his hands.

'No. But you're my family. I'm doing it for all of us and I wouldn't do it if you thought it was the wrong thing.'

'I think it's the right thing. I think it will be great actually. I want to make some changes at work too. You've been carrying the load with Noah and it's not fair. I need to do more. I'm sorry that you had to leave for me to see it.' Tom rubs his fingers over her hands as he speaks.

'I love you,' she says, leaning closer to him so that he can kiss her.

With Tom's arms wrapped around her, the forgotten things take up less space. The promise of life expanding alongside Tom and Noah gives her permission to finally unfurl and live.

Six months later...

'Oh, I look so fat in this dress,' Freya laments as she scrutinizes her profile in the ornate full-length mirror that belonged to their mother.

'You're not fat, you're pregnant,' Ava says as she flounces the bottom of Freya's dress for her.

'Why did you make me wear white? It's so virginal. I think that ship has sailed...' Freya jokes, and then starts belting out the chorus of Madonna's *Like a Virgin,* compelling Ava to join in and start voguing alongside her even though they know it's not the right dance for the song. They giggle in the mirror before composing themselves and Ava goes back to fixing Freya's hair.

'Nobody cares about that stuff anymore. If only virgins got married, the wedding industry would collapse.' Ava shrugs.

'Yeah but I'm a *bridesmaid*. It looks like I'm stealing your thunder.'

At that moment Rachel walks in, also dressed in a simple white silk frock that matches Freya's, minus the baby bump.

'Can you two keep it down please? It's a wedding, *not* a Madonna concert,' Rachel pretends to scold them, and they give her a solemn nod before giggling again.

'How's it looking out there?' Ava asks Rachel.

'Good, everyone's here. Five minutes till kick off.' Rachel turns her attention to her clipboard to tick off the last items on her checklist.

'I knew going into business with you was a good idea.' Ava nods at the checklist. 'You're the queen of organisation.'

Ava has been referring to their small practice as the *dream team*, given the ease at which business has taken off. They've been able to work without the pressure of ridiculous hours and unending corporate grind. Now that the boys are both at school, they've found a rhythm that seems to suit everyone. Working eighty-hour weeks only ever left Ava empty and overlooked by the patriarchal overlords. Being her own boss is empowering in a way she'd always desired but could never quite realise. Rachel embodies a seamlessness in the way she approaches everything, which has calmed Ava's fiery side, allowing her to focus on what she's good at. Rachel's also been instrumental in calming her jittery bride nerves today, which is the ultimate test of a best friend.

'You look amazing.' Rachel smiles at her with glassy eyes before doing up the final button on her dress. The Collette Dinnigan beaded gown had felt too perfect once she'd tried it on and her reflection in her mother's mirror validates her choice. All the yoga she's now obsessed with has paid off too, as the dress seems to cling in all the right places. Her chestnut hair falls in soft waves around her shoulders as she embodies contemporary glamour.

'Ready?' Freya asks.

Ava inhales slowly, 'Yep. I can't wait to remember marrying Tom.'

She had proposed the idea of a vow renewal to Tom a couple of months ago while they were eating pizza, watching Breaking Bad. Reruns apparently, but new for her. She didn't know why the innocuousness of the moment made her blurt out, *Do you want to marry me again?* but she couldn't keep the words inside her. Tom had dropped his half-eaten slice and kissed her in enthusiastic agreement. When Freya offered up the farm for the venue, everything fell into place.

A soft tap on the door brings her back to the moment, as Jeff ushers in Noah, Harry and Pip all dressed up in their wedding finest.

The boys look so grown up in their three-piece suits while Pip twirls around in her *pwincess dwess*.

They line up, each holding onto their mother's hand ready to make their entrance and walk down the aisle.

'You look very bootiful, Mummy,' Noah says, grinning up at her.

'Thank you, baby. You ready to go marry Daddy again with me?'

Noah gives a solemn nod and they make their way outside where the small crowd is seated on white chairs in front of the rose arch. She can see Tom shifting back and forth, clutching his hands together in front of him, and her stomach flips a little.

She begins walking towards him, beaming back at the smiling onlookers; all the while Noah's small hand is tucked inside her own. As she rounds the corner, the flowering daisies sway in a soft breeze, ushering her into new memories.

THE END

ACKNOWLEDGEMENTS

It takes a village to bring a book baby into the world and I feel very grateful for all the people who have helped get me here. Thank you to Carolyn Martinez, Silvana Nagl, Meesha Whittam, Nita Delgado and the entire Hawkeye Publishing family, you have supported me each step of the way, smoothing the road as I go. Thank you to the wonderful Anne Freeman, marketing genius, who is just as fabulous in real life as she seems. Anne, you go above and beyond and I'm so grateful for your mentorship in this process. Thank you all, for believing that this book was worth publishing.

Thank you to my writing buddy, Holly Brunnbauer. Without your encouragement three years ago this book would still be a few scribbled notes hidden in drawer. Thank you for keeping me accountable, reading my early (and very bad) drafts and helping me make them better.

Thank you to the wonderful and generous Jodi Gibson and the entire Write Squad community. You ladies are my writing family where I can show up without feeling like an imposter. Our weekly sessions are a lifeline when I feel like I am just spilling words out into the ether. One of the best things about writing is other authors, and the way you are all so encouraging and generous with your time is something I'll be forever grateful for.

Thank you to all my friends who read early drafts and told me that you loved it. This made me braver and able to show my work to the world. You ladies are my cheerleaders and I love you all.

Thank you to my parents, Michelle and Bryan, for supporting everything I've ever done. When you tell a little girl that she can do anything she sets her mind to, she will. Failure isn't as scary when you a have a safe place to land, and that's what you've always given me. Thank you for loving me like that.

Thank you to my husband, Hamish, and even though you still haven't read this book, I love you anyway. We've been a team for twenty years and life with you is bright. You and the kids are my heart and soul.

Thank you to my three children for making me the luckiest mother in the world. You three are my constant motivation and make my heart full. You teach me more than I will ever teach you. Love you all to the moon and back, times infinity.

And thank you, reader, for picking up my book and giving it your precious time. I appreciate you.

Casey Nott

ABOUT THE AUTHOR

Casey Nott is an author who writes contemporary fiction that celebrates women and explores the challenges they face in modern society. As a former Chartered Accountant and Nutritionist, she's had a wide breadth of life experience from which to draw inspiration. Away from her laptop she's an avid baker and enthusiastic participant in the dark arts (knitting and crochet). Her debut novel, *Forgotten,* was long listed in the 2022 Hawkeye Manuscript Development Competition. She lives in the bayside suburbs of Melbourne with her husband and children, of whom she's quite fond.

You can find her on Instagram @caseywritesstories.

BOOK CLUB QUESTIONS

1. If, like Ava, you woke up forty and couldn't remember the last decade of your life, what milestones would you have missed? How would you adjust to the change?
2. Ava learns how to be Noah's mother whilst grieving for her own. How important is having a mother to one's own motherhood experience?
3. Ava carries a lot of guilt about not being a good enough mother to Noah. Do you think this is relatable to all mothers?
4. There is a shift in Ava and Tom's dynamic when she returns to work. Do you think Tom has been unfair to expect her to give up her career?
5. Freya and Ava have a strong sisterly bond, however Ava's strong sense of responsibility for her little sister sees her drift from supportive to controlling. How do these patterns reverberate throughout the novel?
6. Ava and Rachel's friendship blossoms throughout the novel. What do you think are the elements for a successful adult friendship? How is friendship different at forty compared to twenty-five?
7. How did the novel relate to your life? Are there things you would change about your current life if given the opportunity?
8. What were your favourite scenes in the book? Why did they leave an impression?
9. What do you think happens for the characters after the novel concludes?
10. Did you find the ending satisfying? Did anything feel unresolved?

Book reviews can make or break a book. If you liked what you read today, please do consider posting a review on Goodreads or your favourite forum.

Forgotten is available at www.hawkeyebooks.com.au
and all good bookstores and libraries.

If you enjoyed *Forgotten*, we believe you'll also enjoy:
Returning to Adelaide and *Me That You See* by Anne Freeman
What If You Fly by Camille Booker
Rosanna by Annie O'Moon-Browning
New Year's Eve by Sarah Todman
Where There is a Will by Michel Vimal du Monteil
The Truth About My Daughter by Jo Skinner
Big Music by Gillian Wills